THE Short Forever

continued . . .

BOOKS BY STUART WOODS

THE SHORT
FOREVER

S T U A R T   W O O D S

A SIGNET BOOK

SIGNET
Published by New American Library, a division of
Penguin Putnam Inc., 375 Hudson Street,
New York, New York 10014, U.S.A.
Penguin Books Ltd, 80 Strand,
London WC2R 0RL, England
Penguin Books Australia Ltd, 250 Camberwell Road,
Camberwell, Victoria 3124, Australia
Penguin Books Canada Ltd, 10 Alcorn Avenue,
Toronto, Ontario, Canada M4V 3B2
Penguin Books (N.Z.) Ltd, 182–190 Wairau Road,
Auckland 10, New Zealand

Penguin Books Ltd, Registered Offices:
Harmondsworth, Middlesex, England

Published by Signet, an imprint of New American Library,
a division of Penguin Putnam Inc. Previously published in a Putnam edition.

First Signet Printing, February 2003
10 9 8 7 6 5 4

THIS BOOK IS FOR
ROBERT TOWBIN

1

ELAINE'S, LATE.

Stone Barrington sipped his third Wild Turkey and resisted the basket of hot sourdough bread that the waiter had just placed on the table. Callie was to have been there an hour and a half ago, and he was very, very hungry. She'd called from the airport to say that she was on the ground and on her way, but that had been an hour ago. It just didn't take that long to get to Elaine's from Teterboro Airport, where her boss's jet landed. He glanced at his watch: He'd give her another three minutes, and then he was ordering.

He had been looking forward to seeing her. They'd spent some very pleasant time together in Palm Beach a few months before, on the yacht of his client Thad Shames. She was Shames's majordomo—assistant, cook, social secretary, whatever he needed—and she moved when Shames moved, back and forth between Palm Beach and New York. In New York, she had been living with Stone, and he missed her when she was away.

"Give me a menu," Stone said to Michael, the headwaiter.

"Giving up on her?" Michael asked.

"I am. If I drink any more without some food in my

stomach, you're going to have to send me home in a wheelbarrow."

Michael laughed and placed a menu before him. "Dino's not coming?"

"He should be here in a while; he said he had to work late." He opened the menu, and Michael stood ready, pad in hand. When Stone was this hungry, everything looked good. He'd meant to have fish; he'd gained three pounds, and he needed to get it off, but now he was too hungry. "I'll have a Caesar salad and the osso buco," he said, "and a bottle of the Amerone."

Michael jotted down the order, and as he reached for the menu, Stone looked up to see Callie breezing through the front door. He rose to meet her. She looked wonderful, as usual, in an Armani pantsuit. She gave him a short, dry kiss and sat down.

"I'd given up on you," Stone said. "I just ordered."

Michael handed her a menu, but she handed it back. "I'm sorry, I can't stay for dinner," she said.

Stone looked at her, stupefied. She had kept him waiting for an hour and a half, and now she wasn't going to have dinner?

"Would you like a drink, Callie?" Michael asked.

She shook her head. "No time, Michael."

"You still want dinner, Stone?"

"Yes, please," Stone replied.

Michael retreated.

"So?" Stone asked.

"So what?" Callie replied.

"Is there something you want to tell me?" He wanted an apology and an explanation, but he got neither.

"Stone," Callie said, looking at the tablecloth and playing with a matchbook. She didn't continue.

"I'm right here," he replied. "Have been, for an hour and a half."

"God, this is hard," she said.

"Maybe a drink would help."

"No, I don't have the time."

"Where do you have to be at this hour?" he asked.

"Back in Palm Beach."

Stone wasn't terribly surprised. Thad Shames, a computer software billionaire, had a peripatetic lifestyle, and Callie was, after all, at his beck and call.

"First of all, I'm sorry I'm late," she said. "I had to go by the house and pick up some things."

Stone looked around; she wasn't carrying anything.

"They're in the car," she said.

"What did you have to pick up?" he asked.

"Some things. *My* things."

Stone blinked. "Are you going somewhere?"

"Back to Palm Beach. I told you."

Stone was baffled. "Callie . . ."

She took a deep breath and interrupted him. "Thad and I are getting married this weekend."

Stone was drinking his bourbon, and he choked on it.

"I know you didn't expect this," she said. "For that matter, neither did I. It's just happened the past couple of weeks." She had been gone for two weeks on this last trip.

Stone recovered his voice. "Are you perfectly serious about this?"

"Perfectly, and I'd appreciate it if you didn't try to talk me out of it."

That was exactly what he wanted to try. "I wouldn't dream of it," he said. "If that's what you want."

"It's good, Stone. It isn't like with you and me, but that could never last."

"Why not?" Stone demanded, stung.

"Oh, it's been great. I arrive in town, move in with you; we go to Elaine's and the theater, and around. We fuck our brains out for a week or two, then I go back."

That was exactly what they did, he reflected, but he wasn't going to admit it. "I thought we had more than that going," he said.

"Oh, men always think that," she said, exasperated. "There are things Thad can give me, things I need, things you can't . . ." She left it hanging.

"Can't afford?" he asked. "I live pretty well. Of course, I'm not worth five billion dollars, but I didn't think Thad was, anymore, not after his new stock offering collapsed, and with the way the market has been."

"It's true," she said. "Thad was hurt badly. Now he's only worth three billion."

"What a blow," Stone said.

"It's not the money," she said. "All right, maybe that's part of it. God knows, I'll never have to draw another anxious breath."

"Not about money, anyway."

"Won't you try and understand?"

"What is there to understand? I'm out, Thad's in. It's your life; I can't tell you how to live it."

"If only you'd . . ." She stopped.

Stone didn't want to hear the rest, anyway. "I think it's a little late for 'if only,'" he said. "Clearly, you've thought this out, I'm not going to try to talk you out of it."

"Thank God for that," she muttered, half to herself.

They sat silently for a moment, then, without another word, Callie got up and headed for the door, nearly knocking down Dino, who had chosen that moment to walk in.

Dino turned and watched her rush out the door, then he walked over to Stone's table and sat down. Dino Bacchetti had been Stone's partner when he was still on the NYPD; now he ran the detective squad at the Nineteenth Precinct. "So," he said, "I see you managed to fuck up another relationship."

"Jesus, Dino, I didn't do anything," Stone said.

Dino motioned to Michael for a drink. "That's usually the problem," he said. The drink was placed before him, and he sipped it.

"You want some dinner, Dino?" Michael asked.

"Whatever he's having," Dino replied.

"Caesar salad and the osso buco?"

"Good." He turned to Stone. "After a while, women *expect* you to do something."

"She's marrying Thad Shames."

Dino's eyebrows shot up. "No shit? Well, I'll admit, I didn't see *that* one coming. I guess Thad isn't broke yet."

"Not yet, but he's only worth three billion now."

"Poor guy; couple months, he'll be living on the street. Still, he got the girl."

"Don't rub it in."

"It's what I do," Dino explained.

Stone's cellphone, clipped to his belt, began to vibrate. "Now what?" he said to nobody in particular. "Hello?"

"Stone, it's Bill Eggers." Bill was the managing partner of Woodman & Weld, the prestigious law firm for which Stone did unprestigious jobs.

"Yeah, Bill."

"You sound down."

"Just tired; what's up?"

"You got anything heavy on your plate right now?"

"Nothing much."

"Good; there's a guy coming to see you tomorrow morning at nine, with some work. Do whatever he says."

"Suppose he wants me to kill somebody."

"If this guy wanted somebody killed, he'd do it himself. His name is John Bartholomew, and he's major, in his way."

"I'll be glad to see him."

"You got a passport?"

"Yes." Not that he'd used it for a long time.

"Good. You're going to need it." Eggers hung up.

Elaine came over and pulled up a chair. "Callie left in a hurry," she said. "I guess you fucked it up again."

"Don't *you* start," Stone said.

2

STONE WOKE UP HUNGOVER. HE SHOULDN'T drink that much so close to bedtime, he reflected, and resolved, once again, not to do it again. It was half past eight, and this guy Bartholomew was coming at nine; no time for breakfast. He showered and shaved and got into a suit, then went down to his office on the ground floor.

The ground floor, except for the garage, had been a dentist's office when Stone's great-aunt had still owned the house. After Stone inherited the place and renovated it, mostly with the sweat of his own brow, he turned the dentist's office into his own. His secretary, Joan Robertson, worked at the front of the house, then came a couple of small rooms for supplies and the copying machine, then his own office, a pleasant room at the back of the house, looking out into the gardens of Turtle Bay, a collection of townhouses in the East Forties that opened onto a common garden. Only the burglar bars spoiled the view.

Stone heard the clicking of computer keys stop, and Joan came back to his office. "You're in early," she said.

"What do you mean?" Stone asked, with mock offense. "It's nearly nine o'clock."

"That's what I mean. I'll bet you didn't have time for breakfast."

"You got some coffee on?"

"I'll get you a cup," she said.

"There's some guy named John Bartholomew coming in at nine," he said. "Bill Eggers sent him."

"I'll show him in when he arrives," she said.

Stone shuffled listlessly through the files on his desktop. He hadn't lied when he'd told Eggers that he wasn't busy.

Joan came back with the coffee. He was grateful that her taste in beans ran with his, that she liked the strong, dark stuff that usually got made into espresso. "Did Callie get in last night?" she asked.

"She got in, then she got out."

"Out? You mean, *out*?"

"I do. She's marrying Thad Shames this weekend."

"Good God! I'm shocked!"

"So was I, to tell the truth."

"You let another one get away."

"Joan . . ."

She threw her hands up defensively. "Sorry, it's none of my business. You want me to send a wedding gift?"

Stone brightened. "Good idea. Go find the ugliest piece of sterling that Tiffany's makes and send it to them in Palm Beach with a truly sincere card."

The doorbell rang. "There's your appointment," she said. She left and returned a moment later with a tall, heavyset man in his fifties who, in his youth, had probably played college football.

"I'm Stone Barrington," Stone said, rising and offering his hand.

"John Bartholomew," the man replied, shaking it.

Stone waved him to a chair. "Bill Eggers called last night."

"Did he give you any details?"

"No."

Joan brought in another cup of coffee on a silver tray and offered it to Bartholomew, who had, apparently, placed his order with her on arrival.

Bartholomew sipped it. "Damned fine coffee," he said.

There was something vaguely British about him, Stone thought, perhaps more than just the hand-tailored suit. "Thank you. We drink it strong around here."

"The way I like it," the big man replied. "Never could understand that decaf crap. Like drinking non-alcoholic booze. Why bother?"

Stone nodded and sipped his own coffee.

"We don't have much time, Mr. Barrington, so I'll come to the point. I have a niece, my dead sister's only child, name of Erica Burroughs." He spelled the name. "She's twenty, dropped out of Mount Holyoke, involved with a young man named Lance Cabot."

"Of the Massachusetts Cabots?"

"He'd like people to think so, I'm sure, but no, no relation at all; doesn't even know them; I checked. Young Mr. Cabot, I'm reliably informed, earns his living by smuggling quantities of cocaine across international borders. Quantities small enough to conceal on his person or in his luggage, but large enough to bring him an income, you follow?"

"I follow."

"I'm very much afraid that Erica, besotted as she is, may be assisting him in his endeavors, and I don't want to see her end up in a British prison."

"She's in Britain?"

Bartholomew nodded. "London, living with Mr. Cabot, quite fancily, in a rented mews house in Mayfair." He opened a briefcase and handed Stone a file with a few sheets of paper inside. "Don't bother reading this now, there isn't time, but it contains everything I've been able to learn about Cabot, and something about Erica, as well. What I'd like you to do is to go to London, persuade Erica to come back to New York with you, and, if it's possible without implicating Erica, get young Mr. Cabot arrested. I'd like him in a place where he can't get to Erica. For as long as possible, it goes without saying."

"I see."

"Will you undertake this task? You'll be very well paid, I assure you, and you will lack for no comfort while traveling."

Stone didn't have to think long, and mostly what he thought about was Sarah Buckminster, another relationship he'd managed to fuck up, though it wasn't really his fault. "I will, Mr. Bartholomew, but you must understand that I will be pretty much limited to whatever persuasion I can muster, within the law, and whatever influence with the authorities I can scrape up. I won't kidnap your niece, and I won't harm Cabot, beyond whatever justice I can seek for him, based on crimes that are real and not imagined."

"I understand perfectly, Mr. Barrington. I'm well aware that you are a respectable attorney and not a thug for hire. I'm also informed, by a number of people, Samuel Bernard among them, that you are a resourceful man and that your background as a police detective gives you entrée to certain places."

"Sometimes," Stone admitted, "but not always. There are limits to what an ex-policeman can do."

"I understand. I simply want you to do whatever you can."

"On that basis, I'll go," Stone said. "I'll ask my secretary to book me on a flight this evening."

"That won't be necessary," Bartholomew said, digging into his briefcase and coming up with an envelope secured with a rubber band. He tossed it onto Stone's desk. "You're booked on a two P.M. flight to London, and I've reserved accommodation for you at the Connaught hotel. There's five thousand pounds sterling in the envelope and the name of a man at Coutts Bank in The Strand who will provide you with more, should you need it. Please enjoy whatever food, drink, and guests you may wish to have at the Connaught; the bill will come to me, and you need not keep track of your expenses."

"That's very generous," Stone replied.

"All the relevant addresses and phone numbers are in the file, as is my card. Call me should you need advice or assistance of any sort. I understand that this may take a week or two, or even longer, so don't feel pressed for time. I want this done in the best way possible, regardless of time or cost." He reached into his briefcase, came up with a box, and placed it on Stone's desk. "This is a satellite telephone that will work anywhere in Britain. Please use it to contact me when necessary; my number is programmed into the first digit. All you do is press one and hold it, and I'll be on the other end. Please keep it with you at all times, in case I should wish to contact you."

"All right."

Bartholomew stood up. "Now, I must hurry to an appointment, and you have a flight to catch." He shook hands with Stone, closed his briefcase, and marched out of the office, a man in a hurry.

3

STONE WENT UPSTAIRS AND STARTED
packing. He had no real idea what clothes he might
need, so he overpacked, as he often did, taking three
cases. He was gathering his toiletries when the phone
rang.

"Hello?"

"It's Dino. You all right? You got pretty snockered
last night."

"Yes, I did, but I'm bearing up. In fact, I'm off to
London in a couple of hours."

"For what?"

"Some client of Woodman and Weld has a niece
who's about to get herself in trouble in London, and
I'm supposed to bring her back."

"Who's the client?"

"A man named John Bartholomew." Stone dug in
the file for Bartholomew's card. It bore only a phone
number and a cellphone number. "Sorry, I thought I
had a business card, but it's only a number."

"Anything I can do to help?"

"Yes, you can see if a man named Lance Cabot has a
sheet."

"Just a minute," Dino said.

Stone could hear computer keys clicking.

"Nope, nothing on him, either in our computer or the federal database."

"Too bad, I was hoping for some ammunition. You know anybody at Scotland Yard?"

"Yeah, I think so; let me check the Rolodex." Another pause. "Here we go: Evelyn, with a long E, Throckmorton."

"You're kidding."

"I swear to God, that's his name, and don't forget the long E, otherwise it's a girl's name. He's in that Special Branch thing, with a rank of detective inspector. He was over here last year, looking for an Irish terrorist, and he needed an Italian cop for some help, since the Irish cops wouldn't have anything to do with him."

"Is that what he does? Chase terrorists?"

"Beats me; I didn't get to know him that well, but he owes me a favor, so I'll call him for you."

"Thanks, I'd appreciate that."

"How you feeling about Callie this morning?"

"Okay, though you and Elaine were no help at all."

"I seem to recall there's a lady in London called Sarah Buckminster."

"That crossed my mind."

"She might be just the thing to help you get over Callie."

"I'm already over Callie, but what the hell?"

"Okay, pal, have a good trip. Call me if you get in over your head."

"Yeah, sure."

"I'm always having to pull you out of the shit, you know. What makes you think this trip will be any different?"

"I'll try to get through it without needing rescuing."

"Oh, it's never any bother; you always get into such

interesting shit. Makes my humdrum life just a little more exciting. See ya." Dino hung up.

Stone drove himself to Kennedy Airport while Joan sat in the passenger seat, taking notes on what to do while he was gone. She dropped him at the first-class entrance at British Airways, gave him a peck on the cheek, and drove off in his car. A porter took his luggage into the terminal and left him at the check-in counter.

A young woman looked at his ticket. "I'm sorry, sir, this is the wrong counter."

Stone was annoyed. After Bartholomew's seeming generosity, he'd expected to be in first class.

"You're just down there," she said, pointing to the Concorde check-in.

What a nice man Bartholomew was, Stone thought.

The cabin was tubelike, much smaller than he'd expected, and the seats were no larger than business class, but since the flight was only three hours, it hardly mattered. By the time he'd had a late lunch and read a couple of magazines, they were at Heathrow. He stood in line for immigration, then presented his passport.

"Good evening, Mr. Barrington. Welcome to Britain," the young female officer said. "Are you here on business or pleasure?"

"Pleasure," Stone said. "A little vacation."

"And how long do you plan to stay?"

"Somewhere between a few days and a couple of weeks, I suppose."

"And are you aware that your passport expires the day after tomorrow?"

He was not. "I'm sorry, I didn't notice."

She handed it back to him. "You can renew it at the American Embassy in Grosvenor Square. Enjoy your stay."

Stone pocketed his passport. "Thank you." He followed the signs toward baggage claim and retrieved his cases.

Stone made a point of dressing well when traveling; it seemed to smooth the way, somehow, and British customs was no exception. While a slovenly young man ahead of him had his bags searched, Stone walked through the "nothing to declare" gate and found himself staring at a man in a uniform holding up a sign with his name on it.

"I'm Mr. Barrington," he said to the man.

The man took Stone's luggage cart. "Please follow me, sir."

Stone followed him to a large Mercedes, and a moment later they were on their way into central London. Stone reset his watch, noting that it was nearly eleven P.M., London time, and he was not at all tired or sleepy.

The Connaught was small by hotel standards, discreet, and elegant. At the front desk, he merely signed a check-in form; there were no other formalities.

"I believe the concierge has a message for you, Mr. Barrington," the young man at the desk said. "Just behind you."

"Mr. Barrington?" the concierge said, before Stone had barely turned. "Mr. Bartholomew rang and said that he had arranged privileges for you at these places." He handed Stone a sheet of paper.

Annabel's, Harry's Bar, and the Garrick Club, Stone read. "Thank you," he said to the concierge. "Where would you suggest I go for some dinner at this hour?"

"Well, sir, our restaurant has already closed, and

room service would only have sandwiches this late. I'd suggest Annabel's; it's a short walk, and they go on quite late there." He gave Stone directions. "If you'd like to go straightaway, the porter will be glad to unpack for you."

"Thank you, I will," Stone said. Following the directions, he left the hotel and walked down Mount Street toward Berkeley Square, then turned right. The night was cool and clear, belying what he'd heard about London weather. He crossed a street and followed an iron railing to an awning over a basement entrance, then walked downstairs. He was greeted by a doorman who clearly didn't recognize him, but as soon as he gave his name he was ushered down a hallway.

"Would you like to go straight into the dining room, sir, or would you prefer to have a drink first?" the man asked.

They had entered a beautifully decorated lounge and bar area. "I'd like a drink first," Stone said. He was shown to a comfortable sofa under a very good oil of a dog and her puppies, and he ordered a glass of champagne. He looked around. There were many good pictures and an extremely well-dressed crowd. The women were beautiful in London, he reflected.

As he sipped his champagne, a very handsome couple entered the bar, both obviously a little drunk. They were seated on the opposite wall, and they were both quite beautiful. The girl was tall and willowy, wearing a very short dress, and the young man wore a rakishly cut suit that had obviously not come off the rack. They nuzzled and giggled, and they attracted the attention of other patrons with their behavior.

Stone watched as a barman approached them, and his voice was mildly disapproving. "Good evening, Mr. Cabot," Stone heard him say.

4

STONE WAS SEATED IN A DIMLY LIT dining room with a glassed-off dance floor at one end, and Lance Cabot and Erica Burroughs were seated a few tables away. Although they were drinking champagne with their dinner, they didn't seem to get any drunker.

It was five hours earlier in New York, and Stone's stomach had not caught up with the time change, so he wanted something light. He handed the menu back to the waiter. "May I just have some scrambled eggs with smoked salmon and half a bottle of champagne? You choose the wine."

"Of course, Mr. Barrington," the man said.

Stone finished his dinner before Cabot and Burroughs did. He thought of following them when they left, but he knew where to find them, and, in spite of the time change, he was beginning to believe his wristwatch. He left Annabel's and walked back to the Connaught through the beautiful clear night. A moon had risen, and Berkeley Square was almost theatrically lit, its tall plane trees casting sharp shadows on the grass.

At the hotel, the night clerk insisted on showing him to his room. He found himself in a very pleasant suite, and his clothes had been put away. He soaked in a hot tub for a while until he felt sleepy, then he got into a nightshirt and fell into bed.

It was nearly ten A.M. when he woke, and as he reached for the telephone to order breakfast, he noticed a small electrical box on the side table, displaying buttons for a maid, a valet, and a waiter. He pressed the waiter button, and a moment later, there was a sharp, metallic rap on his door.

"Come in."

A waiter let himself into the room. "Good morning, Mr. Barrington. May I get you some breakfast?"

"Yes, please."

"What would you like?"

There was apparently no menu. "Scrambled eggs, toast, a kipper, orange juice, and coffee, please." He hadn't had a kipper in many years, but he remembered the smoked-fish flavor.

"Right away, sir." The waiter disappeared, to return a few minutes later, rolling a beautifully set tray table.

I'm going to like this hotel, Stone thought, as he dug into his breakfast.

Showered, shaved, and dressed, he presented himself at the concierge's desk. "Can you direct me to the American Embassy?" he asked.

The concierge produced a map. "We're here, and the embassy is just there," he said, "in Grosvenor Square. A three-minute walk."

"And I have to get a passport photo taken."

The concierge pointed to a corner across from the embassy. "There's a chemist's shop there, and they do

American passport photographs, which are a different size from the British ones."

"Good. Now, can you tell me how to find Farm Street?" he asked the man.

The concierge pointed to a spot on the map. "It's quite near, Mr. Barrington; a five-minute walk. Would you like to borrow an umbrella?"

Stone looked toward the door. "It's raining?"

"Happens often in London, sir."

Stone accepted the umbrella and walked outside. A steady rain was falling.

A top-hatted doorman greeted him. "Good morning, sir; taxi?"

"Yes, please." The hell with the walk, in this weather.

The doorman summoned a taxi from a rank across the street, and Stone got into it. "Farm Street," he said.

"Any particular number, sir?" the cabbie asked.

"I want to take a look at a house called Merryvale, but don't stop, just drive slowly past."

"Righto, sir." The cabbie drove off, made a couple of turns, and two minutes later they were in Farm Street, which turned out to be a mews behind Annabel's.

"Here we are, sir," the cabbie said, as he drove slowly past a beautiful little house with flowers growing from window boxes on each of its three floors. "Merryvale."

A small sign on the front door proclaimed as much. Mr. Cabot has elegant tastes, Stone thought. "What would you think it would cost to rent that house?" Stone asked the driver.

"Thousand quid a week, easy," the cabbie replied. "You want me to take you to an estate agent's in the neighborhood?"

Stone thought. He wasn't going to stand conspicuously in the rain in this little mews, waiting for Cabot or Burroughs to emerge. He'd go renew his passport and return later. "Make a U-turn at the end of the street, and let's drive past again," he said.

"Righto," the cabbie said. He drove to the end of the mews and made an amazingly tight U-turn.

As he did, Stone saw a taxi pull up to Merryvale and honk its horn. "Stop here for a minute," he said. A moment later, Erica Burroughs came out of the house, locked the door behind her, and, holding an umbrella over her head, got into the waiting taxi, which immediately drove away. "Follow that cab," Stone said.

The driver laughed. "Twenty-one years I've been driving a cab," he said, "and it's the first time anybody ever said that to me." He drove off in pursuit of Erica's taxi.

Stone watched the city go past his cab window. Shortly, they were in Park Lane, then they turned into Hyde Park. By what seemed to be a rather convoluted route, Erica's taxi took her to Harrod's. She got out of the cab, paid the driver, and ran inside.

Stone was not far behind her. He followed as she went on what seemed to be an extensive but unplanned shopping trip. She wandered through department after department of the huge store, looking at this and that, but the only thing she bought was a pen, in Stationery.

He followed her up the escalator into the book department, where she browsed and bought a novel, then back downstairs into the food halls, which were the most spectacular supermarket Stone had ever seen. She bought a few pieces of fruit, then, suddenly, she turned and came back toward Stone, who was pretending to look at the smoked fish.

She stopped next to him and looked at the fish, too, then turned to him and spoke. "Are you following me?" she asked.

Stone was startled, but there was a small smile on her face. "Of course," he said. "And nobody would blame me."

She laughed. "You were at Annabel's last night, weren't you?"

"I was."

"Were you following me then, too?"

"You'll recall I got there ahead of you."

"And how long have you been following me this morning?"

"Since you left the taxi," he said. "I happened to be right behind you, in another cab."

"Coming from where?"

"The Connaught."

She stuck out her hand. "I'm Erica Burroughs," she said.

Stone took her hand; it was cool and dry. "I'm Stone Barrington."

"What a nice name; it sounds like an investment bank."

"You're not the first to tell me that."

"Since you're at the Connaught, I assume you don't live in London."

"No, New York. I'm just visiting."

"Business or pleasure?"

"Pleasure, at the moment."

She laughed. "You're very flattering, but I must tell you, I'm spoken for."

"I'm desolated."

"However, I'm hungry, standing amidst all this food, and if you're hungry, too, you can buy me lunch."

"I'd be delighted," Stone said, and he was, more than she knew. She was making his job all too easy.

"Follow me," she said. She marched off toward a door, and a moment later they were in another taxi. "The Grenadier, in Wilton Row," she told the driver.

"I take it you live in London?" Stone asked.

"Yes, but only for a few weeks."

"Do you work?"

"Not at the moment; how about you?"

"I'm an attorney."

"With a New York firm?"

"I'm of counsel to Woodman and Weld."

"I know that name; someone there handled my father's estate."

They drove through winding back streets, across Sloane Street, and into Wilton Crescent, a beautiful half-circle of handsome houses, all made of the same stone, then they turned into a mews. At the end, the cab stopped, and they got out. The rain had abated, though it was still cloudy. Stone paid the taxi, then followed Erica up a short flight of stairs and into an atmospheric little pub.

"We'll sit at the bar," she said, grabbing stools for them. "The bar food's the best."

They helped themselves to sausages, Cornish pasties, and cole slaw from a little buffet, then sat down again.

"I'll have a pint of bitter," she said to the bartender.

"Two," Stone said.

They sipped the ale and ate, not talking much. When they had finished their food, Erica took a sip of her bitter.

"Now," she said, "tell me all about you."

"Born and bred in New York, to parents who were both from western Massachusetts; attended the public schools, NYU, then NYU Law School. The summer before my senior year I spent riding around the city in police cars, part of a law school program to give us a look at real life, and I found I liked it, so I joined the NYPD. I spent fourteen years there, finishing up as a homicide detective, then at the invitation of an old law school friend at Woodman and Weld, I finally took the bar exam and went to work for them."

"You were a little old to be an associate, weren't you?"

"I wasn't an associate; I've never even had an office there. I keep an office in my home, and I work on whatever cases Woodman and Weld don't want to handle themselves. It's interesting work. Now, what about you?"

"Born and raised in Greenwich, Connecticut, went to school there, then Mount Holyoke, graduated last spring. Worked at Sotheby's for a while, learning to appraise art and helping with the auctions, then I got a better offer."

This didn't quite jibe with the file on Erica, he thought. "From whom?"

"From my fella. You saw him last night; his name is Lance Cabot."

"One of the Boston Cabots?"

She shook her head. "Denies all knowledge of them. He's from California, but his family came from Canada, not over on the Mayflower."

"And what kind of offer did Lance make you?"

"A thoroughly indecent one, thank you, and I accepted with alacrity. I've been living with him for the better part of a year."

"What does Lance do?"

"He's an independent business consultant, on both sides of the Atlantic."

Yeah, I'll bet, Stone thought. "Wait a minute," he said, "Burroughs, Greenwich; do you have an uncle named John Bartholomew?"

She shook her head. "Nope. No uncles at all; both my parents were only children. Why do you ask?"

"Oh, forget it; someone I know said he had a niece from Greenwich, and I thought the name was Burroughs."

"Not this Burroughs," she said.

Very strange, he thought. "How old are you?" he asked.

"Do you always ask women their age?"

"Always. Their age isn't important; it's whether they'll tell you that's important."

"I'm twenty-two and a half," she said. "And now, shall I tell you why I picked you up at Harrod's?"

"Is that what you did?"

"Didn't you notice? Your following me made it very easy."

"All right, tell me."

"As I told you, I'm spoken for, but I have a very nice girlfriend who's not, and she's on the other side of thirty, which I should think would appeal to you more than a twenty-two-and-a-half-year-old."

"Is she as beautiful as you?"

"Though it pains me to say it, she is more beautiful than I."

"I would like very much to meet her."

"You free this evening?"

"I am, as it happens."

"Suppose we meet you in the Connaught bar at eight o'clock?"

"I'll be there."

"Wear a suit."

"Will do."

"And now," she said, gathering her packages together, "I must run. You stay and finish your bitter; I'm walking from here; it's quite nearby." She hopped off the stool and pecked Stone on the cheek. "Bye-bye." And she was gone.

Stone sipped the now-warm ale and wondered what the hell was going on with John Bartholomew and his "niece."

5

STONE LEFT THE GRENADIER AND
walked back up the mews to Wilton Crescent. No cabs.
He walked a bit farther and found himself at the Berkeley
Hotel, where the doorman found him a taxi.

"Where to, guv?" the cabbie asked.

"There's a chemist's shop across from the American
Embassy. You know it?"

"I do." He drove away. Ten minutes later, Stone was
having his photograph taken by a man with a large
studio Polaroid camera, which took four shots simultaneously. He paid for the photos and walked across
the street to the embassy. As he climbed the steps outside, he saw a familiar-looking form perhaps twenty
yards ahead of him. The man went into the embassy,
and Stone quickly followed.

As he entered the main door, he saw the man get onto
an elevator. Although he got only a glimpse, it seemed
to be John Bartholomew. He started for the elevator, but
a uniformed U.S. marine stepped in front of him.

"You'll have to check in at the desk," the marine
said, pointing to a window surrounded by what appeared to be armored glass.

"Do you know the man who just passed?" Stone
asked. "He got onto the elevator."

"I'm sorry, sir, I didn't notice."

"Can you tell me where to get my passport renewed?"

"Yes, sir. You go out the main door, turn left, walk around the corner to your left, and the passport office is right there."

Stone went to the window first. "Can you tell me if there's a Mr. John Bartholomew in the building?" he said to the woman behind the glass. "I think I just saw him go up in an elevator."

The woman looked at a computer screen that Stone couldn't see, typed something, and turned back to him. "I'm afraid we don't have a Bartholomew working here," she said. She consulted what appeared to be a sign-in sheet. "And no one by that name has entered the building this morning."

"Thank you," Stone said. He wished he could have read the sign-in sheet. He followed the marine's instructions and found the passport office. He filled out a form, gave it and two photos to the clerk, and was told to wait.

"How long should it take?" he asked.

"We're not very busy; perhaps twenty minutes," the clerk replied.

He took a seat and found a magazine.

In a room several floors higher in the embassy, two men studied a television monitor set into a wall with many other monitors.

"Is that he?" one asked.

"Yes, but I think it's all right," the other replied. "I think he's just here to renew his passport."

Stone heard his name called. He was given a form to take to the cashier, where he paid the fee, then returned and collected his new passport. He reflected that what had taken less than half an hour in London would have taken most of a day in New York.

Outside, he couldn't find a cab, so he began to walk back toward the Connaught. He walked down South Audley Street and turned left onto Mount Street. He had gone only a few steps when he saw a familiar name on a shop window across the street. HAYWARD, the gilt lettering said. He crossed the street and entered the shop, shaking his wet umbrella behind him at the door.

A large, well-dressed man got up from a couch. "I recognize the suit, but not the man in it," he said. "I'm Doug Hayward." He offered his hand.

"My name is Stone Barrington, and you're quite right; the suit belonged to Vance Calder. After his death, his wife, who is an old friend, sent all his suits to me. There were twenty of them."

"The cost of alterations must have been fierce," Hayward said.

"They didn't need altering; his clothes fit me perfectly."

"Then I don't suppose I can sell you a suit," Hayward said, laughing.

"I could use a couple of tweed jackets," Stone replied, "and a raincoat. I foolishly didn't bring one."

"Have a look at the rack of raincoats over there, and I'll get some swatches." Hayward departed toward the rear of the shop, where men were cutting cloth from bolts of fabric.

Stone found a handsome raincoat and an umbrella, then he sat down and went through the swatches. A few minutes later, he had been measured.

"How is Arrington?" Hayward asked.

"I saw her in Palm Beach this past winter, and she was well; I haven't spoken to her since then."

"I was very sorry to hear of Vance's death. Did they ever convict anyone of the murder?"

"A woman friend of his was charged and tried, but acquitted. If she really was innocent, then I think it will remain unsolved."

"Very strange. I liked Vance, and, of course, he was a very good customer." Hayward handed him his receipt. "But I suppose he's bequeathed you to me."

Stone laughed. "First time I've ever been a bequest." He shook hands with Hayward, put on his new raincoat, picked up his new umbrella and the Connaught's as well, and walked outside into a bright, sunshiny day. "Not a cloud in the sky," he said aloud, looking around him. Suddenly, he felt exhausted. Jet lag had crept up on him, and all he wanted was a bed. He turned and walked the half-block to the Connaught, went upstairs, undressed, and, leaving a wake-up call for seven, climbed into bed and slept.

The two men in the embassy sat across a desk from each other.

"You really think this can work?" one asked.

"I checked him out very carefully," the other replied. "He's perfect for us."

"If he can make it work."

"Let's give him some time and see. If he can do it, he'll save us a great deal of time and effort and, possibly, ah, embarrassment."

The first man sighed. "I hope you're right."

6

STONE ARRIVED AT THE CONNAUGHT
bar downstairs promptly at eight o'clock, showered,
shaved, and dressed in a freshly pressed, chalk-striped
blue suit. The nap had cleared his head, and he was
sure that, with one more good night's sleep, he would
be over the jet lag. The bar consisted of two oak-pan-
eled rooms filled with comfortable sofas and chairs,
one room with a small bar at one end. He had only just
sat down when his dining companions arrived.

Erica had not lied; her friend was even more beautiful than she. "Stone," Erica said, "may I introduce my
sister, Monica? And this is Lance Cabot."

Stone shook hands all around. Monica Burroughs
was perhaps five-ten, nearly as slim as Erica, and had
deep auburn hair and green eyes. "I'm very pleased to
meet you," he said, and he was not lying.

"Shall we have some champagne?" Lance asked. His
voice was deep, and he seemed to have a mid-Atlantic
accent. A waiter appeared and took the order. A moment later, they were sipping Krug '66.

"I'm astonished to see this on a wine list," Stone said.

"It isn't on the list," Lance replied. "It's a secret, and
I'm sure they have only a few bottles left. Erica tells me
you're a lawyer."

"That's correct."

"And with Woodman and Weld?"

"I'm of counsel to the firm."

"Not a partner?"

"No, most of my work for them is done outside the firm."

Lance regarded him gravely. "It sounds as though you're as much of a secret at Woodman and Weld as this wine is at the Connaught."

"I'm not quite a secret," Stone said. "Like the champagne, I'm available on request."

"Tell me, Stone," Lance continued, "have you ever done government work of any kind?"

"I worked for the government of New York City as a police officer for many years."

"Did you? Erica didn't mention that. What sort of police officer?"

"Every sort, at one time or another. I began as a patrolman and finished as a homicide detective."

"Finished rather young, didn't you?"

"I was retired for medical reasons."

"You look reasonably fit."

"I took a bullet in the knee."

"That's very romantic."

"I can assure you that, at the time, it was not in the least romantic, only painful." Lance was grilling him, and Stone was determined to be polite about it.

"Lance," Erica said, "you're hogging Stone; we'd like to talk to him, too."

Monica spoke up, and her accent was more than mid-Atlantic; it was quite English. "How does one recover from a bullet in the knee?" she asked, and she seemed fascinated.

"With surgery and therapy," Stone said. "It doesn't bother me much anymore. If it becomes troublesome again, I can have it replaced."

"Ah, yes," Monica said, "the modular approach to

human anatomy. I suppose Lance will be having a new liver soon."

Stone and Erica laughed; Lance pretended to.

"And what do you do, Monica?" Stone asked.

"I have an art gallery, in Bruton Street."

"Did you study art somewhere?"

"At Mount Holyoke, like Erica, only a few years ahead of her. I got a master's in art history there, then went to work for Sotheby's. Erica followed in my footsteps, but she lasted only until Lance spirited her away."

"I heard that story at lunch," Stone said. "How long have you lived in London?"

"Nearly ten years."

Lance spoke up. "Long enough to acquire a pretentious accent."

Monica and Erica both shot him searing glances. "Do you really find my accent pretentious, Lance?" Monica asked.

"Oh, very."

"It seems that every time I speak to you, your accent has traveled a hundred miles farther to the east," she said dryly.

Lance flushed a little.

Stone began to feel that all was not entirely well between Monica and Lance, or maybe, between Lance and anybody. "Lance, what made you ask if I'd done government work?"

"Just a hunch," Lance said. "Perhaps there's something a little bureaucratic about you."

Stone laughed. "When I was on the public payroll, hardly anybody thought I was bureaucratic enough. I wasn't thought of as a team player by the NYPD."

"And why ever not?" Lance drawled.

"Because I wasn't, I suppose. I tended to go my own

way, something that's never appreciated in large organizations."

"I know what you mean," Lance said.

"Oh? Are you employed by a large organization?"

"No, but I've had a taste of it," Lance replied.

"And, I take it, you didn't like the taste?"

"You might say that."

"What, exactly, do you do?" Stone asked.

"I consult," Lance replied.

"With whom do you consult, and about what?" Stone asked, glad to be the griller instead of the grillee.

"With a number of people about a number of things," Lance replied. "Monica, will you pass the crisps, please?" Monica slid the little bowl of homemade potato chips toward him. He turned to Erica. "So, how was shopping today? Find anything?"

"Only a pen and some fruit," Erica replied.

Stone was about to ignore the swift change of subject and return to the grilling when Lance looked at his watch.

"I think we'd better go along to dinner," he said.

Everyone began to move toward the door, and Stone gave the waiter his room number for the check. He wondered if Bartholomew would bridle at the appearance of a Krug '66 on the bill.

Outside, they turned right into Mount Street, and Stone fell into step with Monica, behind Lance and Erica.

"We're going to Harry's Bar," she said. "It's just around the corner." She dropped back a few paces behind her sister and Lance. "It's nice to see somebody turning the tables on Lance," she said. "He can be awful."

"It's all right; I don't have anything to hide," Stone said.

"Really? How boring."

Stone laughed. "I'm afraid I'm an open book, as boring as that may be. How about you?"

"I have a great many secrets," Monica replied, "and you will have to ply me with a great deal of champagne and work very hard to learn what they are."

"I'll look forward to it," Stone said, taking her arm.

They walked past the Hayward shop, turned left, and walked another few yards until they came to an unmarked door. Lance rang a bell, and a moment later a woman in what appeared to be a maid's uniform let them in.

"Have you been here?" Monica asked Stone.

"No, in fact it's been many years since I've been in London, so there are a lot of places I haven't been. Just about everywhere, in fact."

"You'll like it; the food is marvelous."

They were led into a dining room hung with many original Peter Arno cartoons, mostly from *The New Yorker* and *Esquire*, Stone thought. The headwaiter seated them at a corner table, and Stone drew the gunfighter's seat, in the corner, which allowed him to view the other diners. He immediately spotted a well-known actor and a man whose photograph he was sure he'd seen in *The New York Times*—something to do with British politics, he thought.

Then he glanced toward the door in time to see two men enter: One was sixtyish, white-haired, very English-looking. The other was John Bartholomew. They were handing their coats to the woman in the maid's uniform.

Stone leaned over and whispered to Erica, who was sitting on his right, "A man just came in who looks very familiar, but I can't place him."

Erica turned and looked toward the door. "The white-haired one? That's Sir Antony Shields," she said.

"He's in the cabinet, I think, but I don't remember which portfolio."

"No, it's the other man who looks familiar."

She looked again. "I've never seen him before," she said. The two men disappeared around a corner to a table out of sight.

So much for Uncle John, Stone thought. He wondered if Lance, whose back was to the door, would recognize him.

7

STONE HAD THE BRESAOLA, THINLY
sliced, air-cured beef, and a pasta dish with seafood.
Lance ordered the wine, and when it came, it was a Le
Montrachet '78. Stone reflected that the cost of the
wines they were drinking on this occasion would pay
for a dozen dinners at Elaine's. Having gotten to know
Lance just a little, he fully expected to end up with the
check.

They dined in a leisurely manner, and with the
wine, Lance became a bit more bearable, even charm-
ing, at times. They were on dessert when Stone saw
Bartholomew and Sir Antony Shields leave the restaurant. Bartholomew had never looked in his direction.
He was tempted to ask Lance if he recognized the
man, but the men were too quickly gone. Stone waved
at the headwaiter.

The man was there in a flash. "Tell me," Stone said,
"the two gentlemen who just left; one was Sir Antony
Shields; do you know the other man's name?"

"I'm sorry, sir, I don't. The reservation was Sir
Antony's, and although I've seen the other gentleman
here before, I never learned his name."

"Thank you," Stone said, and the headwaiter went
away.

The bill arrived, and as Stone started to reach for it, Erica pushed it toward Lance. "You're our guest," she said.

Lance hardly noticed. He signed the bill with a flourish, and they got up to go.

"We're going this way, to Farm Street," Erica said as they went out the door.

"I'll get a taxi for Monica," Stone said, grateful to be alone with her. He shook hands with both Lance and Erica and said good night.

"No cabs in sight," Stone said. "Let's walk down to the Connaught; there's usually a taxi parked out front." Monica agreed, and they strolled down Mount Street, which was shiny from a rain that had come and gone while they were at dinner.

"I think Lance liked you," Monica said.

"I'd be surprised if that were true," Stone replied.

"No, he turned out to be quite friendly toward you, for someone he has nothing to gain from."

"Is he friendlier when he has something to gain?"

"Isn't everyone?"

Stone laughed. "I suppose so."

"And I thought you showed great forbearance, especially early in the evening."

"The remainder of the company was good."

They were nearly to the hotel. "Would you like to . . ." he began.

"Oh, I hardly think the Connaught is the proper place for that," she said, reading his mind. "However, if you're free this weekend, there's a promising house party down in the country. Would you like to go?"

"I'd like that very much," Stone replied.

"Grand. I'll pick you up at, say, three tomorrow afternoon, so we'll miss the worst of the rush-hour traffic."

"Fine. What clothes shall I bring?"

"It's for two nights, so I'd bring some tweeds, a dark suit, and a dinner jacket. That should cover just about anything, except tennis or sailing. The house is on the coast."

They stopped in front of the hotel, and Stone indicated to the doorman that they would like a taxi. "I'll be right here at three o'clock," he said, aiming a kiss at her cheek.

She turned slightly, and he caught the corner of her mouth, and there was just a flick of her tongue.

"Wilton Crescent," she said to the doorman. "I'll point out the house." The doorman told the driver.

Stone put her into the cab and went into the hotel. On the way up in the elevator he thought about John Bartholomew and who he might be. He glanced at his watch. It was only seven o'clock in New York, so he went to his room, undressed, and picked up the telephone. He called Bill Eggers's home, and a maid answered.

"Oh, Mr. Barrington," she said, "they've gone skiing in Chile."

"Chile in South America?" Stone asked.

"Yes, there's apparently snow there this time of the year. They'll be back on Monday."

"Thank you," Stone said, and hung up. He thought some more. Bartholomew had mentioned Samuel Bernard, an old professor of his at NYU Law School. Bernard had been in the OSS during World War II, and he had remained in intelligence when the CIA was founded, serving during the agency's formative years. He had left at the time of the Bay of Pigs disaster, along with a lot of others, including Alan Dulles. Stone found his address book and dialed the number.

"Yes?" The voice was the same, but older.

"Good evening Dr. Bernard," he said. "It's Stone Barrington."

Bernard's voice brightened. "Oh, Stone, how are you?"

"I'm fine, and I hope you're well."

"I'm better than I could justifiably expect to be at my age," Bernard replied, chuckling. "I haven't seen you for a while. What have you been up to?"

"Life has been fairly boring until recently, when it got more interesting."

"Oh? How interesting?"

"That remains to be seen. A man came to see me a few days ago, sent by Woodman and Weld, but he also mentioned your name; said you had more or less recommended me to him."

"Strange," Bernard said. "I don't recall discussing you with anyone recently. What is the man's name?"

"John Bartholomew."

There was total silence at the other end of the line. Finally, Bernard spoke. "John Bartholomew," he said tonelessly. "How very interesting. Can you describe him?"

"Mid-fifties, tall—six-two or -three, athletically built, salt-and-pepper hair, beaked nose, fierce eyebrows. Do you know him?" Stone asked.

"No one knows him," Bernard replied.

"I don't understand."

"Stone, do you remember an Alfred Hitchcock film called *North by Northwest*?"

"Of course; it's a favorite of mine."

"Then you'll recall that, early in the film, Cary Grant is abducted from the Plaza Hotel by foreign agents who have mistaken him for a guest at the hotel. I believe the guest's name was George Kaplan, or something like that."

"Yes, I remember. The Grant character goes across

the country, chasing after Kaplan, but he turns out not to exist. He's a fiction contrived by some American intelligence agency."

"Exactly. Well, in the early fifties there actually was an operation that resembled the one in the film; in fact, I've often wondered if Hitchcock had heard about it. A fictional character was created, given an identity, and checked in and out of various hotels. It was very similar to the film."

"That's very interesting," Stone said, but he couldn't think why.

"May I ask, what did this man want you to do?"

"Well, of course, I must observe client confidentiality, but suffice it to say, as a result of our conversation, I'm now in London. I'm not quite sure what I'm involved in. I saw him earlier today at the American Embassy—at least I think I caught a glimpse of him—and again tonight, at a restaurant, with a man named Sir Antony Shields."

"The Home Secretary," Bernard said. "Something like our Attorney General. He supervises, among other departments, MI5, the British domestic security department, which is analogous to our FBI."

"Well, he's certainly well connected. But why did you tell me about the Hitchcock film?"

"As I said, we ran an operation something like that. Our fictional agent was called John Bartholomew."

Stone felt as if someone had rapped him sharply on the skull.

"The name became, over the years, something of an inside joke, generally referring to a hoax of some sort."

"I see," Stone said, but he didn't see at all.

"Where are you staying?" Bernard asked.

"At the Connaught."

"Let me see what I can learn," he said, "and I'll call you if I find out something."

"Oh, I have a cellphone number," Stone said. "It's one of those satellite things that works in a lot of countries." He gave Bernard the number.

"This may take a while," Bernard said. "Good night." He hung up.

Stone sat on the bed, wondering what he'd gotten himself into.

8

STONE WOKE REFRESHED, HAVING slept well, but all through breakfast he puzzled over Bartholomew, or whatever his name was, and his own assignment in London. Well, he thought finally, I'm an investigator, so maybe I'd better start investigating.

He dug out the phone number of Dino's acquaintance at Scotland Yard and called him.

"Detective Inspector Throckmorton's line," a woman's voice answered.

Stone tried not to laugh at the name. "Good morning, my name is Stone Barrington. Would you tell Detective Inspector Throckmorton that Lieutenant Dino Bacchetti suggested I call him?" He spelled Dino's name for her.

"One moment, please."

There was a brief pause, a click, and a crisp English voice said, "Throckmorton here; is that Mr. Barrington?"

"Yes, Inspector."

"Bacchetti called the other day and said you might turn up. You free for lunch?"

"Yes; may I take you?"

"Name the spot."

"How about the Connaught?"

"I can live with that," he said. "The Restaurant or the Grill?"

"Which would you prefer?"

"Menu's pretty much the same, but the Grill is nicer at lunch, I think."

"Twelve-thirty?"

"See you then," Throckmorton said, and hung up.

Stone booked the table, then showered and dressed and left the hotel. The sun shone brightly, though he was not sure for how long, and he immediately began to enjoy walking. Using his map, he strolled through Berkeley Square, then over to Piccadilly. He turned right at Fortnum & Mason's, the renowned department store and food emporium, and finally came to Jermyn Street and Turnbull & Asser.

He entered the shop, which was filled with brightly colored shirts and ties, looked at both, bought some, bought a couple of the Sea Island cotton nightshirts he preferred, and was sure to get the tax refund forms. He then strolled back to the Connaught, doing a lot of window-shopping in Bond Street along the way.

Evelyn Throckmorton was a small, well-proportioned, handsome man in his forties, wearing a Savile Row suit and a military mustache. He greeted Stone, and they went into the Connaught Grill, which was painted a restful green, and were given a table in an alcove by a window.

"How is Dino?" Throckmorton asked.

"He's very well; we see a lot of each other."

"I've heard him speak of you," Throckmorton said, perusing the menu. "Surprised we didn't meet when I was in New York that time."

"I've been off the force for several years, now," Stone said.

"Oh yes, I remember your last case; Dino and I discussed it in some detail."

Stone didn't care to revisit the Sasha Nijinsky case. "What would you like for lunch?" he asked as a waiter approached.

"The potted shrimps and the Dover sole," the policeman said to the waiter.

"I'll have the same," Stone said. "Would you like some wine?"

"Of course."

Stone ordered a Sancerre, and they chatted a bit until the first course came.

"Now," said Throckmorton, digging into his shrimp, "what can I do for you while you're here?"

"I've been sent over here by a client to look into the activities of an American living in London, and I need the help of an investigator—no, two. I thought you might know of someone reliable."

"I know a lorryload of retired coppers," Throckmorton said. "I daresay I could find you a couple of good men. What will you pay?"

"You tell me."

Throckmorton mentioned an hourly rate, and Stone agreed.

"Anything illegal about this?" Throckmorton asked.

"Not unless surveillance is illegal in Britain."

"Certainly not." Throckmorton chuckled.

"I don't want anyone hit over the head or anything like that. I just want to find out what's going on and report back to my client."

"Nothing wrong with that." He polished off his shrimp and whipped out an address book. "Let me go make a phone call," he said. "I'll be back before the sole arrives."

Stone sat back and sipped his wine. As Throckmorton left, Sir Antony Shields entered the Grill with another man, and they were seated across the room. The man certainly eats well, Stone thought to himself.

Throckmorton returned as the waiter was boning the soles. "There'll be two men here in an hour," he said. "They'll be waiting in the lounge when we're done here. Their names are Ted Cricket and Bobby Jones, like the golfer. They both worked for me at one time or another; they're smart, persistent, and discreet. You'll get what you want from them."

"Thank, you," Stone said. The sole was excellent. "I believe that's your Home Secretary over there." He nodded at the table across the room.

"Yes, saw him when I came back to the table. I've shaken his hand, but I don't really know the bugger, he's too new. Came in with the Labour lot, the second man to hold the office. I'm told he's reasonably bright; he made a name for himself as a barrister, prosecuting as often as defending. That's how we do it over here, you know."

"Yes, I know."

"Likes to see his name in the papers, always has, I'm told, as long as it's favorable. He's gotten a good press so far."

They had dessert and coffee, and Stone signed the bill. They left the Grill and walked out into the main hall of the hotel.

Throckmorton stopped and shook Stone's hand. "Splendid lunch," he said, "many thanks. The two chaps you want are around the corner, there," he said, nodding toward the sitting room. "I don't want to be seen introducing you." He walked through the revolving doors and left the hotel.

Stone walked into the sitting room, and it was immediately obvious whom he was meeting. Cops were cops. They were dressed in anonymous suits, and both wore thick-soled, black shoes. Stone went over and introduced himself.

Ted Cricket was the taller, more muscular man, and Bobby Jones was short, thin, and wiry. They were both near sixty, Stone reckoned, but they looked fit.

"How can we help you, Mr. Barrington?"

"There are two men I want surveilled," Stone said. "The first is named Lance Cabot, and he lives at a house called Merryvale, in Farm Street. He's American, in his mid-thirties, tall, well built, longish light brown hair, well dressed. He lives with a young woman named Erica Burroughs, and she is not to be followed, unless she's with Cabot."

Both men were taking notes.

"The second," Stone continued, "is more problematical, because I don't know his name. He's American, too, somewhere in his mid-fifties, six-two or -three, heavy, maybe two-ten, looks like a former athlete. He has a hawkish nose, thick, salt-and-pepper hair, and bushy eyebrows."

"And where does he live?" Cricket asked.

"That's one of the things I want to know," Stone said. "He's in and out of the American Embassy, through the front door, and that's where you're going to have to pick him up. I want to know where he's staying, who he sees, and where he goes. I don't know if he lives in London or New York, but my guess is, he's in a hotel not far from the embassy."

"Right," Cricket said. "Anything else?"

"I don't know whether the weekend would be productive; why don't you start first thing Monday morning?"

The two men nodded. "And we can reach you here, Mr. Barrington?"

"Yes, and I have a cellphone." He gave them the number.

"We'll report to you daily," Cricket said.

"By the way," he said, "I didn't mention this to Throckmorton, but is it possible to tap Cabot's phone and record all his conversations?"

"Not legally," Cricket said.

"I understand that. Can you do it, or have it done?"

Both men looked wary. Finally, Jones spoke. "I know someone who can do it. But for how long?"

"Let's start with a week," Stone said.

"Could be pricey; I mean, there is a risk."

"I don't mind paying, but I want someone who can do it without risk to himself, you, or me. And I don't want him to know who I am."

"Understood," Jones said. "I'll get onto my man today."

Cricket spoke up. "You understand, I didn't hear any of that."

"Understood," Stone said. "Bobby, why don't you take Cabot, and Ted, you can have the other man."

Both men nodded. They shook hands all around, and the two men left.

Stone looked at his watch; he had half an hour to pack for the weekend.

9

MONICA BURROUGHS ARRIVED AT THE Connaught in an Aston Martin, and the combination of the car and the beautiful woman at the wheel impressed the doorman. Stone's luggage was loaded, and Monica drove up Mount Street to Park Lane and accelerated into the traffic, driving faster than Stone would have under the circumstances.

"Did you sleep well?" Monica asked.

"Very well, thank you."

"I'm sorry to hear it; I thought you'd have lain awake, thinking of me."

"I dreamed of you."

"Something erotic, I hope."

"Of course."

She cut across two lanes of traffic and turned into Hyde Park. Shortly, they were in the Cromwell Road, heading west, as Monica constantly shifted up and down and changed lanes.

Stone tried to relax. "Who are our hosts for the weekend?" he asked.

"Lord and Lady Wight," Monica replied. "He recently inherited the title from an uncle, although he managed the estates for many years while the old man was in a nursing home. The house is a nice old Georgian pile that has just undergone a five-year renovation that cost millions. I can't wait to see it. His lordship made lots and lots of money in property development, so he can afford the title." She glanced at him slyly. "Before he inherited, his name was Sir Robert Buckminster."

Stone sat up straight. "Is he related to a woman named Sarah Buckminster?"

"She's his daughter; know her?"

"Yes." He had known her all too well in New York. They had practically lived together until someone had started trying to kill him, and when a bomb was placed in a gallery showing her paintings, she abruptly left New York, swearing never to return. "I knew her rather well. How do you know her?"

"My gallery represents her work in this country. We had a very successful show last month, sold out the lot."

"Tell me, Monica, did you know that Sarah and I knew each other?"

She smiled a little. "I'd heard your name from her."

"And does Sarah know I'm coming to her father's house for the weekend?"

"No. I wasn't going to tell you about Sarah, either; I wanted to see the look on both your faces, but I couldn't stand the suspense. Now, I suppose, I'll have to be content with the look on *her* face."

This was all too catty for Stone. "Take me back to the Connaught," he said.

"What?"

"I think it would be extremely rude for me to turn up there unannounced, so take me back."

"Oh, don't be such a stick in the mud, Stone; this will be fun!"

"Not for me, and very probably not for Sarah."

"I won't take you back."

"Then let me out of the car, and I'll find my own way back."

"Oh, really, Stone; can't you just go along with this?"

"No, I can't."

"Oh, all right," she said, picking up the car phone and dialing a number. "Hello, Sarah? It's Monica. Yes, sweetie. I have to tell you the funniest thing. Last night, I had a blind date with someone you know, Stone Barrington." She listened for a moment. "No, I'm not kidding; he's over here on business and he met Erica and Lance, and they invited him to dinner." She listened again. "He's very well indeed, and I thought that, if it's all right with you, I'd bring him down for the weekend." She listened. "Wonderful! I'll go get him, and we'll be down in a couple of hours. See you then." She hung up the phone. "There, she said she'd be delighted to see you. Satisfied?"

"I suppose I am," Stone said, but he was still feeling uncomfortable about it.

"I may as well tell you this, too."

"What?"

"Dinner tomorrow night is to celebrate her engagement."

"Swell," Stone said. "Are you sure she said it was all right for me to come?"

"She did, said she'd be delighted. She's marrying a man named James Cutler, who's something big in the wine trade. Sweet man, very handsome."

"Monica, if, when we arrive at the house, Sarah is surprised to see me, I'm going straight back to London."

"Stone, you heard me speak to her. Please relax, it will be all right." They had reached the Chiswick Roundabout, and she turned toward Southampton, flooring the Aston Martin and passing three cars that were going too slowly for her taste.

"How often do you get arrested?" Stone asked.

"Hardly ever."

"Do you still have a driver's license?"

"Of course I do."

Soon they were on the M3 motorway, and Monica was doing a little over a hundred miles an hour.

"Beautiful country," Stone said. "Why don't we slow down and see it?"

"Oh, all right," she said, taking an exit. "We'll go the back roads; it's more fun that way anyhow." Shortly they were on a winding country road that was perfect for sports-car driving, and Monica was driving it very well.

Stone was happier at sixty than at a hundred.

"Do you like art?" Monica asked. "I mean, apart from Sarah's pictures?"

"Yes, I do; my mother was a painter."

"What was her name?"

"Matilda Stone."

"You're kidding! I know her work very well; she did those marvelous cityscapes of New York, especially Greenwich Village."

"Yes, she did."

"I sold one last year for a very nice price. Do you have any of her work?"

"I have four pictures," he said. "And I think they are among her best."

"I don't suppose you want to sell them?"

"No. They're in my house in New York—well, one is in the Connecticut house—and I like them there. I'll never sell them."

"I understand. Are you interested in buying more of her work, if I should come across some things?"

"Yes, of course, if I can afford them."

"I'll let you know." She stopped talking and concentrated on her driving.

Stone was relieved.

An hour and a half later, after a confusion of back roads and odd turns, they drove through an impressive gate and followed a winding road planted with trees that formed a tunnel. They emerged in a large circle of gravel before a limestone Georgian mansion that had been cleaned to within an inch of its existence.

"Wow," Stone said.

"Yes, it's like that, isn't it?"

He was barely out of the car before Sarah came bounding down the stairs to give him a hug and a kiss, holding the hug longer than Stone thought an engaged woman should. She held him at arm's length and looked at him. "You look wonderful," she said. "Hello, Monica." This over her shoulder. Sarah took Stone's arm and led him through the front door, leaving Monica to follow.

1 0

THEY ENTERED A GRAND HALLWAY containing a broad staircase to the second floor. The walls all the way to the ceiling were hung with paintings, portraits—no doubt of ancestors—and English landscapes.

"This is glorious," Stone said.

"Wait until you see the rest of the house," Sarah said; "it's taken years for Mummy and Daddy to restore it."

A houseman appeared, loaded with luggage.

"Miss Burroughs is in Willow, and Mr. Barrington is in Oak," she said to the man. She turned back to Stone. "The guest rooms are all named for trees; there are twelve of them. There had been fifteen, but we used three of them to make room for private baths for all the guests." She led him to their right. "The drawing room is here." She pushed open a door to reveal a huge room furnished with many sofas and chairs. "It's perfect for entertaining." She led him across the hall and opened another door. "This is the library," she said. "We have the books of seven generations collected here, and most of them have been rebound."

Stone stood and stared. The room was paneled in walnut, and a spiral staircase led to an upper level that bordered the huge room. It smelled of leather and old cigar smoke. "Very beautiful," he said, and he meant it.

"Come, I'll show you your rooms." Sarah led the way upstairs and down a hallway to the end. "You have the corner room, overlooking the Solent," she said. "Monica, you're there," she said, pointing to a door across the hall. She opened the door to Oak, and Stone stepped into a large bedroom furnished with a four-poster bed, a chesterfield sofa, and a couple of commodious reading chairs, all very masculine. She led him to the window. "There is the Solent, in all its glory," she said, "and that land on the other side is the Isle of Wight. Well, I expect you'd like to freshen up. Drinks are in the drawing room at six, and dinner will be at eight. We're not dressing tonight; a lounge suit will do." She gave him a big kiss on the lips and disappeared.

Stone watched her go, then stepped across the hall and knocked on the door of Willow.

"Come in."

He opened the door and walked into a feminine counterpart of his own room, all chintz and lace. Monica was unpacking.

"We seem to have separate rooms," he said.

"Oh, that's how it's done at English house parties," she said. "They consider it more fun to tiptoe up and down the halls after lights out. Do you like your room?"

"Very much. You must see it."

She came and put her arms around his neck. "I expect to, late tonight," she said. "I'll do the tiptoeing." She kissed him.

When Stone got back to his room, his clothes had been upacked and put away by some invisible servant.

He sat in an armchair by the window, picked up a copy of *Pride and Prejudice* on the table next to it, and began to read.

At a quarter past six, Stone rapped on Monica's door and walked her down to the drawing room. There were at least twenty people in the room, ranging from their twenties to their fifties. He was surprised to see, among them, Erica and Lance, who waved from across the room. "You didn't tell me they were coming," he said to Monica.

"Didn't I? I meant to, I think."

Sarah came over, leading a tall man in the most severely cut English suit Stone had ever seen. "Stone, this is James Cutler," she said. "James, I've told you about Stone."

"Yes, you have," James said through a clenched smile.

"I'm very glad to meet you, James," Stone said.

Sarah's parents appeared, her father portly, with a complexion that suggested the regular and copious imbibing of port, and her mother a faded blonde with what Stone thought was an exaggerated accent. They were both gracious and moved on when they had done their social duty.

A butler inquired of Stone's and Monica's wishes in drinks, then brought them. Stone had asked for Scotch, thinking they probably wouldn't have bourbon, and he found it dark and smoky, obviously a single malt. Monica took him through the room, introducing him to everybody. Apparently, the Burroughs sisters, Lance, and Stone were the only Americans present.

At dinner, Stone was seated between Sarah and her mother, while Monica was relegated to the other end of the very long table. Stone counted thirty diners. The dining room had a high ceiling and much gilt. They had hardly sat down, when someone's cellphone rang, and a brief hush fell over the table. Lance stood up, blushing, and left the room. A moment later Stone saw him outside the window on the back lawn, pacing up and down in the long English twilight, gesticulating. He wondered what had so upset Lance. When he returned to the table he looked unhappy for a moment, then managed a smile as he resumed his seat.

"I hate those damned things," Lady Wight said, stabbing at something on her plate. "Only an American would bring one in to dinner."

"Mother, not all Americans are so gauche," Sarah said, nodding at Stone.

"Oh, of course not, Stone," her mother said. "So very sorry."

She didn't sound sorry, Stone thought.

After dinner, the men left the women at the table and repaired to the library for port and cigars. Stone passed on the cigar but accepted the port with pleasure. He had not drunk enough vintage port in his life to suit him.

Lance wandered over. "How's it going?" he asked.

"Very well," Stone replied. "Business call at dinner?"

"In a manner of speaking," Lance said, flushing, apparently still angry with whoever had called him. "You know about Wight, of course."

"Not much."

"He's lucky not to be in prison. An office building he put up last year, fortunately in the middle of the night, so no one was killed. The incident prompted an inspection of a dozen of his buildings, and it was discovered that a lot of corners had been cut. Cost the old boy a packet of money and a bad bruise on his reputation. I think he was relieved when inheriting the title allowed him to change his name."

"Mmmm," Stone replied, not wanting to comment.

Half an hour later, the ladies joined them, and everyone talked until past eleven, when people began to drift upstairs to bed.

Stone had just switched off the light and was settling in when the door opened and someone entered. A moment later, she was in bed with him, her hands searching and finding what she wanted. Stone joined in enthusiastically, and after a few minutes they both came noisily, then collapsed. He was half asleep when she left the bed and went back to her room. Just as well, he thought, since he was exhausted and needed sleep.

He had just drifted off when she returned to his bed, snuggling up to him.

"What?" he said sleepily.

"Sorry I took so long," Monica said, throwing a leg over his.

Stone sat straight up in bed. "How long has it been?" he asked.

"I don't know; three-quarters of an hour, I suppose. I had a bath."

Stone fell back onto the bed, realizing what had happened. "Monica," he said, "you're going to have to forgive me. I think I've had too much to drink."

"Oh, surely I can bring you around," she said, feeling for him.

"I'm afraid not," he said. "I hope you'll forgive me. Tomorrow is another day."

"Oh, all right," she said grumpily, and went back to her room.

Stone, before he drifted off again, had the momentary feeling that he was a character in a Feydeau farce.

1 1

STONE SLEPT LATER THAN HE IN-
tended and was still struggling with the time difference. When he came downstairs for breakfast, nearly
everyone had finished. He scraped the last of the
scrambled eggs from a silver serving dish and grabbed
some bacon and toast.

He found a leather chair in the library and settled
into it. As he started on the eggs, Sarah and her fiancé,
James, appeared before him. He struggled to get to his
feet, but Sarah motioned him back into his chair.

"And how are *you* this fine morning?" she asked,
smiling broadly. "I hope you were very comfortable in
your bed last night." She winked, while James looked
on, sure that something was going on, but without a
clue what.

Stone choked down a big bite of eggs. "Yes, sure," he
managed to say without spraying her with food.

"I was certainly very comfortable in bed," Sarah
added unnecessarily.

"Good," Stone said. "What's up for the day?"

"Oh, you're coming sailing with James and me," she
replied, taking James's arm in a proprietary way.
"James is just learning to sail."

James nodded, clearly her prisoner.

"Great; what time?" Stone asked, longing to return to his eggs before they got any colder.

"Five minutes," she said. "We'll meet in the mud room and get you some gear."

"Great," Stone replied, returning to his eggs. They wandered away.

Monica appeared with two cups of coffee and sat down on the rug at his feet. "Good morning," she said. "I hope you're feeling better rested today." Her voice dripped with meaning.

"Yes, thanks. I'm sorry about last night," he said, accepting the coffee and setting it on a small table beside him. "It must be the jet lag."

"We're going sailing shortly," she said.

"I heard." He was shoveling in breakfast as fast as he could. He set down his plate and picked up the coffee. Black. He hated coffee without sugar, but he forced himself.

"I do hope you won't wear yourself out too much today," Monica said, archly. "Perhaps a nap in the afternoon?"

Outfitted with a slicker and a pair of rubber sailing boots, Stone climbed into a Range Rover with Monica, Sarah and her James, and Lance and Erica. Sarah drove like a madwoman, tearing down a narrow, winding track until she skidded to a stop at a dock, where a yacht of forty feet or so lay waiting on a pretty river.

"This is the Beaulieu River," Sarah said over her shoulder to Stone. She pronounced it "Bewley." "Up there a ways is the village of Beaulieu, and the other way is the Solent."

Everyone climbed aboard, Sarah started the engine, and there was much scrambling with lines and sails.

As Sarah motored down the Beaulieu, Stone began hoisting, first the mainsail, then a medium genoa, assisted by James, who clearly didn't know what he was doing and didn't seem to be getting the hang of it. Fifteen minutes later, they emerged from the river into the Solent.

Sarah set a course to the east, and Stone trimmed the sails. "Anybody else on this boat know anything about sailing?" he asked.

They all shook their heads as one person.

"Swell," he muttered under his breath.

The sky was a mix of blue and clouds, and they beat into a stiff breeze of close to twenty knots. Stone zipped up his slicker and wished he had a hat. What with the breeze, it was chilly. They sailed up the Solent, Sarah pointing out the sights, until they were abreast of a town and harbor to starboard.

"That's Cowes," she said, "England's capital of yachting; maybe Europe's."

Everyone looked glumly at Cowes. Sarah seemed to be the only person really enjoying herself.

Stone thought it wasn't too bad. Then Sarah bore away, and he had to let out the sails to go downwind. Off the wind, headed west again, the breeze seemed to diminish, and everyone was more comfortable, even though the yacht was rolling enthusiastically. James climbed out of the cockpit, knelt at the rail, and tossed his breakfast into the Solent. He seemed to feel better then, and he went and stood on the afterdeck behind Sarah, holding onto the backstay to steady himself.

Stone began to enjoy the sail. He hadn't been on a yacht since his trip to St. Marks some years before, and he had never sailed in England.

"Have you done much sailing?" Monica asked.

"At summer camp as a kid," Stone replied. "And I

spent three summers in Maine, as a hand on a yacht. We did a lot of racing up there." He looked up at the mainsail and saw a slight curl as the wind flirted with it. They were sailing dead downwind, and the boom was fully extended.

Stone leaned over and said quietly to Sarah, "You'll be sailing her by the lee in a minute, if you're not careful. You don't want to gybe her."

"I know what I'm doing, darling," Sarah shot back. Then, as if to prove that she didn't, she gave the wheel a slight turn, and the rear edge of the mainsail began to flap.

"Watch it," Stone said, trying not to reach for the wheel to correct her, and then it happened, and fast. The wind got behind the mainsail, and the yacht gybed. The boom whipped across the deck, catching James on the side of the head and catapulting him overboard. He disappeared into the water.

"Christ!" Sarah yelled, fighting the helm. "Gybing back!" She put the helm over.

It took Stone less than a second to think: *Never go after a man overboard; then you'll have two men overboard, and nobody on this yacht can sail, except Sarah.* Then Stone stood up, yelled to Sarah, "Stop the yacht!" grabbed a horseshoe buoy from the stern, and jumped into the water.

The water was colder than he expected. Pushing the buoy ahead of him, Stone kicked his way toward the spot where James had gone under. He shucked off the slicker and took a moment to get rid of his rubber boots, which had filled with water. Moving faster now, he reached what he thought might be the spot where James had gone down. He dove under, feeling, looking, seeing nothing but greenish water. Again and again he dove, until he had no breath left. He came to the surface and looked around him. No sign of James, and the buoy had blown away from him. He treaded water and looked for the yacht. She was lying abeam to the seas, two hundred yards away, her genoa aback and the main flapping free.

He got his second wind and started diving again, and it quickly became apparent that his actions were futile. He was very cold and tired now, the yacht was a long way off, and he didn't know if he could swim that far. He began to try.

He swam slowly, his arms heavy with fatigue. Lance was taking the genoa down on the yacht, and someone, probably Monica, was lying on top of it, trying to keep it from blowing overboard. He thought he heard the engine start. He hoped to God he heard right.

Suddenly, he was only fifty yards from the yacht, and it was headed toward him. Sarah brought the boat to a halt when he was abeam of the helm. "Switch off the engine," he called out weakly. He didn't want to get chewed up by the prop.

Somebody tossed him the other horseshoe buoy, and he grabbed it gratefully. Lance was reaching out to him, grabbing at his clothes.

It took Lance, Monica, and Sarah to haul him aboard, and he wasn't much help. He lay in the cockpit, shivering and gasping for breath.

"Did you see him?" Sarah asked, oddly calm.

Stone shook his head. "He's gone."

1 2

STONE WOKE SLOWLY. THE ROOM WAS dark, but faint daylight showed around the edges of the heavy curtains. Something had woken him, but he wasn't sure what. Then there was a knocking at the door.

"Come in," he said, as loudly as he could, struggling into a sitting position.

The door opened, and Lance Cabot walked in. "Good morning," he said.

"Morning?"

"You've been asleep since we got you back to the house."

"Then it's tomorrow?"

"It's today; the, ah . . . *accident* happened yesterday. How do you feel?"

Stone got a pillow behind him and leaned back against the headboard. "Dull," he said. "I think I'll probably ache a lot when I start moving around."

"The police were here yesterday, but the Wights wouldn't let them near you. They were very concerned about your health. The local doctor came, but you showed no signs of waking up, so he said just to let you sleep it off."

"What time is it?"

"A little after nine. Why don't you come down and have some breakfast? All the guests left yesterday, except you, Erica, Monica, and me. We're all witnesses."

Stone nodded.

"There's going to be an inquest tomorrow morning. The locals hurried it up so they could get it done while we're all here, so we're staying over another night."

"I see."

"I thought you, Erica, Monica, and I ought to get our stories straight."

Now Stone was awake. "Straight?"

"We should be in agreement."

"About what?"

"About what happened."

"Is there any *disagreement* about what happened?"

"That depends on how you see it."

"The yacht gybed, and James went overboard, then I did."

"The yacht didn't gybe; Sarah gybed it. She knew what she was doing."

Stone resisted the thought. "Lance, how much sailing have you done?"

"None, to speak of."

"Then you don't really understand what happened. Boats accidentally gybe all the time; people sometimes get hit with the boom. James was unlucky."

"So that's the story you're sticking to?"

"It's what happened; I was there, too, remember?"

"You weren't on the yacht after James went overboard."

"No. Did something happen then?"

"Very little. Sarah seemed . . . Well, I had the distinct impression that her only real concern was getting you out of the water."

"Tell me exactly what happened after I went in."

"I heard you yell, 'Stop the yacht,' and then Sarah yelled, 'Gybing back.' Or maybe it was the other way around. Why would she gybe back?"

"To get the sails on the same side of the boat."

"But she didn't gybe back," Lance said. "She just turned into the wind."

"That was the right thing to do," Stone said. "When I looked back and saw the yacht, the genoa was aback, and that would stop the yacht."

"Sarah wouldn't start the engine—not at first, anyway. I asked her to, and she ignored me."

"She did start the engine; she came back for me."

"Only after I pointed out that you were still in the water."

"She would have been stunned by what happened," Stone said. "We were lucky she was able to function at all."

"She was as cool as ice," Lance said.

"Lucky for me."

"All right, Stone," Lance said. "You're the lawyer. How should we handle the inquest?"

"Tell the truth; relate the facts as they happened; don't offer any opinions, unless you're asked, then be circumspect. The family is certainly going to have a lawyer there, and—"

"He's already arrived," Lance said. "Sir Bernard Pickering, QC. Very famous barrister, I'm told. A polite shark."

"Then he'll tear you and the others to pieces if you begin to imply that what Sarah did was intentional. Stick to the facts; don't make reckless charges. Have you been questioned by the police?"

"Yes, but not the girls. I told the police they were too upset to talk yet."

"What did you tell the police?"

"I played dumb, told them I don't sail, don't know anything about it."

"Which was the truth."

"After a fashion."

"What do the girls think happened?"

"They don't seem to have a clue."

"Did they question Sarah?"

"No, she's been locked in her room, except to have meals brought in. She won't even talk to her parents, but I think the barrister is probably talking to her by now."

"That's as it should be."

"So you don't think what Sarah did was deliberate?"

"Of course not. I know her quite well, you know, and I've never seen her exhibit any behavior that would cause me to think she might want to kill her fiancé. She was marrying him, after all; if she wanted to be rid of him, she'd have dumped him in a straightforward manner. She's a very decisive girl."

"And you don't think that's exactly what she did?"

"I mean she'd have broken the engagement, told him to get lost. That's pretty much what she did with me, except that we weren't engaged."

"How did all this happen?" Lance asked.

"We'd been seeing each other for a while, had been mostly living together in my house. Somebody from my past turned up—a man my partner on the NYPD had sent to prison for murder some years before. He began killing people close to me, and Sarah was, naturally, very frightened. Then he planted a car bomb outside a gallery where Sarah was showing her paintings. We managed to get everybody out before it went off, but after that, she just wanted to leave the country as quickly as possible. She asked me to come with her, and initially, I agreed, but then, at the airport, I changed my mind. She got on the airplane and, as far as I know, never looked back. I didn't hear from her again after that."

"Cool and decisive," Lance said.

"That doesn't make her a murderer."

"I guess not." Lance stood up. "I'll take your advice, Stone. I don't suppose anything I could say at the inquest would make a great deal of difference."

"Not after the barrister got through with you," Stone said.

"He wants to talk to you; you'd better get dressed and come downstairs." Lance left the room and closed the door behind him.

Stone sat and thought about the scene on the boat for a minute. Lance couldn't be right, could he? Of course not. He got up and headed for a shower.

1 3

STONE SHAVED, SHOWERED, DRESSED, and went downstairs; the house was very quiet. He walked into the library and found a man sitting before a fire reading a leather-bound volume. "Good morning," he said.

The man rose; he was of Stone's height but much slimmer, balding, with pale gray eyes. "Good morning." He held out his hand. "I'm Bernard Pickering. I expect you're Barrington."

Stone shook the hand. "Yes."

"I've ordered us some breakfast," Pickering said, nodding at a small table at the end of the room that had been set for two. As if on cue, a maid entered the room bearing a silver tray. "Come," Pickering said, leading the way.

"I understand you're a lawyer back in the States," Pickering said, pitching into his eggs.

"That's right."

"Have you done any criminal work?"

"Yes, and I was a police officer for many years before I began to practice law."

"And you're a partner, now, in Woodman and Weld?" the barrister asked, rasing his eyebrows.

"I'm of counsel. I work out of my own office."

"I see," Pickering replied, though clearly he didn't.

"I do much of their criminal work."

Pickering's eyes narrowed. "Yes, I see." Now he really did. "Well, that should make our conversation easier. I'm glad you're someone who will understand the, ah, limits of my questions."

"You mean the limits of my answers, don't you?"

"Quite so. A death of this sort is always a delicate matter, and, if we handle it properly, we can dispose of the entire incident at this inquest."

"I hope so," Stone replied.

"I'm a bit concerned about Mr. Cabot's attitude."

"We talked about it. I don't think he'll be of particular concern to you."

"James Cutler's body came up in a fisherman's trawl in the middle of the Channel, late last night. It's being examined now."

"I expect that death will be determined to have been caused by blunt trauma to the head or drowning, or both," Stone said.

"Very probably. Will you give me your account of the events of yesterday?"

Stone related his story quickly, without embellishment.

Pickering nodded as he spoke. He took no notes. "Tell me, Mr. Barrington," he said, "are you an experienced yachtsman?"

"I've done a lot of sailing, but not recently."

"Are you aware that the standard procedure in such an event is for the crew not to enter the water to help?"

"Yes, I'm aware of that, and I considered it before going after James."

"And what was your thought process, may I ask?"

"If someone goes into the water after a man overboard, then there are two men to be rescued, instead of one, but in this instance I believed that the blow from the boom would have rendered James unconscious, and that he would be unable to help himself."

"Mmmm," Pickering muttered in an affirmative fashion. "I expect you did the right thing. Did you see or touch Cutler after you went in?"

"No, I swam to where I thought he might be and dove for him, but I never saw or touched him."

"Are you familiar with the tides in the Solent?"

"No."

"The tide turned while you were sailing toward Cowes, so by the time you came off the wind and sailed toward the Beaulieu River, the tide would have been ebbing, and you might have had a couple of knots under you."

"That would have made no difference in my search, since James, the yacht, and I would have all been equally affected by the tide."

"Good point," Pickering said. "Did Sarah say anything to you during this incident?"

"No, she didn't have time before I went into the water, and I was in no state to have a conversation with her after they got me aboard again."

"Good," Pickering said, almost to himself. "Do you recall any display of attitude or emotion on her part after you were back aboard?"

"No, I was shivering too badly to notice, then I must have fallen asleep or passed out. I don't remember being brought from the yacht back to the house."

"Good," Pickering repeated. "Well, I think that's all; we can enjoy our breakfast now."

"Have you spoken to Sarah?"

"Yes, about an hour ago."

"How is she?"

"Grieving, feeling guilty that she may have done

something to cause James's death. That's preposterous, of course."

"It's not preposterous, but in my judgment, for what it's worth, the whole thing was an accident."

Pickering gazed over Stone's shoulder and out the window. He seemed to be considering something. "Tell me, Stone," he said finally, "if I may call you that . . ."

"Of course."

"What do you know of Sarah's personal circumstances?"

"Not much. I haven't seen her for a year or so, since she left New York."

"I understand you were, ah, close, while she was there?"

"Yes, that's true."

"Have you had any contact with her since she left New York?"

"None at all, until we met here on Friday evening."

"No letters or phone calls? Email?"

"No."

"And how did you come to be here this weekend?"

"I was invited by Monica Burroughs."

"Did you know that the house party was to be at the home of Sarah's parents and that the occasion was the announcement of her engagement to James Cutler?"

"Not until we were driving down here from London."

"So Sarah was surprised to see you?"

"No, I asked Monica to call her and explain that I was coming."

"Had Monica not planned to tell her?"

"I don't believe so."

"Why ever not?"

"I believe that Monica had intended my visit as a surprise."

"I see." He did not.

"I think it was probably mischievous on her part."

"Oh, I see." Now he did.

"But in any case, embarrassment was avoided by all because of Monica's call to Sarah."

"Good."

"Do you think I could see Sarah? Is she up to it?"

"I suppose she is, but I'd rather no one who will be testifying tomorrow speak to her until after the inquest."

"Would you tell her, then, that I asked after her and that I send my condolences?"

"Of course I will. I have one other question for you, Stone, and I would like this part of our conversation to be kept in the strictest confidence for the time being."

"All right."

"Are you aware that Sarah is James Cutler's heir?"

"You mean she's the beneficiary of his will?"

"Very nearly the sole beneficiary."

"Is that sort of arrangement before a marriage common in this country?"

"It is not. I doubt if it is in the States, either."

"In the States—or in New York, at least—they would be more likely to have a prenuptial agreement limiting Sarah's benefits in the event of a divorce—or James's, depending on Sarah's circumstances."

"Sarah's circumstances are that she is a well-regarded painter with a nice income from her work, but she possesses no serious assets, except a long lease on her London flat. Whether she will inherit much from her father depends on the outcome of a number of lawsuits filed against him in connection with the collapse of an apartment building last year."

"Was James particularly well off?"

"Let's just say that Sarah is now the largest independent importer and distributor of wines in the United Kingdom, and she has widespread holdings in various French and Italian vineyards. She also now owns something upwards of a hundred and fifty wine shops and two hundred pubs. I doubt if she has much interest in running such a business, but it would bring a very large price if sold to one of the big wine and spirit conglomerates. Are you beginning to get my drift?"

"I believe I am," Stone said.

Stone spent the remainder of the day reading more of Jane Austen in the library and joined the others for dinner, except Sarah, who dined in her room. Dinner was a quiet, almost somber affair, with little conversation. Everyone went to bed early, and Stone was not visited by anyone after retiring.

1 4

STONE LEFT THE HAMPSHIRE COUNTY Council building and found Monica waiting for him outside with the motor running. His baggage was already in the boot of the car, and he had said his good-byes to Lord and Lady Wight, but not to Sarah, who was still sequestered, pending her testimony to the coroner's jury.

"How did it go?" Monica asked, putting the Aston Martin in gear and driving away.

"As planned, I think; Pickering seems to have everything well in hand."

"I was surprised at how subdued he was when he questioned me," she said. "He has a reputation as a tiger in court."

"I think he went out of his way to give the impression that he was unconcerned about the outcome. He would not have wanted the coroner to think that he was defending Sarah of a charge."

"Then he's clever."

"Yes, he is."

"Did he need to be?"

"It never hurts, if a lawyer can avoid being seen to be clever."

They drove in silence for half an hour. Finally, Monica spoke again. "Lance seems to think that Sarah did it deliberately."

"None of the evidence I'm aware of supports that view."

"So you think it was an accident?"

"Yes." And he would continue to prefer to think that. Then he thought about Sarah's late-night visit to him two nights before. A fling on her part, nothing more, he told himself.

She dropped him at the Connaught. "Dinner this week sometime?"

"Let me call you; I don't know yet how long I'll be here."

She handed him a card. "Home, gallery, and cell-phone."

He thanked her and followed the porter into the hotel.

"You have a number of messages, Mr. Barrington," the concierge said, handing him some small envelopes.

Stone waited until he was back in his suite to open them. Two were from John Bartholomew, or whoever he was, one was from Dino, and one was from Bill Eggers at Woodman & Weld. Stone dialed the New York number for Bartholomew. The number rang, then was interrupted, then rang again.

"Yes?"

"It's Stone Barrington."

"I've been trying to reach you, but the phone I gave you wasn't working."

Stone looked over and saw the phone resting on its charger. "I'm sorry; I forgot to take the phone with me when I went away for the weekend."

"I read about your weekend in the morning papers," Bartholomew said.

Not the New York papers, Stone thought. Barthol-omew was still in London.

"Hello?"

"I'm still here."

"What have you learned?"

"That Cabot calls himself an independent business consultant."

Bartholomew made a snorting sound. "Of course."

"And that Erica Burroughs is not your niece."

Now it was Bartholomew who was silent.

"And her mother is not dead, though her father is."

"It's not necessary for you to know everything," Bartholomew said.

"Perhaps not, but it's necessary, if we're to continue this relationship, that what I do know is true and not a lie."

"My apologies," Bartholomew said stiffly. "What do you want to know?"

"Why do you want Lance Cabot in an English jail?"

"I can't tell you that."

"Is your interest in him personal, or are you work-ing for someone else?"

"Both."

"Who are you?"

"Do you wish to continue to represent me in this matter?" Now Bartholomew was angry.

"I don't much care one way or the other," Stone replied evenly, "but I don't like to be kept in the dark about the motives for my investigation."

"I'm afraid it will have to be that way for a time, but I'd like very much for you to continue."

Stone made his decision. "All right, I'll continue." Until I find out what the hell is going on, he thought.

"Good. But please keep the phone I gave you on

your person at all times. I don't like not being able to reach you."

"All right."

"Contact me again when you have something to report."

"All right."

Bartholomew hung up without further ado.

Stone called Bill Eggers.

"Hi there, you called while I was in Chile?"

"Yes, I did. You're going to Chile for the weekend, nowadays?"

"At the invitation of a client who has a Gulfstream Four."

"You're a lucky man. Who is the man you sent to see me last week?"

"How do you mean, 'who'?"

"What's his real name, for a start."

"I thought it was Bartholomew."

"It's not; I know that much. How did he come to you?"

"A client referred him."

"Who's the client?"

"I'm afraid that's confidential."

"Where is the client located?"

"In Washington; you can infer what you wish from that."

"I will. Do you have any idea what Bartholomew really wants?"

"I don't even know what he *told* you he wants."

"He told me a cock-and-bull story, and I'm annoyed."

"I hope you haven't done anything rash."

"Like quit?"

"Yes."

"Not yet, but I'm going to, if he keeps lying to me."

"Stick it out, Stone. I can't tell you why you should, but I'd appreciate it."

"Oh, all right, Bill."

"Thanks. I'll remember." He hung up.

Stone called Dino.

"How you doin'?" Dino asked cheerfully.

"I had a strange weekend."

"Tell me."

Stone told him.

"And she inherits the guy's business?"

"Apparently so. What do you think?"

"You know what I think," Dino chuckled, "but I have a more suspicious mind than you do."

"I think I prefer not being suspicious right now."

"I'll be willing to bet you hear from Sarah before the day's out."

"She's grieving," Stone said.

"Yeah, sure. I gotta go; anything else?"

"Nope."

"She's going to call you." Dino hung up.

Stone stood up and stretched, and the phone rang. He picked it up. "Hello?"

"It's Sarah," she said.

1 5

SHE SOUNDED PERFECTLY NORMAL—
not depressed, not upset, just Sarah.

"How are you feeling?" he asked.

"Perfectly all right, thank you."

"What was the outcome of the inquest?"

"Accidental death," she replied. "Had you expected another outcome?"

"No, I was sure that would be the verdict."

"Sir Bernard seemed to think I might have purposely gybed the yacht; is that what you think?"

"No, and I told him so."

"Did he say to you that I might have done it on purpose?"

"No, and I don't think he believes that—not from anything he said in our conversation."

"What about Lance? Does he believe I killed James?"

"Lance doesn't know anything about sailing; he didn't really understand what happened. I explained it to him, and he seemed satisfied."

She was silent for a moment. "There's something I have to tell you."

"All right."

She seemed to be having trouble getting it out. Finally she spoke. "I didn't intentionally cause James's death, but I'm not really very sorry he's dead. Does that sound awful?"

Stone avoided a direct answer. "Please tell me what you mean."

"I wouldn't have gone through with it—the marriage, I mean."

"Then why were you having an engagement party?"

"My parents pressed me, told me I was getting old. I'm thirty-two, for Christ's sake!"

"Maybe they just want grandchildren."

"Oh, they do, that's true. I liked James, but I was never in love with him. They kept saying what a perfect match we were, and I suppose it did look good on paper, at least. I guess we could have made it work, produced the grandchildren, bought a country house, given good dinner parties. But I just didn't want it."

"I'm sorry you had to go through that," Stone said, because he couldn't think of anything else to say.

"Have you seen this morning's papers?"

"No," Stone said. They had been stuck under his door when he returned to his suite, but he hadn't even looked at them yet.

"We're all over them, and the tabloids are hinting that I killed James for his money! Can you imagine?"

"Well, yes, considering . . ."

"We weren't even married; how could they say I killed him for his money?"

"Well, there is his will."

"What?"

"His will; he made a will. Surely you're aware of that."

"Aware of what? I don't know anything about a will."

"Apparently, James recently made a new will, making you the primary beneficiary."

There was a stunned silence at the other end of the line. "That's preposterous! Why would he do a thing like that before we're married?"

"I don't suppose we'll ever know," Stone replied. "But according to Sir Bernard Pickering, that's what he did."

"Why is it that everyone knows this but me?"

"I thought you did know it; I don't know how Pickering found out, unless he prepared the will."

"Pickering is a barrister; he wouldn't do wills; a solicitor would have to do that."

"Who is James's solicitor?"

"I have no idea . . . Wait a minute, yes I do; I was introduced to him at a party a couple of weeks ago."

"Do Pickering and the solicitor know each other?"

"I don't know; I suppose it's possible."

"Could they work out of the same law firm?"

"Solicitors and barristers are in different firms."

"Have you heard from the solicitor?"

"No."

"I expect you will shortly, if there's any truth to all this."

"Tell me exactly what Pickering told you."

"He said you were now the largest independent importer of wines in Britain and that you now owned a lot of wine shops and pubs."

"Hold on a minute; someone is rapping on my door." She put the phone down and returned after a moment. "It's a letter from James's solicitor," she said. "Hand delivered."

"What does it say?"

"I haven't opened it."

"Open it."

"Oh, Stone, this is so crazy."

"Open the letter and read it to me." He heard the ripping and rustle of paper.

"'Dear blah, blah, blah, condolences, etcetera. It is my duty to inform you that, shortly before his death, Mr. Cutler made a will, in which you are an important beneficiary. I would be grateful if you would call at this office at your convenience so that we may discuss this matter. Yours very sincerely.' It says 'important beneficiary.' That doesn't sound like I inherit everything."

"Maybe it's British understatement."

"Oh, God, I can't deal with this now; I have to arrange a funeral for James in London; he didn't have any family to speak of—both his parents are dead, and he had no brothers or sisters, so it all falls to me."

"Is there anything I can do to help?"

"Stone, will you go and see this solicitor and find out about this?"

"I think it might be better if you had your own solicitor go."

"I don't have one, and I hate Daddy's. Just go and talk to him; I'll tell him you're coming."

"All right. Is there anything else?"

"Let me give you his phone number and address."

Stone wrote it all down, and Sarah's London number as well.

"I'm coming up to London tomorrow, and I'll call you then."

"All right. I'll be around here. Oh, let me give you a portable phone number, too." Stone retrieved the phone from its charging cradle and read off the number, which was taped to the telephone.

"I'll call you tomorrow," she said, "and I'll call the solicitor now."

"All right; tell him I'll wait to hear from him." Stone hung up and went to retrieve the papers. The story was on the inside pages of both the *Times* and the *Independent*, and it was brief in each case. It didn't seem out of the ordinary to Stone. The phone rang. The solicitor, he thought. "Hello?"

"Mr. Barrington, it's Ted Cricket; Bobby Jones and I would like to come and see you, if that's all right."

"Yes, fine. When's good for you?"

"How about six o'clock this evening at your hotel?"

"That's good for me. I'll see you both at six in the same place we met the first time."

"Good, sir." He hung up.

Stone hung up, too, and the phone rang immediately. "Hello?"

"Is that Mr. Barrington?"

"Yes."

"My name is Julian Wainwright; I am solicitor for the estate of James Cutler."

"Oh, yes, Sarah Buckminster said you'd call."

"Miss Buckminster tells me you'll be representing her in the matter of the Cutler estate. I'm a bit confused; you're an American, are you?"

"That's right, but I'm not representing her as an attorney, only as a friend. Sarah is very busy with making funeral arrangements at the moment, and she asked me to see you about the letter you sent her today."

"All right, then; will sometime this afternoon be good?"

"Yes, fine."

"Say, four o'clock?"

"That's fine. I have your address."

"I'll see you at four, then." He hung up.

Stone hung up, too, and sighed. How did he get roped into this?

1 6

THE SOLICITOR'S OFFICE WAS IN PONT
Street, near Harrod's, and Stone was on time. So was
Julian Wainwright; Stone was shown immediately into
his office.

"Been over here long?" Wainwright asked, showing
him to a chair.

"Just a few days," Stone said.

"Known Sarah long?"

"We knew each other when she lived in New York."

"Forgive me, I'm just trying to understand why she
sent you to receive this news."

"I thought I explained that on the phone," Stone
said. "She's busy making funeral arrangements, and,
of course, she's upset about the events of last weekend."

"Ah, yes," Wainwright said, shuffling some papers
on his desk. "Well, I expect you'll want to know the
contents of James Cutler's will."

"That's why I'm here," Stone reminded him.

"It's like this," Wainwright said. "James left be-
quests to Eton College, Magdelan College at Oxford, to
Oxfam—that's a large charity over here—and to his
club, the Athenaeum. The total of those was three hundred thousand pounds." He paused, seeming to have

a hard time reading the neatly typed document before him.

"Go on," Stone said.

"The remainder of his estate, James left to Sarah Buckminster." He took a deep breath and sighed.

"You seem in some way unhappy about this," Stone said.

"I must tell you, I counseled James against it. He came in to make a will which would take effect on his marriage to Sarah. We went over everything very carefully, the full list of his assets. I was quite all right with it all, but when he came back to sign the will, after it had been typed, he noted that the will would take effect on their marriage, and, rather offhandedly, he asked that it be changed to have immediate effect. When I questioned this, he said, 'Oh, hell, I'm marrying the girl in a few months' time, just do as I ask.' So I had the page retyped, and he signed it."

"Was the will properly attested to and witnessed?"

"Of course," Wainwright replied, sounding offended.

"Are you satisfied that the will represents his true intentions at the time he made it?"

"As unwise as his intentions may have been, yes."

"Then I don't see any problem."

"You've read this morning's papers?"

"The *Times* and the *Independent*."

"Not the tabloids?"

"They don't have the tabloids at the Connaught."

"Well, they've as much as accused Sarah of murdering James for his money."

"Then I should think she'd have a very good libel suit against the tabloids," Stone said.

"Quite," Wainwright replied.

"Tell me," Stone said, "when James made this sudden decision to have his will take effect immediately, did he in any way intimate that Sarah was aware of this decision?"

"No, he didn't."

"And his decision seemed to you to be made on the spur of the moment?"

"Yes."

"Are you aware that Sarah was unaware of the will until I told her about it this morning?"

Wainwright's considerable eyebrows shot up. "No, I was not. And, may I ask, how did *you* become aware of the contents of the will?"

"I was told by Sir Bernard Pickering," Stone replied, watching for a reaction, and he got it.

Wainwright gulped but seemed unable to speak.

"Are you and Sir Bernard acquainted?" Stone asked.

"We are next-door neighbors in the country," Wainwright replied.

"And when did you convey the intent of the will to Sir Bernard?"

Wainwright was perspiring now. "I was having dinner at his home on Saturday evening, when he got the call from Lord Wight, requesting his services. I thought it my duty to make him aware of the circumstances."

"For which I'm sure he was grateful," Stone said. "What is the date on the will?"

"Two weeks ago."

"And during that time, did you divulge the contents to any other person, apart from Sir Bernard?"

"I did not."

"To your knowledge, did James Cutler tell anyone else?"

"Not to my knowledge."

"Do you believe he might have told Sarah about the will?"

"I suppose it's possible."

"How long did you represent James Cutler?"

"More than twenty years; we were at Eton together."

"Were you good friends?"

"Very good friends."

"Given your knowledge of your friend and client, do you think it is likely that he would have told Sarah of the contents of the will?"

Wainwright thought for a moment, then shook his head. "No, I do not. James was very closemouthed about that sort of thing."

"That being the case, can we agree that, since Sarah was unlikely to know the contents of the will, there would be no motive for her to intentionally cause his death?"

"I . . . believe we can," Wainwright replied.

"Then I think it would be appropriate for you to issue a public statement to that effect."

Wainwright looked puzzled. "I don't think I've ever issued a public statement about anything."

"Do you know someone at one of the large newspapers?"

The solicitor brightened. "Why, yes, I was at school with a fellow at the *Times*."

"Then I think a phone call to him and a brief interview on the subject would suffice, and your friend would be grateful to you for the story."

"That's rather a good idea," Wainwright said, looking pleased.

Stone avoided chuckling. A largish percentage of the law firms in New York would have retained a publicist for such a chore. "Is there anything else that Sarah should know about the will?"

"No, I don't think so."

"I think she should see a list of James's assets and liabilities," Stone pointed out.

"Oh, of course." He shuffled through the papers on his desk. "I had him prepare a financial statement in conjunction with signing the will." He handed some papers to Stone. "And a copy of the will for Sarah."

Stone looked quickly through the documents. "He didn't have any debt to speak of."

"None more than thirty days old."

"And you are the executor?"

"At James's request."

"Sir Bernard suggested to me that his holdings might easily be sold to one of the wine and spirits conglomerates."

"As a matter of fact, James had a rather rich offer from one of them less than three months ago, but he wasn't inclined to accept it."

"I very much doubt that Sarah will have any interest in running these businesses. Perhaps after the funeral, you might contact that company and see if they're still interested."

"I will certainly do that," Wainwright replied.

"By the way, what was the offer?"

"Four hundred ninety million pounds sterling."

Stone did the math. Around three-quarters of a billion dollars. "Did James build this business from scratch?"

"Oh, heavens, no. He was the fourth generation of Cutlers in the business, but he greatly enlarged the business during his tenure."

"One other thing, Mr. Wainwright: Are there any disaffected siblings or maiden aunts who might challenge this will?"

"None. James was an only child, as was his father before him."

"Any large charities to whom promises had been previously made?"

"None."

"Then you see no reason why this will should not be promptly probated?"

"None at all. Tell me, is Sarah currently represented by a solicitor?"

"No, she's not." Stone stood up and shook Wainwright's hand. "Thank you for being so frank with me. I'll convey what you've told me to Sarah, who I'm sure will have some instructions for you, in due course."

Wainwright looked pleased at the prospect.

Stone left the solicitor's office and started looking for a cab in Sloane Street. Sarah Buckminster was going to be a very happy starving artist, he reckoned. He glanced at his watch. And now he had to get back to his own business.

1 7

STONE WAS ON HIS SECOND CUP OF
tea in the Connaught's lounge when Ted Cricket and
Bobby Jones appeared, exactly on time. When he had
seated them and their tea had been served, he sat back
and waited for their report.

"As you requested," Ted Cricket began, reading
from a notebook like a good cop, "I positioned myself
outside the United States Embassy at eight A.M. this
morning and waited for the appearance of a gentleman of the description provided by you on Friday last.
Such a gentleman appeared just after ten A.M. and
went into the embassy. He emerged at twelve thirty-
nine P.M. with another gentleman, who was American
in his dress, and I followed them to a restaurant and
pub called the Guinea, in a mews just off Berkeley
Square. They remained there for nearly two hours,
then returned to the embassy.

"At half past four, the first gentleman emerged from
the embassy again and, on foot, proceeded to a house
in Green Street, a short walk from the embassy. He let
himself in with a key, and I surmised that the house is
his residence in London. To check this, I knocked on
the door of the basement flat, where a caretaker lives,
and asked him questions regarding the occupants of

the building. He was extremely reluctant to talk to me until I gave him to understand that I was a police officer; then he became marginally more cooperative.

"He divulged, in an oblique manner, that the house was owned by the American government, and that it consisted of four flats occupied by various transient government officials. He knew the gentleman I was following, who occupied the third-floor flat, only as Mr. Gray. Mr. Gray has occupied the third-floor flat for at least four years, though he is often away, and he keeps a considerable wardrobe in the flat. He is apparently unmarried, though he sometimes receives lady guests in the flat. He receives no mail there, and I am inclined to believe that Gray is not the gentleman's real name.

"I am also inclined to believe that Mr. Gray is not, formally speaking, an accredited American representative to Her Majesty's government. He has all the earmarks of a spook." Cricket stopped talking.

"I'm inclined to agree," Stone said. "I'm also inclined to think that it would be fruitless, not to mention dangerous, to attempt to bug Mr. Gray's flat, because if he is a spook, his organization will have taken steps to prevent such an action."

"Agreed," Cricket replied.

"The question now is, how do we find out his real name?"

"I had a thought about that, Mr. Barrington," Cricket said. "Why don't I have his pocket picked?"

Stone smiled. "I think that's a wonderful idea. Can you get it done without his knowing?"

"I know a person who can," Cricket replied confidently. "Mr. Gray might even enjoy the experience."

"I take it your pickpocket is female."

"Indeed, yes."

"Go to it."

Cricket turned to Jones. "Bobby, what do you have for Mr. Barrington?"

Jones produced his own notebook. "I began surveillance of the Farm Street house at seven A.M. this morning. By mid-morning, it became apparent to me that the house was not occupied, except by a cleaning lady who arrived at eight and departed at ten, so I had my man go in and wire the place for sound while I stood guard. He was out by one P.M., and now all the phones serve as taps for us, whether they are in use or not. The microphones are voice-activated and are recorded automatically by a machine in a garage about forty meters from the house. I'll check it daily for anything of interest.

"I continued my surveillance of the house, and a little after three P.M. Mr. Cabot and Miss Burroughs returned and went into the house with some luggage. Less than an hour later, two men arrived outside in a car and knocked at the door. They were large gentlemen, and in spite of extensive tailoring and barbering, they struck me as right out of the East End. They rang the bell, and when Mr. Cabot emerged, they pulled him out of the house and began to rough him up, in the manner, I would say, of debt collectors for a loan shark or a bookmaker. Since I assumed you did not wish the man harmed, I approached, identified myself as a police officer, and asked Mr. Cabot if he required any assistance.

"He said he did not. I asked if he wished to make a charge against either or both of the gentlemen; he said he did not. I took the gentlemen aside and suggested that if I caught them in the neighborhood again I would have them in the nick very shortly. They got into their car and left. By this time, Mr. Cabot was already back inside the house.

"I then went to the garage and listened to the tape recording of what was said in the house. Miss Burroughs asked Mr. Cabot who had been at the door, and he replied, quite coolly, I thought, that some people had knocked at the wrong door. After that their conversation was of a mundane nature, and I reset the recorder. I waited within sight of the house until it was time to come here and see you."

"Very good, Bobby," Stone said. "Were you able to overhear any of the conversation between Cabot and the two men?"

"No, I'm afraid I was out of earshot. I expect they might be leery of returning to the house, but if they should telephone Cabot, we'll have a recording of the conversation."

"Do you have any further instructions for us, Mr. Barrington?" Cricket asked.

"You already know what to do about Mr. Gray; my main concern is to know his real identity. As for Mr. Cabot, Bobby, I'd like to maintain the surveillance on him for a few more days. I want to know who he sees during the days—I don't think we need bother with his evenings. I'm particularly interested to know if he has any criminal contacts. After his encounter with the muscle, I wouldn't be surprised. And, of course, I'd like a daily report on what your recorder picks up."

"Of course," Jones replied. "If anything that sounds remotely interesting is recorded, I'll dub it off onto a portable so you can hear it."

"Very good," Stone said, rising. "I'll look forward to hearing from both of you."

"Mr. Barrington," Cricket said, "may I make a suggestion?"

"Of course."

"I think it might be good for Bobby and me to swap

targets every day. That way, the gentlemen are less likely to spot the tail."

"By all means," Stone said. "Change whenever you wish."

He shook hands with the men, and they left.

Stone returned to his room, and as he entered, the phone rang.

"Hello?"

"It's Sarah; I'm in London. Can we have dinner tonight?"

"All right. Where would you like to meet?"

"Where do you suggest?"

"It's your town."

"There are some press people hanging around outside my flat."

"Then I don't think you should be seen with me; that would just add fuel to the flame."

"I can get out a back way, I think. Why don't I come to the Connaught? I don't think they would follow me inside, and if they did, they'd be thrown out."

"All right."

"What's your suite number?"

"Ah, let's meet in the restaurant."

"Eight-thirty?"

"That should be all right. I'll book the table now."

"How did your meeting with James's solicitor go?"

"It went well; I'll tell you about it tonight."

"Bye-bye." She hung up.

Stone called downstairs and booked the table, then he soaked in a hot tub for a while and lay down for a nap. As he drifted off, he wondered who had sent the hoods to deal with Lance Cabot.

18

SARAH WAS LATE. STONE SAT AT THE corner table in the handsome Connaught restaurant, with its glowing mahogany paneling, and sipped a vodka gimlet as slowly as he could manage. The restaurant quickly filled with people, and still Sarah did not arrive. He knew that if she phoned, the front desk would get a message to him, and he wondered why she had not.

Then she came into the dining room, looking flustered. Mr. Chevalier, the maître d', showed her to the table, and Stone stood up to receive her, pecking her on the cheek.

"God, I need a drink," she said, breathless. A waiter materialized at her elbow. "A large Johnnie Walker Black," she said to him, "on ice." The waiter vanished and returned with the drink.

"Take a few deep breaths," Stone said.

"It didn't work, going out the back way," she said, pulling at the drink. "I had planned to get a taxi, but they were laying for me in the mews, and I had to duck into the garage and drive my car. I went twice around Belgrave Square at high speed, with them on my tail, and I finally lost them at Hyde Park Corner, when some traffic cut them off. God, these people are awful!"

"I'm glad you finally evaded them," Stone said. Then, near the restaurant's door, a flashgun went off. Some people in the restaurant turned and looked in the direction of the photographer, but Stone noted that others hid behind their menus or napkins. Apparently, not all the couples in the restaurant were married, at least, not to each other.

The flashgun went off again, but two waiters were grappling with the photographer, pushing him into the hallway. He was complaining loudly about freedom of the press and making as big a fuss as possible, but gradually his voice faded as they got him into the lobby, then out the door. Stone saw the man outside a window, jumping up and down, trying to spot his prey, then a police officer appeared and led him away by the collar.

"Apparently, I didn't lose them," Sarah said. "I hope to God his pictures don't come out."

"I wouldn't count on it," Stone said.

"Did you see the tabloids? They know your name. Apparently, there was a reporter at the inquest, though I didn't see any photographers. Apparently, there aren't any newsworthy rock stars or politicians anymore, so they've settled on me. I've never had an experience like this." She signaled the waiter for another drink.

"Slow down," he said. "You've still got to drive home, you know." The waiter came and brought menus.

"I can't deal with it; you order."

Stone turned to the waiter. "Surprise us." The waiter vanished.

"Just keep breathing deeply," he said. "Don't rely on the whiskey to calm you down." He took the drink from her hand and placed it on the table. "Now, would you like to hear about my meeting with Julian Wainwright?"

"Yes, please; I'd like something else to think about."

"Well, you've a lot to think about," Stone said. "First, let me ask you some questions: Did James say anything to you about making you his beneficiary?"

"No. Well, he mentioned something in passing, like, 'Of course I'll have to make a new will,' but I assumed he meant after we were married."

"Were you aware of the day he went to sign the will?"

"Yes, because we had seen his solicitor the night before. I knew he was going there."

"Did you discuss the will at all?"

"No, he just said he was going to see Julian; he implied that he had a number of things to discuss with him. There had been an offer for his companies some time back, and I think they were going to talk about that."

"Yes, Julian mentioned that." Stone patted his pocket. "I have the will and James's financial statement, and I'll give them to you later, but the thrust of it is that he left three hundred thousand pounds—"

"Good God! He left me three hundred thousand pounds?"

"No, he left that much to his schools and to charities. He left everything else to you."

She stared at him blankly. "You mean his business?"

"Yes."

Her eyes welled up a little. "I don't know anything about running a business; I don't want it. Tell Julian to take it back."

"Take it easy, now, that's not how it works. You don't have to run the business."

"I don't?"

"Remember the offer that James was discussing with Julian?"

"Yes."

"I asked Julian to investigate whether discussions might be reopened."

"So you think Julian can sell it?"

"Yes."

"What a relief!"

"Do you want to know how much it's worth?"

"Yes, please."

"The offer was for four hundred and ninety million pounds."

Her mouth dropped open. "Surely you mean thousand."

"No, million."

"But that's . . ."

"A lot of money."

"Oh, my God."

"Of course, there will be taxes to pay and other fees, but you should come out of this with a substantial amount of cash or stock."

"I think I'd prefer cash," she said absently, as if her mind were elsewhere.

"And there were other things—James's house in London and a country house, investments. He was a very wealthy man."

"I knew he was well off," she said, "but I had no idea, really. He never talked about it much, the way a lot of businessmen do. I thought he was in it because he loved wine so much, and because his father before him was."

"And his grandfather and great-grandfather, apparently."

"He didn't even mention that."

"Do you know the two houses?"

"Of course. They're both in wonderful locations, but they need a complete redoing."

"I'm sure you'll enjoy that."

Their dinner arrived, and they talked less as they dined. Stone thought the food was sublime, as was the wine Mr. Chevalier had chosen for them. "I don't think I'll ever look at a menu here again," Stone said.

"Stone, I never had a chance to ask you: Why are you in London?"

"A client asked me to come and look into something for him."

"Something? What thing?"

"I can't tell you that; client confidentiality."

"Of course, I should have known. Is it one of those wonky investigation things you get into?"

"Sort of. Tell me, how do you know Monica and Erica Burroughs?"

"I've known Monica for years; she sells my work."

"Of course, I knew that."

"But I met Erica only recently, when she and Lance came over."

"Do you know Lance well?"

"Not really, but he's very nice."

"What does he do?"

"Something mysterious; I could never figure it out."

"Neither could I."

They ate on, finishing with dessert and coffee.

"I think I'd like a brandy," she said.

"Careful, you're driving, and I hear they're tough about that in this country. I want you to get home in one piece, and without getting arrested."

"I can't go home," she said. "They'll be waiting for me."

"Can you go to a friend's?"

"I can't even leave the hotel; they're bound to be waiting outside. I'll stay with you." Her foot rubbed against his leg under the table.

"No, you won't," Stone said. "First of all, you're supposed to be in mourning."

"I'm not a widow!"

"Near enough. Second, they have a photograph of us together; if you don't leave the hotel, they'll make a very big thing of that. What you have to do is, walk out of the hotel like a citizen, get into your car, and drive home. Ignore any questions or photographers, and lock your doors. Live your normal life, except stay out of men's hotel suites. You can't become a fugitive; they'll go away eventually. Once the funeral is behind you, they'll lose interest."

"I hate this," she said.

"It won't last forever."

"I mean, I hate not being able to sleep with you."

"You've already done that, remember?"

She giggled. "I'll bet you thought I was Monica."

"No comment." He pushed back from the table and walked her to the lobby. "Now, shake my hand," he said. "They could be anywhere."

She shook his hand, then stole a peck on his cheek.

"Oh, you should have these." He handed her the will and the financial statement, and she tucked them into her bag. "Bye," she said, then walked out.

As soon as she was out the door, flashguns began popping.

19

BOBBY JONES STOOD ON GREEN STREET, half a block from the house where John Bartholomew resided. He wore a suit and a cloth cap and, in spite of the warm weather, a raincoat. Bobby had learned, after years of surveillance, how to stand for long periods of time without becoming too tired. He wore thick-soled black shoes, and inside were sponge pads to cradle his feet. He had been there since eight a.m. It was now nearly half past nine.

Bartholomew came through the front door and down the steps, then turned toward Grosvenor Square and the American Embassy.

Bobby crossed the street and followed, keeping the half-block distance. He had expected Bartholomew to go straight to the embassy, but instead, the man crossed the street and began walking east along the little park at the center of the square. Well, blimey, Bobby thought, he's on to me already. Bobby didn't follow; instead, he walked to a bench that offered a good view of the square, checked to be sure Bartholomew wasn't looking at him, shucked off the raincoat, turned it inside out, and it became tweed. He stuffed his cloth cap into a pocket, sat down, opened his newspaper, and set his half-glasses on the tip of his nose, so he could look over them. In a practiced fashion, he would glance at Bartholomew, then down at his paper, turning a page occasionally, then look back at his quarry.

Bartholomew proceeded around the square at a march, swinging an umbrella and taking in the sunny morning like a tourist. He crossed the street again, but instead of walking into the embassy through the front door, he continued straight along the street toward the entrance of the passport office, disappearing around the corner of the building.

Bobby sat his ground, resisting the urge to run to the corner to see if he had gone inside. Bartholomew would go inside, Bobby was sure; the man worked there, didn't he? What he would do now was go upstairs, then peer out the window to see if his tail was still here. Bobby, accordingly, got up, crossed the street, and went into the little chemist's shop on South Audley Street, where he browsed for a few minutes, then bought a small tin of aspirin. Finally, he returned to Grosvenor Square, walked to the farthest point from the embassy, and took a seat on another bench to wait for lunchtime.

Bartholomew looked from his window down into Grosvenor Square. "He's gone," he said to his companion. "But I'm sure he was tailing me."

"You're getting paranoid in your old age, Stan," the man said. "Who would want to follow you anymore? The Cold War is over."

"Maybe for you," Bartholomew replied.

At twelve o'clock sharp a handsome blonde woman in a black silk raincoat approached Bobby's park bench. "Mr. Jones?" she asked.

Bobby stood. "Yes, indeed," he replied.

"I'm Moira Bailey, Ted Cricket's friend."

"Glad to meet you," Bobby said, shaking her hand. "Let's take a stroll around the park, shall we?"

"Love to." She took his arm.

They walked up and down the little park, always keeping the front door of the embassy in sight. "I'll point him out when he leaves," Bobby said, "then he's all yours."

"Right," Moira replied.

They had to wait for three-quarters of an hour before Bartholomew appeared, walking with another man, no doubt the American that Ted Cricket had spotted him with the day before.

"He's the taller of the two," Bobby said. He handed her a card. "Here's my cellphone number; let me know when you're done."

"Right," Moira replied, then set off down the square, keeping Bartholomew in sight.

Bartholomew and his friend walked down into Berkeley Square, then down an adjoining mews and into a restaurant. Moira waited two minutes, then followed them in.

The two men were standing near the end of a crowded bar, each with a pint of bitter. Bartholomew was leaning on the bar, pulling his suit tight against his body. Nothing in the hip pocket, she thought. Then he fished his wallet from an inside coat pocket and took out a five-pound note to pay. Oh, thanks, she thought, taking it all in. She saw the ladies' room door past them, up a couple of steps, and she walked toward it, catching Bartholomew's eye and interest along the way, offering him a little smile. She went into the ladies', freshened her makeup, and went out again. Bartholomew had stationed himself where he could watch her come out. She smiled at him again, then put a foot out, missed the first step, and began to fall forward.

Bartholomew took a step forward, his pint in his left hand, stuck out an arm, and, grazing a breast, caught her in his right arm.

She deliberately did not regain her feet right away, leaning into him, staggering him a couple of steps away from the bar.

"There," he said, lifting and setting her on her feet again.

"I'm so sorry," she said breathlessly. "My heel caught on the step."

"It's quite all right," Bartholomew said. He still had his arm around her. "I think you should have a drink with us and regain your composure."

"Oh, I wish I could," she said. "You seem very nice, but I'm on my way to a rather important appointment. I just came in here to use the ladies'."

"Oh, come on," Bartholomew said. "What'll it be? Harry?" he called to the bartender.

"No, really, I can't," Moira said. "I'd love to another time, though." She didn't want to be there when he discovered his wallet was missing.

"Give me your number, then."

She fished in her handbag and came up with a card, identifying her as Ruth Hedger. "You'll most likely catch me in the early evenings," she said. "Do you have a card?"

"Name's Bill," he said. "You can remember that, can't you?"

"Surely," she said. "Thank you for saving me from a nasty fall." She turned her large eyes on his like headlights, making him smile. "Bye-bye." She continued down the bar, knowing his eyes were on her ass, and out into the mews.

Once outside, she walked back to the square and turned a corner, making sure Bartholomew had not followed her, then she took a tiny cellphone from her pocket, checked Jones's card, and punched in the number.

"Yes?" Jones said.

"I've got it."

"Where are you?"

"In Berkeley Square."

"You know Jack Barclay's?"

"Yes."

"Go and look at a Rolls; I'll be there in five minutes."

She hung up and walked along the east side of the square toward the Rolls-Royce dealer. She walked inside, immediately attracting a young salesman, who looked her up and down rather indiscreetly, she thought.

"May I help you?" he asked.

She glanced at her watch. "I'm meeting my husband here; we wanted to look at a Bentley."

"Right over here," the young man said, taking her elbow and steering her toward a gleaming white automobile. "This is the Arnage, in our Magnolia color," he said. "Eye-catching, don't you think?"

"It's gorgeous," she said, catching sight of Bobby Jones over his shoulder. "Oh, there he is!" She waved and smiled brightly.

Bobby approached them. "Hello dear," she said, pecking him on a cheek. "Isn't this a beautiful Bentley?"

Bobby looked at the car sourly. "You'll have to be content with your Mercedes," he said. "Let's get out of here." He took her arm and guided her toward the door, with never a glance at the salesman.

20

AFTER BREAKFAST STONE LEFT THE
Connaught and began to wander aimlessly around
Mayfair, window-shopping and thinking. He was
making precious little progress in his investigation of
Lance Cabot, and even less in his investigation of his
client, John Bartholomew, or whoever he was. Still, he
had been in England for only a few days; perhaps he
was being impatient.

Finally, his impatience led him into Farm Street,
where he saw Ted Cricket standing at the far end. He
did not approach the house, but he motioned for
Cricket to go to the next mews, and they met there.

"Anything to report?" Stone asked.

"Not yet, Mr. Barrington," Cricket replied, "but then
I didn't expect for anything to happen. They haven't
left the house yet, and when I checked the tape, there
had only been a couple of phone calls, both for Miss
Burroughs, both innocuous."

"Heard anything from Bobby?"

"Not yet, but I expect we'll have some results before
the day's out. We have your cellphone number, if anything of note occurs."

"Thanks, Ted; I'll talk to you later." Stone walked
back up the mews and slowly back toward the Con-

naught. He passed the Hayward tailor shop, but didn't go in; it was too soon for fittings on the jackets he had ordered. His pocket phone rang.

"Hello?"

"Mr. Barrington, it's Bobby Jones."

"Yes, Bobby?"

"I have what you wanted; can we meet?"

"I'll be at the Connaught in two minutes."

"So will I, sir."

Stone encountered Bobby at the front door, and they went in together and sat down in the lounge. Bobby reached into his raincoat pocket and presented Stone with a large wallet.

Stone received it in a handkerchief and lightly turned it over. It was of alligator, and it must have cost a bundle, Stone thought. He looked inside and found more than five hundred pounds, mostly in fifty-pound notes. One side of the wallet held three credit cards, an ATM card from Barclays bank, an international health insurance card, and half a dozen calling cards, all in the name of Stanford Hedger, Mayfair House, Green Street. The credit cards were in the same name. "Well," he said, "at least we have his name, now."

"The lady pickpocket said he introduced himself as Bill, so Hedger could be a false name, too."

"If it is, he's gone to a great deal of trouble to establish that identity. Since we know he lives at the Green Street address, I'm inclined to think that Hedger is his real name."

"Maybe so, but these buggers have a thousand names, if they want them."

"Bobby, can you dust this for fingerprints and have them checked with the international database?"

"I have a friend who can," Bobby replied. "Of course, my prints are on it, as are the pickpocket's."

"How long will it take?"

"A day or two, depending on how busy my friend is."

"All right."

"What do you want me to do with the wallet after that?"

"Wipe all the prints off it and stick it through the mail slot of Hedger's building. Maybe he'll think someone found and returned it."

"All right, sir; I'll be on my way then." Bobby took the wallet back in a handkerchief of his own, tucked it into a raincoat pocket, and left.

Stone went upstairs. It was just coming onto nine o'clock, New York time, and he called Bill Eggers, who he knew came in early.

"Eggers."

"Hi, it's Stone."

"Hey. What's up?"

"Does the name Stanford Hedger mean anything to you?"

"Sounds familiar," Eggers said, "but I can't place it. Who is he?"

"That's what I want to know. I think it may be Bartholomew's real name. By the way, he works for the government, probably in intelligence."

"That doesn't surprise me, based on who sent him to me, but I can't elaborate on that."

"I see."

"I hope you do."

"Of course I do, Bill, but should you get some information that doesn't compromise your relationship with a client, will you pass it on to me?"

"Okay, I can do that."

"Talk to you later."

Stone thought it might not be too early to call his old professor, Samuel Bernard.

"Yes?" The voice was surprisingly weak.

"It's Stone Barrington, sir; how are you?"

"Oh, I've had a bad couple of days, but I'm better now."

"Is this not a good time to talk?"

"No, no, go right ahead. What can I do for you?"

"Does the name Stanford Hedger mean anything to you?"

"Indeed it does," Bernard replied without hesitation.

"Who is he?"

"When I knew him, and later, when I only knew *of* him, he was considered one of the agency's brightest young men."

"Tell me about him."

"He was a bit impulsive, perhaps even wild, but that doesn't hurt one's reputation in the Company, if the results are good. Of course, if one makes a mistake . . ."

"Did Hedger make a mistake?"

"He did, and I can't tell you about it, except to say that it cost the lives of half a dozen operatives in a Middle Eastern country. Fortunately for Hedger, none of them was American, or he would have been in real trouble."

Stone wasn't sure what else to ask. "Is there anything else you can tell me about him?"

"There was a wife, in his youth, but she died in an automobile accident. Hedger was driving, and he was said to have been broken up by the event, though I never knew him to be broken up by anything. He had a level of self-confidence that is usually only found in maniacs, and that seemed to make him impervious to most disastrous events, like his Middle Eastern debacle. I shouldn't think it took him long to get over his wife's death."

"Anything else?"

"He was extraordinarily brave, in the physical sense, which, I suppose, comes with his level of self-confidence. I doubt if he believed that anyone could ever do him harm. He garnered a couple of medals for valor, and that stood him in good stead in the agency. Still, careful people never trusted him, and there are always a lot of careful people in the Company."

"What about those who were not so careful?"

"There are always those in the Company, too, and they always found uses for Hedger. Later, when he rose to supervisory levels, he attracted younger men who seemed to share his attitudes. He was kept busy keeping them out of trouble, which some saw as his just reward."

"Do you have any idea what he might be involved with now?"

"I shouldn't think he's involved with anything. He's dead."

That brought Stone up short. "Are you sure?"

"He died in an explosion in Cairo about two years ago—one caused by an Islamic fundamentalist suicide bomber."

"Was his body identified?"

"Some body parts were, I believe. If you'll forgive me, Stone, I have a visitor, who's on the way upstairs now. I'll call you if I think of anything else. You're still at the Connaught?"

"Yes, sir, and thank you."

Stone hung up the phone, baffled more than before.

2 1

THE FUNERAL SERVICE FOR JAMES CUT-
ler took place at the Catholic church in Farm Street,
which Stone remembered being mentioned in the novels of Evelyn Waugh. All the people present at the house
party the weekend before attended, plus a great many
others, many of whom Stone surmised were business
acquaintances of the deceased. Julian Wainwright was
prominent among them, looking suitably sorrowful.
When the service was over, many of those present ad-
journed to the house occupied by Lance Cabot and
Erica Burroughs, which was conveniently nearby.

A light lunch was served, and Stone had a glass of
wine. He wandered idly through the house looking at
pictures and taking in the place. It was handsomely
decorated, and Stone wondered if Lance had had it
done or if the house came that way when it was rented.
As he strolled down a hallway, he heard Lance's voice
through an ajar door, apparently to the study.

"Let me make this as clear for you as I possibly can,"
Lance was saying, "if you persist in this, if you send
anyone else for me, I'll kill them, then I'll find you and
I'll kill you. That is a solemn promise." Then he
slammed the handset down onto the receiver.

Stone ducked into a powder room and closed the

door. He wanted to hear all of that conversation, and fortunately, he had the means to do so quite nearby. He ducked out of the house and found Bobby Jones down the street.

"Good day," Jones said.

"I want to hear what's on the recorder," Stone said.

"Of course; I'll take you there."

Stone followed the little man to a garage nearby. Jones unlocked a small door in the larger one and closed it behind them. He went to a cupboard at the rear of the garage, unlocked a padlock, and opened the door to reveal a small tape machine. "How far back today do you want me to go?"

"The last conversation," Stone replied.

Jones rewound the tape, and the sound of voices backward and at speed could be heard, then stopped. He punched a button and the recorder began to play.

"*Hello?*" Lance's voice.

"*I want it,*" another male voice said. "*You're all out of time.*" The quality of the connection was poor, as if the call were coming from some Third World country.

"*Let me make this as clear for you as I possibly can,*" Lance said, and the rest was as Stone had heard a moment before.

"Let me hear it again," Stone said.

Jones rewound the machine, and Stone listened carefully. The voice was American, he thought, but he could not be sure, and it didn't sound like Bartholomew. "Once more," Stone said, and listened.

"Sounds like he's got somebody on his back," Jones said, resetting the machine.

"Yes, it does."

"Sounds like money to me."

"Could be. Could be almost anything of value— even information."

"I suppose so, but I'm a copper right to the bone, and I tend to think in the simplest terms, especially where a threat to kill is involved."

"You could be right," Stone admitted. "By the way, I checked with a knowledgeable friend in New York, and Stanford Hedger has been dead for two years."

"You could have fooled me," Jones said, letting them out of the garage and locking the door behind him. "What do you make of that?"

"Well, one of two things, I guess: either Hedger isn't dead, or he's dead and Bartholomew is using his identity for some purpose."

"This is far too thick for me," Jones said. "Give me a nice homicide any day; I never know what to make of these spooks."

"You've had experience with them before?"

"Yes, but only with the blokes on our side—MI6. The trouble with trying to figure them out is you never know what they want, and if they explained it to you, you probably wouldn't understand it."

Stone laughed. "I see your point. I have a feeling, though, that whatever is going on here is taking place outside the bounds of any official action. It sounds awfully personal to me."

Stone said goodbye to Jones and returned to the party. As he entered the house, he encountered Lance, who had an empty glass in his hand.

"Where did you go?" Lance asked, motioning him to follow toward the bar.

"Just for a stroll; I felt like some air."

"I know the feeling," Lance replied. "These wakes can be oppressive."

"It was good of you to have it here."

"I'm happy to help out Sarah at a difficult time." He

got a drink from the barman and led Stone out into a small garden. They sat down on a teak bench.

"Lovely house," Stone said.

"I had nothing to do with that," Lance said. "It came as you see it, right from the agency. The owner is with the Foreign Office; he's in India or someplace."

"Good break for you."

"The rent isn't a good break. Tell me, is what I've been reading in the papers true?"

"I don't know; what have you been reading?"

"That Sarah is going to inherit James's estate."

"That much is true," Stone said. "I've seen the will."

"How much?"

"Hard to say; difficult to put a value on the business." So far, he hadn't told Lance anything that wasn't public knowledge.

"I suppose Sarah will sell it."

"I don't know if she's had time to think about it. I imagine there'll be quite a lot of legal work to be done before it's settled."

"This turn of events brings me back to what I initially said to you about the boating *accident*."

"You still think it wasn't an accident?"

"I have a suspicious mind."

"Well, I've looked into it a bit, and so has Sir Bernard Pickering, and to my knowledge, no information has arisen to indicate that Sarah even knew about the contents of James's will."

"But you can't say definitively that she did or didn't know."

"I don't think anyone can, but it's my best judgment, based on what Sarah has told me and on my knowledge of her character, that she did not know."

"You sound as if you're testifying at a trial."

"You sound as if you're conducting one."

Lance laughed. "Fair enough."

"How well did you know James?"

"I'd met him two or three times."

"What did you think of him?"

"I thought that, like a lot of men, he was very smart about business and very stupid about almost everything else."

"You mean about Sarah?"

"Yes. She obviously didn't love him."

Stone nodded. "I think you're right; she was under a lot of pressure from her parents to marry him. I don't think she would have gone through with it."

"I do."

"Why?"

"Because Sarah impressed me as someone who would not have let an opportunity like James get past her."

"That's a pretty cynical view. How well do you know Sarah?"

"Not all that well, but I'm a pretty good judge of character."

This conversation was going nowhere, Stone thought. He decided to change the subject. "Do you know someone named Stanford Hedger?"

Lance turned and looked at him for a moment. "No, I don't," he said. Then he got up and walked back into the house, leaving Stone on the garden bench.

22

STONE RETURNED TO THE CONNAUGHT, and as he entered, he caught sight of Ted Cricket sitting in the lounge, having a cup of tea. Stone joined him.

Cricket looked grim. He reached into a pocket and handed Stone a single sheet of paper.

Stone unfolded it.

The fingerprints on the wallet were checked against all available databases. Only in the United States was there an apparent match, but no identity was provided. Instead, a message appeared onscreen, stating: "This record is unavailable, for reasons of national security." I have returned the wallet to the Green Street house, as per your instructions.

This letter constitutes my resignation from the assignment. Mr. Cricket will present you with my bill. Please do not contact me again.

It was signed by Bobby Jones.

"I understand about the fingerprints," Stone said to Cricket, "but what's wrong with Bobby?"

Cricket handed him another sheet of paper, outlining Jones's fee and expenses. "He'd be grateful for cash," Cricket said.

"Of course," Stone replied, reaching for the envelope containing Bartholomew's expense money. He handed Cricket the cash, including a generous bonus. "Thank him for his help, will you?"

"Of course."

"Now tell me what's going on with Bobby."

"When Bobby returned the wallet, he was apparently followed from the house by two men. They dragged him into an alley and beat him badly."

"Jesus, is he all right?"

"He will be, eventually. He's in hospital at the moment."

"I want to go and see him."

"He doesn't want to see you, Mr. Barrington. He regards the beating as a message from Mr. Bartholomew to stay away from him and from you."

"I'd like to pay any medical bills."

"We have a National Health Service in this country."

Stone peeled off another thousand pounds from Bartholomew's money and handed it to Cricket. "Then please give him this; if he needs more, let me know."

Cricket pocketed the money. "I'm sure he'll be grateful."

"What about you, Ted? Do you want out of this?"

"No, sir; I'd like to stay on it in the hope of meeting the two gentlemen who did this to Bobby."

"I understand, but I can't promise that will happen."

"It will, if I continue to follow Bartholomew."

"I don't want you to get hurt, too, Ted."

"Believe me, Mr. Barrington, it is not I who will be hurt."

"Ted . . ."

"Let me deal with this, please. I know what I'm doing."

"I don't want anyone killed."

"I've no intention of doing that."

"I don't want Bartholomew touched."

"I won't promise you that."

"This isn't how this was supposed to go."

"I understand that, but it went that way."

"I'll continue to pay you to watch Lance Cabot," Stone said. "But I don't want you near Bartholomew. Don't follow him again."

"In that case, I'll have to leave your employ, Mr. Barrington." He handed over another sheet of paper. "Here's my bill."

Stone paid it.

Cricket stood up and offered his hand. "I'm sorry it turned out this way, Mr. Barrington; I know you're a gentleman and that you didn't intend for anything like this to happen."

"Thank you, Ted, and I wish you luck."

"And the very best to you, Mr. Barrington. Oh, by the way, I'll leave the tape recorder going in the garage for the time being."

Stone shook his head. "Don't bother; I'll be returning to New York, as soon as I take care of a couple of loose ends."

"Then I'll have the equipment removed," Cricket said. He turned and left the hotel.

Stone went to the concierge's desk and asked to be booked on a flight to New York the following day, then he went to his suite. He took out the little satellite phone, positioned himself near the window, and from the phone's memory, dialed Bartholomew's number.

It was answered on the second ring. "Yes?"

"It's Stone Barrington."

"What do you have to report?"

"You and I have to meet right away."

"I'm in New York."

"We both know that's a lie; you're staying at a house in Green Street and visiting the American Embassy every day."

There was a grinding silence for a moment, then Bartholomew said, "The Green Street house in an hour."

"No; someplace public."

"All right, the Garrick Club, at six o'clock, in the bar; I'll leave your name at the door."

"I'll be there." Stone hung up. He stretched out on the bed and tried to nap. Jet lag took a long time to completely go away.

The Garrick Club porter directed Stone up the stairs, which were hung with portraits of dead actors, costumed for their greatest roles. The whole clubhouse seemed to be a museum of the theater. Stone found the bar at the top of the stairs, and in this room, the portraits were of actors more recently dead—Noel Coward and Laurence Olivier and their contemporaries. The bar was not crowded, and Bartholomew stood at the far end.

"What are you drinking?" he asked.

"Nothing, thank you."

Bartholomew shrugged. "As you wish. Let's go in the other room." He led the way to an adjoining reading room and settled into one of a pair of leather chairs. "Now, what's so important?"

Stone fished an envelope from his pocket and handed it over. "This is the remainder of the money you gave me, and an accounting of what I spent. I'm returning to New York tomorrow."

"But you can't do that," Bartholomew said, alarmed.

"Watch me. I've had enough of your lies, Mr. Hedger, if that's your real name."

"*You* stole my wallet?"

"I had it done. And you're responsible for putting a retired policeman in the hospital."

"He was working for *you*? I had no way of knowing that."

"I should warn you that there's another retired policeman, a much larger one, looking for you right now, and I wouldn't want to be in your shoes when he finds you."

"Oh, Christ," Bartholomew said, tugging at his whiskey. "What the hell were you doing having me followed and my pocket picked?"

"I like to know the truth about the work I do, and I wasn't getting it from you."

Bartholomew rubbed his face with his hands.

"What is your real name?"

"That's not important," Bartholomew said. "You're better off not knowing, believe me."

"As you wish. Since Stanford Hedger is dead, I'll assume that's just another alias." His eyes narrowed. "Or maybe not. You *are* Hedger, aren't you? And you just want someone to think you're dead."

"How the hell do you know about that?"

"I have my resources, Mr. Hedger." Stone decided to fire a guess. "Tell me, was Lance Cabot one of your bright young men at the Company?"

Hedger shot him a sharp glance. "You're wandering into an area where you shouldn't be."

"I've been in that area since I arrived in London," Stone replied. "Thanks to you. What was it you really wanted to accomplish when you put me onto Lance Cabot's back?"

"You're better off not knowing."

Stone guessed again. "It wasn't exactly official Company business, was it?"

Hedger shook his head slowly.

"What was it about?"

"All right, I'll tell you; I guess I owe you that. But you breathe a word of this, and you'll be in more trouble than you can imagine."

For a moment, Stone thought he probably shouldn't know this; then he changed his mind. "Tell me," he said.

2 3

HEDGER, IF THAT WAS HIS NAME, leaned back in his chair and sipped his whiskey. "It was a Middle Eastern operation," he said, "and those are always a mess. We had—still have—a shortage of Arabic-speaking operatives, locals who blend in—and that always makes things difficult. Even when you recruit them, you can never really put any trust in them; you never know if they're doubling for Hamas, or some other radical organization.

"Cabot fit in really well out there; his Arabic was outstanding—so good that he could impersonate an Arab on the phone, if not in person; he wore the region like an old shoe. So much so that I began to suspect him."

"Of what? Of being an Arab?"

"Of course not; the man looks like a California surfer, doesn't he?"

No, Stone thought, but he understood what Hedger meant. "If you say so."

"I began to feel that he was too much taking the part of the people who were supposed to be the opposition. He didn't like the Israelis we dealt with—thought they were too smart and too devious—and he seemed charmed by Arab custom and even by their fanaticism.

He said that's the way he would be if he were a Palestinian. That sort of comment doesn't go down well with one's colleagues, you know?"

"I can imagine."

"Lance developed some Palestinian contacts—a man and a woman—whom he trusted, but I didn't. He kept making the case that we should take them inside, tell them more. I wouldn't do it. I always felt that, the moment we turned our backs, they'd be on the phone to Yasser Arafat or somebody, and that we'd end up paying the price. Well, we did."

"Did trust them?"

"To an extent. And we paid the price. We put together an operation—I can't tell you exactly what, but it was supposed to disrupt the leadership of a particularly virulent organization. Lance and I went to Cairo, where our people there put together two explosive devices that were to be carried into buildings by our two operatives, concealed somewhere, then left with timers set. We arranged a meeting in a safe house, and both operatives showed up, but Lance didn't. He called and said he'd be late. I explained to these two people how the devices worked, and showed them how to set the timers. I waited as long as I could for Lance, then I sent them on their way. Five minutes later, the safe house exploded. The operatives had brought something with them. Lance was, apparently, watching from across the street, and he was on the scene very quickly.

"I was unconscious and was taken to a safe hospital. When I woke up and figured out what had happened, I told my people to tell Lance I had died. That's how Stan Hedger came to be dead."

"Does Lance still believe you're dead?"

"No, certainly not. We ran into each other in Paris

last year, so that was that. Lance left the Company shortly after the Cairo debacle and went private."

"What does that mean?"

"It means he used the contacts he'd made in the Middle East while serving the Company to serve himself. He began trading in arms, drugs, Japanese automobiles, whatever he could get his hands on, buy or sell. He's still dealing with the two operatives who nearly killed me."

"I can see how your people might be unhappy with him."

"Unhappy, yes, but officially, he can't be touched."

"Why not?"

"Because he can't be proved to have committed a crime, or even to have sold me out. Contrary to popular belief, the Company no longer blithely assassinates people who have annoyed it. Never did, really."

"But you still want to hurt him."

"I want him out of circulation. He's a danger to people he once served with, like me, and he's not exactly working in his country's best interests."

"So you're doing this privately, without Company cooperation?"

"Why do you think I hired you?"

"Well, I'm afraid you've thrown a monkey wrench into my investigation of Lance."

"How so?"

"There were two retired cops working for me, remember? They were taking turns surveilling you and Lance. Now one's in the hospital, and the other has quit. He's the one who wants to meet up with you in a dark alley."

"I'm really very sorry about the whole thing with the man being hurt," Hedger said, sounding sincere. "In my business, you do not deal kindly with strangers who follow you and pick your pocket."

Stone felt a pang of guilt. That was something he should have considered. "In any case, I don't see how I can be helpful to you after all that's happened. Lance knows who I am; we've socialized. I can hardly sneak up on him. And I've used my only police contact to hire these two men, one of whom is now badly hurt. I don't feel I can go back to my contact and ask him for more help."

Hedger looked thoughtful. "You say you and Lance have become friendly?"

"'Friendly' may be too strong a word. We know each other; I like his girl and her sister."

"Oh, yes, Monica took you down to Lord Wight's place, didn't she?"

"Yes."

"And you knew Wight's daughter from New York?"

"Yes."

"Well?"

"Rather well."

"So you have a plausible social history, as far as Cabot is concerned?"

"Yes."

"Then I can't see any reason why you shouldn't continue to investigate him, but more from the inside."

"For one thing, I mentioned your name to him yesterday."

"What?"

"I asked him if he knew someone called Stanford Hedger; he said no, then walked away."

"Why the hell did you do that?"

"I was still trying to figure out who you were, remember? If you had told me the truth—"

"Does he know why you asked about me?"

"No."

"All right, here's what you do: At the first opportunity, tell Lance everything that's happened—about my hiring you, and all that, right up to this meeting. But you tell him you quit, that you were disgusted with my lying to you."

"What would that accomplish?"

"It would disarm his suspicions. Don't tell him that you know anything about Cairo or his having been in the agency; just tell him our conversation stopped at the point where you handed me back my money and quit."

Stone thought about this. It was an intriguing situation, and he did not like Lance for doing the kind of business he was doing.

"You'd be doing a good turn for your country, if that means anything to you," Hedger said, pushing the hook in a little deeper.

"I don't know."

"Give it another week," Hedger said. He removed another, fatter envelope from his pocket and tossed it into Stone's lap. "Live it up a bit; see more of London and Monica, Erica, and, above all, Lance. I just want to know what he's up to, so I can stop him doing it."

"Tell me the truth; do you intend to kill him?"

"Stone, if I'd intended that, he'd have been dead two years ago."

"All right," Stone said finally. "Another week, and that's it."

"It's all I ask. How about a drink, now, and some dinner downstairs? Have you ever visited this club? Know anything about it?"

Then Bartholomew/Hedger, who was suddenly not such a bad guy after all, launched into a history of the Garrick Club and a list of its famous members.

Stone was charmed, a little, and he accepted Hedger's dinner invitation.

2 4

STONE WOKE THE FOLLOWING MORN-
ing with a hangover, the result, he was sure, of the
great quantity of port that he and Hedger had shared
at the Garrick Club. They had dined in the club's main
dining room, a long, tall hall with acres of walls filled
with fine portraits, the room's red paint browned by
decades of tobacco smoke. Stone had spotted a former
American secretary of state and half a dozen well-
known actors, and Hedger had pointed out government officials, barristers, and journalists among the
crowd. Stone had been impressed.

Now he was depressed. He made a constant effort
not to overindulge; he had failed, and the result was
worse than jet lag. The phone rang—more loudly than
usual, he thought. "Hello?"

"Good morning, it's Sarah," she said brightly. It was
the first time they had spoken since the funeral.

"Good morning," Stone struggled to say.

"You sound hungover."

"It's jet lag."

"No, you're hungover, I can tell. You always
sounded this way when you were hungover." She had
him at the disadvantage of knowing him well.

"All right, I'm hungover."

"And how did this happen?"

"How do you think it happened? The usual way."

"And in whose company?"

"A business associate's—not a woman—and at the Garrick Club. And don't start coming over all jealous."

"I am jealous, but the Garrick is my favorite London men's club, so I'll forgive you."

Stone, in his condition, couldn't make any sense of that. "Thank you."

"Now, you and Erica and Lance are coming down to the country for a few days. I have a meeting with Julian Wainwright this morning, then I'll pick you up at the Connaught. Please be standing out front with a bag in your hand at twelve o'clock sharp."

Stone struggled to think. He needed an opportunity to get closer to Lance, and here it was. "Are the tabloids still following you?"

"They vanished immediately after the wake at Lance's house."

"Do I need a dinner jacket?"

"Always a good idea at an English country house."

"All right, I'll be ready at twelve."

"Of course you will." She hung up.

Stone took some aspirin, had breakfast, and soaked in a hot tub for half an hour. Feeling more human, he read the papers, then the phone rang again. "Hello?"

"Mr. Barrington?" A female voice.

"Yes."

"It's Audie, at Doug Hayward's. Your jackets are ready for a fitting; when would you like to come in?"

Stone glanced at his watch. "Ten minutes?"

"Perfect; see you then."

Stone threw some things in a bag, told the concierge to cancel his flight to New York, left his bag with the doorman, and walked up the block to Hayward's shop. The tailor got him into a collection of loosely stitched pieces of cloth that only slightly resembled a jacket, made some marks, then ripped out the sleeves and made some more marks—twice, once for each jacket.

"Good," Hayward said. "How long are you staying in London?"

"I'm not sure."

"I can probably have these ready for your last fitting in a week, if you're still around."

"I suppose I will be. Doug, do you know a man named Lance Cabot?"

"I've made a lot of clothes for him."

"Know much about him?"

"He pays my bills; that's about it."

"Oh."

"You hungover this morning?" Hayward asked.

Stone nodded.

"Have a pint of bitter at lunch; that'll set you right."

Stone nodded again. He left the shop and walked back to the Connaught. Sarah was sitting out front in what appeared to be a toy car. It was little more than a bright orange box, with a tiny wheel at each corner. She stuck her head out the window.

"You're late, and your bag's in the boot."

"What boot?" Stone asked, walking around the car.

"Get in!"

The doorman held the door open for him.

"Now I know how the clowns at the circus feel," he said, folding his body and getting awkwardly into the vehicle. Surprisingly, he fit and was not uncomfortable.

Sarah threw the car into gear, revved the engine, and drove away up Mount Street at a great rate, the car making a noise like an adolescent Ferrari. A moment later, they were in busy Park Lane, whizzing through traffic.

Stone looked out the window and saw the pavement rushing past, and it seemed closer than he had ever been to it. He had the feeling that, if they hit a bump, he would scrape his ass on the tarmac.

"Ever been in one of these?" Sarah asked.

"A Mini? I've seen them around London."

"A Mini Cooper," she said. "Very special, from the sixties. I had this one restored, and it's *very* fast." She changed down, accelerated across two lanes, and careened into Hyde Park.

Stone winced. Why was it his lot in this country to ride with women who drove as if they had just stolen the car? "Try not to kill me," he said.

"Frankly, you look as though death would come as a relief," she replied. "What were you drinking?"

"Port."

"Ahhhhh. Goes down easily, doesn't it?"

"All too easily."

"And who was your host?"

"A man named . . . Bartholomew." He still didn't feel comfortable calling him Hedger.

"English or American?"

"American, but an anglophile."

"Thus, the port."

"Yes."

"How did you like the Garrick?"

"It's beautiful."

"They're just about the last of the old London clubs that still bar women from membership," she said. "I rather admire them for it; I think I enjoy going there more because it has an entirely male membership."

"Hmmpf," Stone said. He was drifting off.

He came to in a hurry a few minutes later, as he was

thrown hard against his seat belt. He looked out the windshield to see the narrow road ahead filled with sheep. One came up to his window and briefly pressed its nose against the glass, and it was eye to eye with him. "Where are we?" he asked.

"In the middle of a flock of sheep," Sarah replied. "They have the right of way in the country."

"I mean, where are we?"

"Halfway there. You hungry?"

Oddly, he was. "Yes."

"There's a pub round the bend; we'll have a ploughman's lunch." She drove on when the sheep had passed, then turned into a picturesque country pub. They went inside, picked up their lunch—bread, cheese, and sausage, and a pint of bitter each, then made their way into a rear garden and sat down.

Stone drank deeply from the pint. "There, that's better," he said.

"The bitter will set you right," Sarah said.

"That's the second time today I've been told that."

"And we were both right, no?"

"Yes, you both were. What do you know about Lance Cabot?"

"I told you already—not much."

"Remember everything you can. Anything ever strike you as odd about him?"

"Only that he seems to fit in awfully well with English people. People I know don't even seem to regard him as a foreigner."

"Have you ever seen him with anyone you didn't know?"

She thought. "Once, in a London restaurant, I saw him across the room, dining with a couple—man and woman—who looked foreign."

"What kind of foreign?"

"Mediterranean."

"That's a big area."

"Turkish or Israeli, perhaps."

"Describe them."

"About his age, well dressed, attractive—the woman, particularly. She was quite beautiful, in fact."

"Could you hear them talking?"

"No, but they didn't seem to be speaking English. I couldn't read their lips, and I'm quite good at that, even from a distance. I don't know if I told you, but as a child I had some sort of flu or virus that resulted in a sharp hearing loss. My hearing came back after a few months, but during that time I became adept at reading lips. Most people couldn't tell I was hard of hearing."

Stone nodded in the direction of a young couple sitting on the opposite side of the garden. "Tell me what they're talking about."

Sarah squinted in their direction for a moment, then giggled. "She's lying to him," she said.

"How?"

"She's saying they were just friends, that they never slept together, and he believes her, but she's lying."

"How do you know?"

"I can just tell."

"You're a woman of many talents," he said.

"I thought you already knew that."

"I had forgotten how many."

"Don't worry," she said, "I'm going to remind you."

2 5

THEY DRESSED FOR DINNER AND DINED in a smaller room than last time, at a round table, the heavy curtains drawn to shut out the night, in the English fashion. Stone didn't understand why the Brits did that; he enjoyed the long summer twilights.

The talk ranged through politics, sport, and the relationship between the English and the Americans. Stone noticed that Lord and Lady Wight, during this part of the conversation, seemed to feel that Lance was on their side of things, while Stone and Erica occupied the other. It was as Sarah had said; the Brits were very comfortable with Lance, considering him one of their own. Stone couldn't figure out why.

Port was served with Stilton at the end of the meal, and Stone sipped warily from his glass, his hangover having only just disappeared. At some invisible signal, the ladies rose and left the room. Stone nearly went with them, but Lance signaled him to stay.

"Over here, the ladies go somewhere, and the gentlemen stick around for cigars," Lance explained, lighting something Cuban.

Stone despised cigars—smoking them or smelling somebody else smoking them.

Wight did not light a cigar, but sniffed at Lance's.

"My doctor has taken me off them," he said. "Bloody cruel, if you ask me." He looked at a pocket watch from his waistcoat. "If you gentlemen will excuse me, I'm turning in early. My respects to the ladies." He got up and left.

They sat quietly for a moment, Stone playing with his port, Lance puffing his cigar and staring at the windows, as if he could see through the thick drapes and out into the night.

"You asked me a strange question the other day," he said finally. "I'd like to know why."

"About Hedger?"

Lance nodded almost imperceptibly.

"I have a lot to tell you about that," Stone said.

Lance waved the cigar, as if motioning him onward.

"Last week a man showed up in my office, recommended by Woodman and Weld, and introduced himself as John Bartholomew."

Lance shot him a glance.

"I take it you understand the significance of that name," Stone said.

Lance shrugged slightly.

"He told me that he was concerned about his favorite niece—his dead sister's child—that she had run off to England with someone of whom he suspected evil things. He retained me to come over here and see if I could disentangle the girl from the clutches of this ogre. Normally, I wouldn't take on such an assignment, but he had passed muster with Woodman and Weld, and they had urged me to help him, so I came."

"And how did he expect you to deal with this ogre?" Lance asked, blowing smoke in Stone's direction.

Stone waved it off with his napkin. "I told him up front that I would not participate in harming him, and that I would not kidnap his niece. He said he would be content if I could get the ogre put into jail."

Lance laughed, choking on his cigar smoke. "And how did he expect you to do that?" he was finally able to ask.

"He told me that you were supporting yourself by smuggling drugs into Britain—on your person, no less. I had a police contact; when I confirmed Bartholomew's charges, I intended to put him onto you."

"And now that you have been unable to confirm this information, what are your intentions?"

"I have none. I resigned from Bartholomew's employ yesterday."

"Oh? Why, pray tell?"

"I discovered that he had been lying to me."

"And how did you do that?"

"I hired two former policemen—one to follow Bartholomew—"

"I imagine that came to naught," Lance chuckled.

"Not entirely. My policeman had his pocket picked; that's how I learned that his name is Stanford Hedger."

"I don't imagine Stan took kindly to that."

"He did not. Some of his acquaintances put one of my policemen in the hospital."

Lance nodded sagely. "Figures. What about the other one?"

"Oh, he was assigned to follow you; actually, the two of them took turns. I had your phones tapped, too."

Lance turned and looked at Stone for the first time. "You *what*?"

"Don't worry, I didn't learn anything. The conversations were very boring. Except for one, that is."

"And what was that about?"

"Apparently, someone wants something from you, and you don't want to supply it. I believe you threatened to kill anyone who pressed the issue."

Lance was obviously thinking back over that conversation. "No names were mentioned, as I recall."

"That's correct."

"So, having left Stan's employ, you're back at square one?"

"No, square one was in New York, and now I'm in England and rather enjoying myself. I'm simply a tourist now; I returned Hedger's expense money to him, having deducted a sum for the benefit of the injured policeman."

"What else did Stan tell you about me?"

"He told me of your former, ah, business connection. He told me about the explosion in Cairo, in which, he believes, you were complicit."

"Ungrateful bastard," Lance said. "I saved his life, you know. I was about to walk into the building when it blew, knocking me down, and I dragged him out of the ruins, unconscious, and got him to a hospital."

"Did you think he was dead?"

"That's what I was told the following day. Then, last year, he turned up at a dinner party in Paris, where I was also a guest. Quite a surprise, I can tell you."

"I can imagine. Why does Hedger want you in jail?"

"He doesn't want me in jail; he wants me dead. It would be easy to arrange, of course, if he could get me into a jail; then he could hire somebody to put a shiv in my liver."

"Why wouldn't it be easy to make you dead?"

"Because I know too much about him, and he doesn't know who else I've told. For all he knows, there's a neat little manuscript tied up with red ribbon, waiting in a safe-deposit box at my bank."

"Is there?"

"Too bloody right there is."

"Then it's ironic that he wants you dead for the very same reasons he can't afford to kill you."

Lance grinned broadly, the first time Stone had ever seen him do so. "I like the paradox," he said.

"Tell me some of what you know—not enough for Hedger to want me dead, of course. How does he operate?"

"Oh, Stan manages to use his official connections to arrange unofficial profits for himself."

"Funny, that's what he said about you."

"I use every connection at my disposal," Lance said readily. "The difference is, I waited until I had left our mutual employer to use them, whereas Stan is still employed and using his contacts to the hilt. There are rules about that."

"But if you haven't already made his activities known to his employer, why would you now?"

"That's what worries Stan, apparently. Personally, I don't give a shit what he does to make a buck, as long as it doesn't endanger my own prospects. What Stan fears is that, in competing with him in business, I might turn him in, to get him out of the way. He could end up in prison if I did, you know. At the very least, he'd be bounced out of his job, and without any pension or benefits. He's only a few years away from retirement, and he wants all that, in addition to the illicit wealth he's accumulated over the years."

"These activities have made him rich, then?"

"Not rich enough for Stan's liking," Lance replied. "I think he wants to live like a potentate when he retires."

"Is there that much to be made?"

"You wouldn't believe me if I told you."

"Try me."

"How much do you know about Stan?"

"I've learned that he was something of a wild man in the Company, at least in his youth, and that at least some of his superiors didn't trust him."

"That's accurate information," Lance said, "as far as it goes."

"It's about all I know, so far," Stone said.

"All right, I'll tell you about Stan."

Stone leaned forward, eager to learn.

2 6

LANCE CABOT GOT UP AND LED STONE into the library, then settled into a leather sofa, inviting Stone to join him.

"What about the ladies?" Stone asked.

"They're in the drawing room nattering away," Lance said. "If they want us, they'll hunt us down." He had brought the decanter with him, and he refreshed Stone's port glass and his own.

Stone waited patiently for him to begin.

"Stanford Hedger got out of Yale in the early sixties," he said, "and he went straight into the Company, having been recruited well before graduation by a professor who later recruited me. It was a good time to join up; he was just completing his training when the Cuban invasion came along—hadn't had a posting yet, so he couldn't be blamed for what happened at the Bay of Pigs. But a lot of his superiors were blamed, and a lot of them left the Company, leaving an unusual amount of room for early promotion. Stan was good at languages; he had French, Russian, German, and more than a smattering of Arabic. Later he came by Hebrew, which impressed the Israelis. He was still at the military language school in Monterey, California, when the Bay of Pigs invasion came to grief. It's a wonderful school; they teach you things like perfect military German or Russian, the idea being that when they got ready to put somebody over a border, he'd blend in.

"Stan got put across what was then the East German border, dressed as a colonel—Stan looked a lot older than he was. He wrought havoc on the other side; he'd walk into a military command when the senior officer was out, flash some bogus orders signed by the Soviet commander, issue a lot of ridiculous orders, and it would take them days, sometimes weeks before they'd get everything straightened out again. He was one step ahead of them for three or four months, then, as they were closing in on him, he hit a West German worker on the head, stole his clothes, and rode back into West Berlin on the S-Bahn, the elevated railway that took several thousand essential workers back and forth to the East from the West every day. It was a bravura performance, almost entirely solo, and it brought him to the attention of the higher-ups—got him decorated, it did."

"Not a bad start for a bright young man."

"It was a lot better than not bad, and it helped that Stan came out of a background that the agency loved and trusted—Choate, Yale, and half a dozen of the very best clubs. His father worked for Wild Bill Donovan in the OSS during World War Two, and by that time he was the head of an important New York brokerage house. If you'd tossed the two dozen top men at the Company in a room together and told them to design the perfect agent, they would have come up with Stan."

"What came next for him?"

"Vietnam. By 'sixty-five, he was on the ground there, in Laos, Thailand, wherever he could do the most good. He was one of two or three guys who invented Air America, the CIA-fronted airline that flew people, equipment, drugs, and all sorts of contraband all over Southeast Asia. He made some money out of that, legend has it."

"Was he motivated by money?"

"Not at first, probably, but agents in that sort of situation suddenly start seeing it lying around on the ground in neatly tied bundles, and it's hard not to pick up some of it. Stan spent it as fast as he made or stole it, though; he had an establishment in Saigon that included a townhouse that had formerly belonged to a French governor, a chauffeured Rolls-Royce of a certain vintage, and a mistress who was said to be the most beautiful and the most sexually adventurous female for a thousand miles in any direction. He entertained on a scale not often seen outside the loftier regions of French society—a superb cellar had come with the house—and his guests included everybody of importance who came through the city: journalists, presidential advisors, senior military figures. It was said that the only reason Hanoi never tried to blow the house to smithereens was that all the servants were Viet Cong, and they reported everything that happened there. Stan, of course, maintained he was running them as double agents."

Stone had to laugh.

"When the whole thing finally came crashing down, Stan got out on the last helicopter leaving the embassy. You remember a photograph of an American slugging somebody who was clinging to the chopper as it rose?"

"Yes."

"Look closely, allow for age, and you'll see that it was Stan. It made him more famous than ever, in certain circles."

"What happened to the mistress?"

"Funny you should ask. Stan abandoned her at the end, but it's said that, within a week of the fall of Saigon, she was living with the commandant of what had suddenly become Ho Chi Min City. She had the house all ready and waiting for him. Eventually, she got out of the country and ended up in LA, where she is now running the most exotic bordello the town has ever seen. I'll give you the number, if you're going to be out there anytime soon."

"You never know. What did he do after Vietnam?"

"He had a number of dull postings after that, kept his head down until nobody remembered whose fault Vietnam had been. I met him in the early eighties, when I arrived at the Farm."

"What farm was that?"

"The Farm is the training school for the covert side of the agency, and by that time, Stan was running it. It's the intelligence equivalent of an army officer becoming the commandant at West Point."

"I see."

"I think Stan saw something of himself in me—though, of course, a slightly dimmer bulb—so he did a lot of mentoring with me and got me into the Monterey school."

"What language?"

"Arabic; I initially learned it in bed from a Lebanese girlfriend at Yale, and after the Monterey school, I was very good with it. Stan saw that I got a Middle Eastern assignment, a good one. I still can't tell you much about that, but it involved slinking around various deserts, in mufti, listening a lot. I was limited by my Western appearance, but I did all right. I became something of a specialist, too, at listening in on interrogations and interpreting not just language, but all of the subject's words and actions. The downside was, I had to watch the interrogations through a two-way mirror, and they were never pretty."

Stone didn't want to think about that.

"The friction with Stan started when I began to develop my own sources and collaborators. He was working out of the Cairo embassy by then, his cover being something like agricultural attaché, and he ran a tight ship. When I wouldn't share my contacts with him or anybody else, he began to ride me. I was mingling a lot in the upper reaches of Middle Eastern society, too, so some of my sources were very well placed. I'd write reports giving a lot of good information, which Stan would always say was worthless because I wouldn't ascribe it to a verifiable source. Then I began getting reports past him, directly to Langley, which is against Company policy, and that drove him nuts. The Company has a chain of command, just like the military, and if you violate it, you have to be very, very careful. Stan's problem was that my information in these reports nearly always turned out to be accurate, and it made Stan look bad that he hadn't passed them on to Langley himself."

"I can see how that might annoy him."

"Then the explosion of the safe house happened, and after he recovered from that, I've been hearing from old friends, he became diminished in the eyes of his superiors and something of a has-been in the eyes of his inferiors. That's when he really started going for the main chance."

"And he hasn't been caught at it?"

"Stan's too smart to get caught in the usual ways. Somebody would have to turn on him, and that's why he worries about me. Sometimes I think that if I could sit down at dinner with him, I could put his mind at rest, but he regards me as as much of a business competitor now as a threat to his personal security."

"I can see that it's a difficult situation," Stone said.

Lance looked sad. "One of us is not going to survive this situation," he said. Then he looked grim. "And it isn't going to be me."

Then the ladies came looking for them.

"I think you're going queer for Lance," Sarah said. She was lying on top of Stone, having just drained him of most of his precious bodily fluids.

"What?" Stone managed to say, still panting.

"The two of you went into this huddle after dinner, and I think you'd still be there, if I hadn't come in and dragged you away." She began toying with his penis.

"You're not going to find any joy there," Stone said. "Not after what you've just put me through. I may take weeks to recover."

"Nonsense," she said, squeezing. "You're recovering already."

Stone groaned.

"I'm going to make you forget about Lance," she said, traveling down his torso with her tongue, until she had him in her mouth.

She was absolutely right, Stone thought. Lance was right out of his mind.

2 7

STONE HAD FINISHED BREAKFAST AND
was reading the London papers in the morning room
when Sarah came in.

"And how are we this morning?" she asked, in the
manner of a visiting nurse. She pecked him on the
forehead.

"I don't know about you," he said in a low voice,
"but I can hardly walk."

"You're out of shape," she laughed. "We'll have to
get you fit again. Come on, we're going to the market."
She tugged him out of the chair, grabbed a basket by
the front door, and led him outside, where an ancient
Morris Minor estate car, nicely kept, awaited them.

"Where's everybody else?" Stone asked, as Sarah
started the car.

"Erica's sleeping in; Lance wanted a drive, so I
loaned him the Mini Cooper."

"Where'd Lance go?"

"I dunno; just for a drive." They passed through the
gates of the estate, and Sarah turned toward the village.
Shortly, they had stopped in front of a small grocery.

Down the block, Stone spotted the bright orange
Mini Cooper. "You go ahead and shop," he said to
Sarah; "I want to have a look at the village."

"All right; meet me at the car in half an hour; I'll be done by then." She went into the grocery.

Stone started down the street toward the Mini Cooper. It was empty, and he looked around, wondering where Lance might have gone. Then he saw him enter a pub across the street. Stone glanced at his watch; it was just opening time. He dawdled down the street, wondering why Lance would be in a pub before lunch. Wasn't there enough booze back at the house? He considered going inside himself, but Lance's behavior was unusual enough that he preferred not to be seen following him. He ducked into a news agent's across from the pub, bought a *Herald Tribune,* and pretended to read it. No more than a minute had passed when he saw two people get out of a parked saloon car and head for the pub.

Stone had never seen them before, but their appearance struck a chord. They were Mediterranean in appearance, and the woman was quite beautiful. That matched the description of the people Sarah had seen with Lance in a restaurant, and he remembered Hedger's saying that two of Lance's contacts in Cairo had been a young couple. Stone tucked the newspaper under his arm and crossed the street.

The pub had stained-glass windows, and Stone peered through one. He saw the three of them seated at a corner table, and he moved around to the side of the building for a better view. He found another window, one with clear glass, partly protected by curtains. He could stand and look inside through a small opening in the drapes without being seen by Lance and his friends.

There was a very earnest conversation going on, which stopped abruptly when a barmaid brought drinks to the table, then resumed as soon as she had gone. Lance was making a point, tapping a forefinger hard on the table, leaning forward for emphasis. The couple seemed uncomfortable, and the woman placed her hand on Lance's arm, in a calming motion. He jerked away from her and brought his palm down hard on the table, apparently very close to losing his temper. The couple sat back and listened, not arguing. Then Lance threw some money on the table, got up, and walked out.

Stone flattened himself against the wall until he was sure Lance had left the pub, then started toward the front of the building. From around the corner, he heard the distinctive sound of the Mini Cooper revving, then driving away in a hurry. Stone went into the pub.

The couple were still there, ignoring their drinks, looking worried, talking animatedly. Stone stood at the end of the bar nearest them and ordered a lemonade.

"I don't care," the man was saying. "This is getting dangerous."

"We have to do this," she said. "What choice do we have? How else are we going to make this kind of money?"

"Why do we have to take all the risks?" he asked.

"We're not taking *all* the risks; Lance is doing his part."

"Let's get back to London," the man said, standing up.

Stone turned his back to them, pretending to examine a photograph of the pub on the wall next to him. He didn't want them to register his face; he might run into them again.

When they had been gone long enough to get to their car and drive away, Stone left the pub and walked back to the Morris Minor. Sarah was just com-

ing out of the grocery with a cart filled with bags, and
he helped her stow them in the rear of the estate car.

They were back in plenty of time for lunch, and found
Erica had joined the living. After they had eaten, Lance
took Stone into the morning room and sat him down.

"I've done some looking into your background," he
said, "and I like what I've learned."

"What have you learned?" Stone asked.

"I've learned what sort of policeman you were and
what sort of lawyer you are now. I'm impressed with
the variety and depth of your experience."

"Thank you," Stone said, not sure what to make of
this.

"I think you and I might do some business together.
Interested?"

"What sort of business?"

"Profitable."

"How profitable?"

"Very."

"How illegal?"

"Entirely aboveboard," Lance said. "And the money
will be made quickly."

"In my experience," Stone replied, "fast money is usually made at the expense of the law and at the risk of
prison. I'm not interested in either of those possibilities."

"I assure you, this would be a straightforward business transaction."

"Why do you need me to accomplish this transaction?"

"First, there's some legal work in New York; I need
to create a corporation and open banking and brokerage accounts in the corporation's name."

"Any attorney could do that," Stone said. "Why me?"

"Because you're here, and I'm not in New York," Lance replied. "It's as simple as that."

Stone had a feeling it was not at all simple. "I'd have to know all of what you intend to do and how you intend to do it."

"Not just yet."

"I'm sorry," Stone said, "I won't be involved unless I know what I'm getting into."

"I promise, you'll only be doing what any New York attorney would be doing."

"You mean, what I don't know won't hurt me?"

"That's quite true."

"I've always found that truism to be a lie," Stone said. "It's what you don't know that can destroy you."

"I can't tell you everything just yet," Lance said.

"Let me know when you can, and then we can talk about it," Stone replied. "Whatever you tell me will be bound by attorney-client privilege *as long as it's legal*, and if we should agree to disagree, you'd have nothing to fear from my talking about your deal."

Lance stared at him for a moment. "You're not a very trusting person," he said.

"Let's see," Stone said. "What I know about you so far is that you're ex-CIA and that you're involved in, shall we say, unconventional business dealings. And you have a serious enemy who is still inside the Company and who wishes to see you in jail or, perhaps, worse. Does that about sum it up so far?"

"You're taking Stan far too seriously," Lance said.

"I'm not sure you're taking him seriously enough," Stone said.

"I assure you, I'm giving him the attention he deserves."

Stone shook his head. "I'm not willing to talk about this, until you're ready to talk to me a lot more."

Lance considered this. "All right," he said. "I'll be back to you as soon as I can." He got up and left the room.

Stone wondered if he wasn't getting near the time when he should be calling Detective Inspector Throckmorton. Not just yet, he decided finally.

2 8

STONE ARRIVED BACK AT THE CON-
naught and checked his mail and messages, among
which was one from Doug Hayward to come back for
a fitting. Quick, he thought.

He changed clothes, then left the Connaught and
walked up Mount Street toward Hayward's shop. In
the middle of the block he stood, waiting for traffic to
subside enough for him to cross, but before he could
move, a large black car pulled up in front of him and
stopped. He could not see through the darkened windows, and as he tried, a rear door opened and a large
man reached out, took him by the lapels, and jerked
him forward into the commodious rear compartment
of the car. Before he could say anything, he was on the
floor, with large feet holding him down, one on the
nape of his neck.

"What is this about?" Stone managed to croak, even
though his neck was held at an odd angle.

"Shut up," a man's deep voice said.

Stone shut up.

The car drove for, maybe, twenty minutes. Stone
tried to keep track of the time and the turns, but he
couldn't see his watch, and, not knowing the street
plan well enough, he couldn't figure out where they

were going. They seemed to drive around three or four traffic circles, and shortly after the last one, they made a right turn and stopped. The two men in the rear seat hustled Stone through an open door in a narrow back street and into a darkened hallway. They marched Stone along, making a couple of turns, then he was propelled forward into a small room, bouncing off the rear wall, and the door was slammed behind him.

"You have one minute to strip off all your clothes, or we'll do it for you," the deep voice said.

Stone thought about this for half a minute, then he got out of his clothes and laid them neatly on a bench along one wall. His eyes had become accustomed to the gloom, and he could see that he was in a windowless room with a steel door. There was a bucket in a corner and the bench, no other furniture. A moment later, a small door in the larger one opened, then closed, then the two men came into the cell, took away his clothes, and slammed the door behind them.

Stone thought about it. These people did not seem like the police. Surely the London police had procedures about arrest and detention, just as the New York department did, and what he was experiencing did not seem to conform to any set of procedures in any civilized country. This was more like something out of a World War II film about the Gestapo, or a spy novel.

Perhaps three minutes passed, then the cell door opened again, and someone threw his clothes at him.

"Get dressed," the deep voice said. "You have one minute."

Stone was tying his necktie when the door opened again and he was half escorted, half dragged down another series of hallways, then pushed into a brightly lit room, the door slamming behind him.

Blinking rapidly, he discovered that all the room

was not brightly lit, just the part containing a wooden stool. The other side of the room, some twelve or fifteen feet away, contained a table behind which sat three men. They were in deep shadows and he could see only their forms, not their faces. It seemed to be arranged as some sort of Stalinist tribunal.

"Sit down, please, Mr. Barrington," a smooth male voice said.

Stone went and sat down on the stool. There was something odd about the man's voice, but he couldn't figure it out.

The smooth voice spoke again, and Stone figured it was coming from the man in the middle, who was bald, with a bullet-shaped head. "Tell us, please, if you have ever heard the following names, in any context: Robert Graves?"

"What?"

"Robert Graves."

"Yes. The poet."

"Any other context?"

"No."

"Maureen Kleinknect?"

"No."

"Joanna Scott-Meyers?"

"No."

"Jacob Ben-David?"

"No."

"Erica Burroughs?"

"Yes."

"In what regard?"

"A friend of a friend."

"How well do you know her?"

"I've had lunch with her once, dinner with her a couple of times, in a group."

"Lance Cabot?"

"I've had enough of this," Stone said. "Who are you, and what do you want?"

"I've just told you what we want, for the present. Lance Cabot?"

"If you are acting in some sort of official capacity, tell me now; otherwise, you can go fuck yourself."

"Lance Cabot?"

Stone said nothing.

"If you would prefer it, Mr. Barrington," the smooth voice said, "I can arrange for the two gentlemen who brought you here to come and persuade you to answer."

Stone said nothing. The voice was very English, but the speaker was not. There was an underlying accent.

"Just once more; Lance Cabot?"

"He is the companion of Erica Burroughs; I've seen him when I've seen her."

"How does Mr. Cabot earn his living?"

"He styles himself a business consultant; I have no idea what that means."

"Did you know him before arriving in London?"

"No."

"Ali Hussein?"

"Pardon?"

"Ali Hussein?"

"Never heard of him."

"Sheherezad Al-Salaam, also known as Sheila."

"Nor her."

"Sarah Buckminster?"

"Yes."

"Go on."

"I knew her when she lived in New York; we renewed our acquaintance after I arrived in London. Don't you read the papers?"

"Monica Burroughs?"

"The sister of Erica. Art dealer. Spent part of one weekend in her company."

"John Bartholomew?"

"No."

"John Bartholomew?"

"I don't know anyone by that name."

"Mr. Barrington, don't try my patience."

Stone said nothing. The man made a small movement with one hand, and Stone heard a buzzer ring in another room. A moment later, the door opened and the two thugs entered.

"John Bartholomew?" the smooth voice asked.

"Yes."

"Tell us."

"Mr. Bartholomew visited me in New York and asked me to come to London to persuade his niece to return with me to the United States."

"What is the name of his niece?"

"Erica Burroughs."

"And why did he want her returned to America?"

"He said he was concerned that her boyfriend might involve her in illegal activities."

"What sort of activities?"

"Drug smuggling."

Stone heard a low laugh. "What is the real name of John Bartholomew?"

Stone tried to sound puzzled. "Real name? I know him only by that name."

"Are you still in his employ?"

"No."

"Why not?"

"I discovered that Miss Burroughs is not his niece, and that he seemed to have other motives for hiring me."

"What motives?"

"He seemed to have some animus for Mr. Cabot."

"For what reason?"

"He did not confide that to me. When I discovered he was lying to me, I resigned from his employ."

"Have you seen him since that time?"

"No."

There was a scraping noise from the table in front of him, and Stone realized that the contents of his pockets were on the table. A hand picked up the satellite telephone and held it in the light for Stone to see.

"What is this?"

"It's a telephone."

"What kind of telephone?"

"A cellphone, like any other." Stone heard beeps as a number was tapped into the phone. A moment later, a phone rang in another room. The phone was returned to the table.

"Describe John Bartholomew."

"Six feet three or four, heavyset, dark hair going gray, sixtyish."

"Nationality?"

"American, as far as I know."

"Why do you carry a false passport?" A hand held it in the light.

"If it's false, then they're handing out false documents at the passport office in the London embassy of the United States of America. If you'll check the date of issue, you'll see I got it last week."

There was some whispering among the three men, then the smooth voice spoke again. If you have left Mr. Bartholomew's employ, why do you remain in Britain?"

"Tourism."

"Mr. Barrington, you are trying my patience again."

"A woman, as well."

"What woman?"

"Sarah Buckminster. Don't you read the papers?"

"You are interested in her?"

"Yes."

"In what way?"

"Miss Buckminster and I lived together in New York. We have renewed our acquaintance."

"Ah."

"Yes, ah."

"Miss Buckminster has recently become very rich."

"Ah, you do read the papers."

"Are you interested in her money?"

"What do you think?"

"Ah."

"If you say so."

"Mr. Barrington, I can't say that I like your attitude."

"I can't say that I like being abducted on a public street, imprisoned, and interrogated by a group of people who have read too many bad novels."

"Mr. Barrington, this is your final opportunity to tell us what we want to know."

"Have I denied you anything so far? I have no idea what you want to know."

"According to your papers, you were once a policeman."

"That's correct."

"Surely you conducted interrogations."

"Many times."

"Didn't you always find out what you wanted to know?"

"No, I didn't; unlike you, I was constrained by the law."

"We are constrained by nothing."

"No kidding."

The man made a motion with his hand; one of the

two thugs stepped forward, swept Stone's belongings into a paper bag, and stepped back.

"Get rid of him," the smooth voice said.

Stone did not like the sound of that. Before he could move, the two men were on him, one at each arm, dragging him back down the series of hallways, outside, and into the car. Once again, he was facedown on the floor of the limousine, with a foot on his neck.

The car drove away, turning this way and that. Stone lay still, knowing that he had no chance until the car stopped and they took him out. Then he would give them the fight of their lives.

Twenty minutes later, the car came to a halt; Stone was picked up and bodily tossed into the gutter. As he started to rise, the paper bag with his belongings hit him in the back of the head. By the time he got to his feet, the car had turned a corner and was gone. People looked at him oddly as he dusted himself off and returned his belongings to his pockets. He looked around. The Hayward shop was across the street; he was back where he had been abducted.

He walked across the street and into Hayward's. Doug Hayward rose from a leather sofa, and a small dog began to bark at Stone.

"Shut up, Bert," Hayward said. "Come on back, Stone; we're ready for you."

Stone silently followed Hayward to the rear of the shop and the dressing room, where he removed his jacket.

"Stone," Hayward said, "are you aware that you have a footprint on the back of your shirt collar?"

2 9

STONE LET HIMSELF INTO HIS SUITE
and got out the satellite telephone. He pressed a
speed-dial button and waited.

"Yes?"

"I have to see you now."

"Can't do it; how about tomorrow?"

"I'll be in New York tomorrow, if I don't see you
now."

A brief silence. "Where?"

"The lounge at the Connaught will do. Ten minutes."

"All right." He rang off.

Bartholomew/Hedger bustled into the lounge and sat
down next to Stone, who was sipping a cup of tea.

"Some tea?" Stone asked.

"What is it?"

"Earl Grey."

Hedger made a digusted noise and raised a finger to
a waiter. "Bring me a pot of English Breakfast," he said.

Stone waited while the tea was brought.

"All right, what?" Hedger said.

"Earlier today, I was grabbed by two men, stuffed

into the back of a car, driven to an unknown location, stripped, searched, and interrogated by three men. By one man, really; the other two just sat and listened."

Hedger stared at him. "What the hell are you talking about?"

"Didn't you hear anything I said? I want an explanation."

"Why do you think I know anything about it?"

"I believe you are a member of a group who indulges in such activities; you were my first thought, even though they asked me about you."

Hedger held up a hand. "What did they want to know about me?"

"Whatever I knew; your name, for instance."

"Did you tell them?"

"No."

"If they didn't know my name, how did they ask about me?"

"They asked about John Bartholomew. Obviously, they didn't get the joke. They wanted to know Bartholomew's real name."

"What did you tell them?"

"I told them about our initial meeting and told them I had left your employ."

Hedger looked relieved. "All right, now I want you to take me through this incident, step by step, and tell me exactly what happened and exactly what they asked you."

"It was a big car, black, with blackened windows; a limousine, I believe. Plenty of room for me to lie face-down on the floor with some palooka's foot on my neck."

"Describe the two men who took you."

"Big, muscular."

"What did they say to you?"

"Shut up."

"What?"

"They told me to shut up. Oh, one of them told me to undress, once we reached their location."

"Accent?"

"Pretty hard to determine from the words 'shut up,' but I'd say British."

"Class?"

"I didn't ask them where they went to school."

"No, *class;* social class: upper or lower?"

"Jesus, I don't know, but it's hard for me to believe that members of the upper class indulge in broad-daylight kidnapping. Lower, I guess."

"What about the other men, their accents?"

"Only one of them spoke. His voice was smooth, cultivated, definitely upper class, but there was some sort of accent underneath it."

"You mean a foreign accent?"

"You know the actor Herbert Lom?"

"Yes."

"An accent like that, sort of—foreign, but British upper class at the same time. It's as if he were born elsewhere but educated here."

"Do you know anyone else, an Englishman, with the same kind of upper-class accent?"

Stone thought about it. "James Cutler," he said, "and his solicitor, Julian Wainwright." Also Sarah and her parents, but he didn't mention that.

"Do you know where Cutler and Wainwright went to school?"

"Eton, I believe."

"Ah."

"Ah, what?"

"Just ah. That would indicate someone fairly high up in the food chain."

"What food chain?"

"The food chain in whatever country he's from. They don't ship out butchers' sons to be educated at Eton."

"Oh."

"Tell me exactly what they asked you."

"It was a list of names, nothing else."

"What were the names?"

"Robert Graves was the first."

"The poet?"

"They asked me if I knew the name in any other context."

"Who else?"

"Two women's names—an Irish first name, and the last name was odd—Klein something or other."

"Maureen Kleinknect?"

"Yes, that's it. Who is she?"

"It doesn't matter; she's dead. What was the other one?"

"Joanna with a double-barreled last name."

"Scott-Meyers?"

"Yes."

"Go on."

"Then there was Erica and Monica Burroughs, Lance Cabot, Sarah Buckminster, and you."

"And what did you tell them about each of these people?"

"The bare minimum."

Hedger sat back in his chair and sipped his tea. "Once again, describe the two men who dragged you into the car. This time I want every detail."

"I told you—big."

"What else?"

"Come to think of it, they both had dark skin—not *very* dark, but a little, and black hair."

"Describe the three men who interrogated you."

"They were seated behind the lights in the room, in shadows, so I could only see silhouettes."

"Tell me about the silhouettes."

"The two on the ends were just shadows, lumps, but the one in the middle—the one doing the interrogating—was bald, with a bullet-shaped head. That was all I could see of him, really."

"That's interesting; you were very good to pick that up, in the circumstances."

"Thank you. Now give me a good reason why I should continue to work for you while this sort of thing is going on."

"Two reasons. First, this won't happen again; they believe they have everything you know. Second, I'm doubling your hourly fee."

Nobody had ever doubled his hourly fee before; Stone was impressed, still . . . "That won't do me any good, if I'm dead."

"They're not going to kill you."

"Why not? What's their motive for keeping me alive?"

"These people are from a foreign country—probably a foreign intelligence service, or at least some clandestine group. It's a lot of trouble to kill people and dispose of their bodies, and they won't do anything that will call attention to themselves. Anyway, if they'd wanted you dead, you'd already be dead."

"I don't know . . ."

"Think about it; what do you know that you haven't already told them?"

"Not much, just your name."

"Exactly, and they don't believe you know that. They believe they've milked you dry, so you're of no further use to them. They'll leave you alone, now."

"If you say so," Stone replied doubtfully.

"Trust me," Hedger said.

Yeah, sure, Stone thought. But double his hourly fee sounded awfully good. It wasn't until Hedger had left that Stone remembered that he had forgotten to mention the two Arab names he'd been asked about. What were they . . . Ali and Sheherezad, also known as Sheila? He couldn't remember the last names.

3 0

STONE'S NEXT THOUGHT WAS TO HAVE the same discussion with Lance Cabot that he'd had with Stanford Hedger. Rain had begun to beat against the Connaught's windows, so he retrieved his new raincoat and umbrella from his suite, and the doorman got him a cab. It was only a short way to Farm Street, but Stone was not going to dance over there in the rain.

The cabbie was just turning into Farm Steet, when Stone stopped him. "Just hold it right here for a minute," he said. Lance Cabot and the couple he'd met with in the village pub were leaving the house, getting into a cab of their own. "Follow that cab," Stone said, "but not too closely." He could see the driver in the rearview mirror, rolling his eyes.

"Right, guv," the cabbie said. "It's your money; I'll follow them to Cornwall, if you like."

"I doubt if they'll go that far."

Lance's cab set off. Stone's driver reversed for a few yards, then drove up another mews. Stone thought the man had lost the other cab, until it appeared ahead of them. "Very good," he said to the driver.

"It's what I do," the cabbie said. "You know about The Knowledge?" Lance's cab turned into Park Lane, and Stone's followed.

"What knowledge is that?"

"The Knowledge is what every London cabdriver has to have before he gets a license. You drive all over town on a motorbike for a year or two, taking notes on addresses, public buildings, pubs, theaters and tube stops—whatever you see; you go to classes at night; and finally you take the exam. A question would be, like, 'A passenger wants to go from Hampstead Heath to Wormwood Scrubs Prison. Describe the shortest route, and name every cross street, public building, and tube stop along the way.' Miss one cross street, and you've missed the question. Miss too many questions, and you've failed the exam. Get it right, and you have The Knowledge, and you get your license."

Lance's cab drove around Hyde Park Corner, through Belgrave Square, on to Sloane Square, and started down the King's Road. Stone glanced at side streets as they passed and wondered if he could ever memorize them all. "That's pretty impressive," he said.

"I had a mate once, went through all that, passed The Knowledge, got his license, then he went out to celebrate that night, had a lot to drink, and got stopped by the police on the way home and Breathalyzed. Lost his license; he'd taken two and a half years to get it, and he kept it only a few hours."

"Poor fellow," Stone said. They were past World's End now, continuing down the King's Road, past dozens of antique shops. A large, black car overtook Stone's cab and drove on.

"Who's in the other cab?" the cabbie asked. "If you don't mind my asking."

"My wife's boyfriend, I think," Stone replied.

"Don't you worry, guv, I won't lose the bastard."

Up ahead, Lance's cab was signaling a left turn. The black car turned, too. It was starting to look familiar to

Stone. Lance's cab approached a large building that had probably once been a warehouse but now bore a large sign declaring it to be an antiques market. Down the block, Lance's cab came to a halt, and its three occupants got out. The black car stopped half a block behind them.

"Stop here," Stone said. The cabbie stopped. Stone watched as two large, swarthy men got out of the back of the limousine and followed Lance and his companions into the building.

"Is there another entrance to this place?" Stone asked.

"Just around the corner, there, in the King's Road," the cabbie said.

Stone got out of the cab and handed the driver a ten-pound note.

"Thanks, guv," the driver said. "You want me to wait for you? Won't be easy getting a cab in this weather."

Stone handed him another tenner. "Wait ten pounds' worth, and if I haven't come back, forget it."

"Righto, guv."

Stone walked around the corner and into the building. The place was a warren of antique shops, some large and rambling, some no more than a yard or two wide. It was uncrowded, with only a few shoppers wandering about. He had to make an effort not to window-shop; he worked his way quickly through the building, looking for Lance, and then he saw him and his two friends turn a corner down a long corridor and walk toward him. Stone ducked into a shop and pretended to look at a piece of statuary. After a two-minute wait, when they hadn't passed the shop, he looked down the corridor again; they had disappeared.

Must have gone into a shop, Stone thought. He made

his way slowly down the corridor; then he saw a small sign, hung at right angles to a shopfront: A&S ANTIQUITIES—MIDDLE EASTERN SPECIALISTS. Ali and Sheila? Stone stopped and peered through a corner of a window. The woman was sitting at a desk writing on a pad. He could see the back of Lance's head in a small office behind her. Stone wondered how long it would take for the two men to find them and what would happen when they did. It wouldn't be good, he thought.

He stood back from the window and read the phone number painted on the shop window, then went back the way he had come. When he was at the King's Road entrance, he called the number on his satellite phone.

"A&S Antiquities," the woman's voice said.

"Let me speak to Lance at once," Stone said.

"I beg your pardon? There's no one here by that name."

"He's in the back room with Ali, and this is an emergency. Put him on and quickly!"

"Yes?" Lance's voice said, warily.

"It's Stone Barrington. Two very large Middle Eastern gentlemen are in the building looking for you at this moment. I've met them before, and they are not friendly."

"What are you talking about?"

"If I were you, I'd get out of there right now. I have a cab waiting at the corner, near the King's Road entrance to the building. You don't have much time."

Lance's voice could be heard, but muffled, as if his hand were over the receiver, then he came back on. "We'll be right there," he said.

Stone put the phone in his pocket and ran through the rain to the cab, not bothering with his umbrella.

"Where to, guv?" the cabbie asked.

"Just wait. We're being joined by some other people."

"Whatever you say, guv."

A moment later, Lance and his two friends dived into the cab. "Get us out of here," Lance said to the driver. He turned to Stone. "Now," he said, "what's going on?"

They drove past the black limousine. "You recognize that car?" Stone asked.

"No."

"The two gentlemen I described were in it; they followed you from your house."

"How do you know that?"

"I was on my way to see you when you came out of the house; they followed you, so I followed them."

"Why would you do that?"

"I had a rather unpleasant encounter with them and some friends of theirs earlier today," Stone said. "I wanted to spare you the same experience, or worse."

"Who are they?"

"I had hoped you could tell me. The man they work for is bald, with a bullet-shaped head."

"Does that sound familiar?" Lance asked Ali and Sheila.

Both shook their heads.

They had driven around the block and were now on the opposite side of the antiques market building. As they drove toward the King's Road, a section of the building exploded outward, followed a split second later by a huge roar. The cabbie, without a word, executed a speedy U-turn.

"I believe that was your shop," Stone said to Ali and Sheila.

Lance was suddenly on a cellphone, punching in a number and waiting impatiently for an answer. "Erica," he said, "I want you to leave the house right this minute; go to Monica's gallery; take nothing with you. Do you understand? I'll explain later; just get out of there immediately!" He ended the call and turned to Stone. "Thank you," he said.

"Not at all," Stone replied. "But now perhaps you'll tell me what the hell is going on."

3 1

LANCE STARED OUT THE CAB WINDOW at the rainy streets. He had not answered Stone's request. "Tell me about your encounter with these people," he said.

Stone related his tale of being abducted and interrogated. When he had finished, Lance still said nothing for a long moment. "Sounds like the Mossad to me."

"We've got to get out of the country," Ali said. "They just proved that to us."

"No, not yet," Lance replied, still looking out the window. Once Erica is out of the house, they won't know where to find us."

"Where are we going?" Sheila asked.

Lance opened the partition and gave the driver an address. "To Monica's gallery; we'll figure it out there."

The gallery was in Dover Street, off New Bond Street; it was a wide building with a limestone front and had a single word, BURROUGHS, painted on the front window. Stone was impressed; he'd imagined something smaller.

"Can you wait for us?" Lance asked the cabbie.

"As long as you like, mate," the cabbie replied. He lowered his voice. "The other bloke knows you're having his wife off, you know; I can't wait to see what happens."

Stone heard this and laughed.

"What is he talking about?" Lance asked as they turned toward the gallery.

"I had to tell him something," Stone said. They went inside.

Monica Burroughs was sitting at a desk in the large gallery, talking to Sarah Buckminster, who was seated next to her, looking at some slides. "Oh, hello," she said, as Stone and Lance approached.

"Is Erica here?" Lance asked.

"No, is she supposed to be?"

Lance went to the window and looked out into the street.

Sarah came around the desk and pecked Stone on the cheek. "What's up? Lance looks worried."

"There's been a little trouble," Stone said. "Lance asked Erica to meet him here."

"What sort of trouble?"

"I'll tell you later."

Lance was pacing up and down, checking outside often. He came to where Stone and Sarah stood. "I'm going to go and get her," he said.

"Wait a few minutes," Stone replied. "She's probably on her way; she wouldn't be there when you got there."

As if to prove his point, Erica came through the front door, breathless. "I'm sorry to take so long; I couldn't get a cab in this rain. What's happening?" she asked Lance.

"We have to move, and right away," Lance replied.

"Why?"

"There's been . . . some trouble; I don't want to go into it right now, but our house isn't safe at the moment. We can go back later and pick up some things."

Erica looked at Stone. "Will *you* tell me what's going on?"

"It's best if you just do as Lance says for the moment," Stone replied. "Lance, do you have anywhere to go?"

"I'm thinking," Lance said. "I suppose we could find a small hotel somewhere."

"James's house," Sarah said suddenly.

"What?" Lance asked.

"James's house; there's no one there but the housekeeper; there's plenty of room for, what, the four of you?" She nodded toward Ali and Sheila.

"Are you sure that will be all right, Sarah?" Lance asked.

"Of course." She began rummaging in her large handbag. "I've got the key here somewhere." She came up with it, handed it to Lance, and gave him the address, in Chester Street.

"Thank you, Sarah," he said, kissing her on the cheek. "Come on, everybody, let's move."

Stone walked out with them and gave the cabbie a fifty-pound note. "Thanks for your help," he said. "Forget about all this, especially where you're taking these people."

"What people?" the driver asked. "Thanks, guv; good luck." He handed Stone a card. "There's my cellphone number, if you need me again."

Lance slammed the door, and the cab took off. Stone went back inside the gallery.

"Now, will you tell me what happened?" Sarah asked.

"Lance's friends Ali and Sheila have—had an antique shop in a market in the King's Road. It was bombed a few minutes ago, and he's concerned for their safety, and his own and Erica's."

Monica spoke up. "What has Lance gotten Erica into?"

"I don't know the details," Stone said. "I expect we'll hear about it in due course, but they'll be safe at James's house, I'm sure."

"Will the police be coming 'round?" Monica asked.

"No, I don't think so."

"That's all I need, to have a lot of policemen crawling all over my gallery."

"Monica, you are unconnected with all this," Stone said. "In the extremely unlikely event that a policeman should drop by, just tell him everything you know, up to, but not including, the past ten minutes. You don't know where Erica is, all right?"

"All right," Monica said uncertainly.

"More likely than the police is that someone more . . . unofficial . . . might ask Erica's and Lance's whereabouts, and your answer should be the same. That's very important."

"All right," Monica said. "And who would these unofficial people be?"

"Whoever bombed Ali and Sheila's shop. And by the way, you've never heard of either of them."

"That suits me just fine," she replied. "I didn't like the look of them. And Lance didn't even introduce them."

"I'd better phone James's housekeeper and let them know that Lance is coming," Sarah said. She picked up the phone on Monica's desk and began dialing.

Monica took Stone aside. "Tell me the truth," she said. "Is somebody going to throw a bomb through my gallery window?"

"Monica, really, you have nothing to be concerned about."

"Should I call the police?"

"Certainly not; what would you tell them?"

"I don't know; I could ask for protection, or something."

"Protection from whom? You're better off ignorant of this whole business. Practice being ignorant."

"I always knew Lance would get Erica into some sort of trouble."

"What made you think that?"

"Lance is always getting these mysterious phone calls on his cellphone, or going off to meet people in pubs or other odd places. He doesn't have an office, like a normal businessman; he travels at odd times and on short notice, and Erica thinks this is all perfectly normal."

"Lots of people do business out of their homes," Stone said. "I, for one, and a lot of what you've just said would apply to me, too."

Monica laughed. "I wouldn't want you mixed up with her, either. Mixed up with me, on the other hand, would be different. When are we going to have that dinner?"

"I think we'd better postpone that indefinitely," Stone said.

Sarah hung up the phone and joined them. "That woman—Mrs. Rivers, James's housekeeper—is a pain in the ass; I'm going to fire her at the first opportunity."

"What's the problem?"

"She didn't want them in the house, said Mr. James wouldn't approve. I had to explain to her that she isn't working for Mr. James anymore, she's working for Miss Sarah, and she'd better get used to it in a hurry. I went over there yesterday to start cleaning out the place, and she behaved as if James were coming back momentarily, as if he'd been out of town on business. I've asked Julian Wainwright to write her a letter telling her that she's now in my employ, but I suppose she hasn't received it yet."

"Relax," Stone said. "All this will work itself out with time. I'm sure it won't be hard to find another housekeeper, if Mrs. Rivers can't accustom herself to her new circumstances."

"I hope so," Sarah replied.

Stone had a thought. "Monica, do you by any chance have a key to Lance and Erica's house?"

"Why, yes," Monica replied. "Why?"

"I think it might be a good idea for me to go over there and make sure everything is undisturbed."

Monica went to her desk, opened a drawer, and handed Stone a set of keys. "There's everything," she said, "front door, garage across the road, even the wine cellar."

"I'll talk to you later," Stone said to them both, and he headed for the street to find a taxi. He couldn't let an opportunity like this pass. He left the gallery and, in the pouring rain, started looking for a taxi.

3 2

STONE GOT OUT OF THE CAB AT THE bottom of Farm Street; he might as well have walked, he reflected, it had taken him so long to get a cab. The rain was still falling steadily, and the sky was unnaturally dark for the time of day. Lights were coming on in the houses of Farm Street.

He moved slowly up the little street, looking for men on foot or in cars. He did not want to encounter the two large men in the black car again, if he could help it. The street was empty of people, and all the parked cars were empty. With a final look around, Stone ran up the steps of the house and let himself in.

Grateful to be inside again, he stuck his umbrella into a stand to drain and hung his wet raincoat on a peg inside the door. The house was quite dark, with only minimal light coming through the windows from outside. Stone drew the curtains on the street-side windows and switched on the hall light to get his bearings, then switched it off again.

He had a brief look at the drawing room, switching the lights on and off again, then turned to the study, where he figured anything of interest to him would most likely be. He switched on a lamp on the desk, and the beautiful old paneling glowed in the light. There were many books, most of them bound in leather, and the desk seemed quite old, probably Georgian. Stone tried the drawers and found them unlocked. He sat down at the desk and began to go methodically through the drawers.

The contents were what might be expected in any prosperous home—bills, credit card statements in Erica's name, but none in Lance's. In a bottom drawer he found several months of bank statements, this time in Lance's name. They were from The Scottish Highlands Bank, of which Stone had never heard, and he learned from examining them that Lance wrote very few checks. There were no canceled checks in the statement, but the printout identified each payee, and they were mostly for rent and household expenses. Those that weren't were in larger amounts—five to ten thousand pounds—and were made payable to cash. Lance seemed to walk around with a lot of money in his pockets. All the deposits into the account were from wire transfers from two banks—one in the Cayman Islands and one in Switzerland. Lance would transfer twenty-five thousand pounds at a time into the account. These were substantial amounts, but not those of a multimillionaire; Lance, apart from his high-end address, seemed to live rather simply. There was no evidence of car ownership, clubs, or expensive purchases.

Erica's credit card statements revealed mostly purchases of clothing and small household items. Her deposits came from a New York bank and were more on the order of ten thousand dollars at a time, and less frequent than Lance's. Stone returned everything carefully to the drawers, leaving them as he had found them. He looked around the study again. There were no filing cabinets, and a small closet held only some stationery and a fax machine.

Stone switched off the study light and went up-stairs. There were two floors of bedrooms, and the ones on the top floor seemed unused. The second floor contained a large master suite only, with a king-sized bed, two baths, and two dressing rooms. Though Erica had accumulated a lot of clothes, Lance seemed to own no more than he could pack into two or three suitcases. He switched off the lights and went downstairs, dis-appointed.

He had expected to find something—he wasn't sure what, but something that would tell him more about Lance's business dealings. There was so little as to seem unnatural, not even a briefcase, and Lance had not been carrying one earlier in the day. Nobody could do any sort of business so lightly equipped, which made Stone think Lance must have an office some-where else in London.

He checked the kitchen and had one final look around, preparing to leave. Then, looking at the keys Monica had given him, he found one labeled "wine cellar," which she had mentioned. He looked around for a door and found one under the stairs. The light switch gave no joy, and he felt his way down the steps to the bottom, where he found another door. Feeling for the lock, he inserted the key and turned it. As he stepped into the cellar, something brushed against his cheek, and he grabbed it: a string. He pulled it, and a single light bulb came on. The wine cellar was about twelve by fifteen feet and quite full of bottles. He checked a few and found some lovely old clarets and burgundies; whoever owned the house had been lay-ing them down for years; you couldn't just walk into a shop and buy them anymore.

He stood in the middle of the cellar and looked at each of the four walls. Why was the cellar so small, when the house was so much larger? He examined the walls, which were covered by racking from floor to ceiling. Walking slowly around the room, he checked between each stack of racks, and finally he came to a pair that seemed somehow unlike the others. The racks were all fixed to the wall, except these two, which moved when he shook them. Pressing an eye to the crack between one rack and its immediate neighbor, he saw the dull glint of dim light on metal. A hinge, maybe?

He moved along one rack farther, peering into the small spaces between them, and he saw a flat piece of metal that seemed to connect two racks. It was recessed too far to reach with his fingers, and even his pen was too fat to fit between the racks. He looked around and saw a small table containing a decanter and a corkscrew.

He picked up the corkscrew, which was of the waiter's type—small, flat, with a folded knife blade at one end. He opened the knife and poked it between the two racks, finding the strip of metal. It moved when poked, and he tried inserting the blade underneath the strip and pushing upward. Almost to his surprise, the metal strip moved easily. It had been holding the two racks together; now, with it out of the way, Stone pulled on the two racks and they quite easily swung into the cellar like double doors. He could now see that each rack had a solid wood back that was fixed to the wall by four heavy hinges.

Behind the two racks was another door that, surprisingly, seemed to have no lock. Stone turned the knob and pushed it open, revealing a small room of about eight by ten feet. He found a light switch, and a fluorescent fixture brightly illuminated the space. He had found Lance Cabot's office. The room was equipped with everything a home office requires—office supplies, file cabinets, and a multipurpose printer/copier/fax machine, connected to a substantial-looking computer with a flat-screen monitor.

Stone tried the filing cabinets: locked. He switched on the computer and waited for it to boot up. Finally a screen appeared, demanding a password. Stone tried Lance, Cabot, Erica, Monica, Ali, Sheila—all the names he knew to be connected to Lance. None worked. Frustrating. He could do this all night and get nowhere. The steel desk on which the computer keyboard rested was locked, too, every drawer, and there was nothing visible or searchable in the office that could tell him anything. Indeed, except for the secret location of the room, it was like any other home office—well equipped, but utilitarian. Nothing exotic—no high-frequency radios, no mysterious equipment. Of course, with the Internet, who needed long-range radios these days?

Stone knew a little about picking locks, and he looked around for something he might use for a lockpick. Nothing but a letter opener and some paper clips. He examined the desk lock and got a small surprise. He had expected standard office locks, the kind that anybody with some picking skills could open, but these were more substantial. Each was an inch or so in diameter, and when he examined the small space between each drawer and desk, the bolts were larger than usual. It would take a much greater expert than he to deal with these locks, which had no commercial names on them. It appeared that the old locks had been drilled out and replaced with the larger, more secure ones. The locks on the filing cabinets were identical.

As Stone sat staring at the desk, wondering what to do next, he heard a noise above his head. It occurred to him that he was sitting directly below the main foyer of the house, and what he had heard was a footstep, followed by the sound of the front door closing.

There was no way out of the cellar, except the way he had come, and that opened into the foyer. Quickly, Stone turned off the wine cellar light, then pulled the two rack/doors closed and secured the metal strip. Then he closed the office door, fearful that light might escape around the door, and switched off the lights. Nothing to do now but be quiet and wait.

3 3

STONE LISTENED AS AN OCCASIONAL
footstep struck the wooden floor above, instead of a
rug, and it became apparent that more than one person was in the house, and, from the sound of the heavy
steps, they were men. They moved in and out of rooms
on the floor above, and then they stopped. Either they
were standing still or walking on rugs.

Then Stone heard a noise in the wine cellar, and dim
light appeared around the edges of the door to the little office. He could hear voices now, though they were
muffled, and the men appeared to be speaking a foreign language. He put an ear to the door, trying to hear
better, but it didn't help much. Then there was a
louder voice and two sharp reports, which Stone knew
could only be gunshots. They were not very loud, but
not silenced, either—probably a small-caliber handgun. A moment later, there were two further shots, and
he knew what that meant. The light disappeared from
around the door, and then there was nothing but silence, until he heard footsteps in the foyer, and the
sound of the front door opening and closing.

Stone checked his watch, the hands of which glowed
in the dark, and waited a full five minutes. Then he
switched on the office light. Something made him look

down, and he did not like what he saw. Blood was seeping under the door. He pulled it open slightly and listened; not a sound. He opened the door, raised the latch holding the wine racks shut, and pushed. They moved a couple of inches, then stopped against something soft.

Stone got as low as he could, put his shoulder against the racks, and pushed hard. Slowly, whatever was blocking the racks moved, and he was able to open them wide enough to step through. Light from the office fell on a man's back. Stone stepped between the racks and over the body and found the ceiling light. Not one, but two bodies lay on the floor of the wine cellar; they were the two men who had abducted him, and each of them had two new orifices in his head.

Stone inspected the wounds; small caliber, he thought, probably a .22 pistol, maybe a .25. He checked the coat pockets of the two corpses and came up with two Greek passports. Greek? What the hell did that mean? Nobody was mad at the Greeks, were they? Who would shoot two Greeks in a wine cellar in Mayfair? And why would a bunch of Greeks abduct and interrogate him?

His first impulse was to go upstairs and call the police, in the person of Detective Inspector Evelyn Throckmorton, but then he had second thoughts. How could he explain his own presence in the house? If he tried, he'd have to explain everything he'd done since he'd arrived in the United Kingdom, including the identity of his client. Also, his client had not asked him to search this house; he'd done it on his own. He would make a terrible witness, too, having seen nothing and having heard only footsteps and gunshots.

Discretion, in this case, was definitely the better part

of valor. He stepped over a body, back into the office, and wiped anything he might have touched. Then he closed the office door, wiped the knob, and secured the two wine racks in place. He wiped the knob of the wine cellar door and went upstairs, wiping anything else he might have touched in the house. Finally, he put on his raincoat, retrieved his umbrella from the stand, opened the door a crack, and peered up and down the mews. It was dark now, and streetlights were on, but the mews was empty. He let himself out, wiped the doorknob, inside and out, closed the door behind him, and walked down Farm Street in the direction of Berkeley Square.

He had reached the square before he saw anyone else, and he kept the umbrella low to keep anyone from remembering his face. Deciding against a taxi, he walked across Berkeley Square and up the little hill into Dover Street. The gallery was closed and dark. He dropped the keys to the Farm Street house through the mail slot.

What now? He wanted to talk to Lance. He walked up to New Bond Street, then to Conduit Street, found a cab at the Westbury Hotel, and gave the driver the Chester Street address that he'd heard Sarah give Lance. As the cab made its way through the West End, he thought about the two dead men on the wine cellar floor at Lance's house. How long would it be before anyone found them? Lance clearly didn't intend to go back to the house anytime soon. Was there a housekeeper or a cleaning lady? If so, would she go down to the wine cellar? He retraced his own steps, thought about the time line from a policeman's perspective. He was without an alibi from the time he left the gallery until he got into the taxi at the Westbury. How long was that? An hour at the most. Where else could he have been for an hour? Monica and Sarah knew he had the keys to the house, including the wine cellar. But no one would have any reason to question them, would they?

He thought about the cases he had solved as a cop by interviewing people at the periphery of a case. Any thorough investigation would get to them soon enough. Should he get out of the country? No, that would be the worst thing he could do. The cab stopped in front of the Chester Street house; Stone paid the driver and rang the bell. Erica answered the door.

"Oh, Stone, come in," she said, giving him a peck on the cheek. "Where have you been?"

Already, he needed an alibi. "I was at the gallery for a while, then I did some window-shopping." In the pouring rain? That was weak; he'd have to do better than that if the police questioned him.

"Come on in; Lance is on the phone." She showed him into the drawing room, which was empty. The place was handsome and spacious, but it looked as though it had been decorated by a bachelor with the help of a maiden aunt; the furniture was comfortable, but dowdy, and the curtains were too elaborate. "Awful, isn't it?" Erica asked cheerfully.

"Fairly."

"Can I get you a drink?"

"Yes, please; bourbon, if there's any in the house; Scotch, if there isn't."

She went away and came back with a double old-fashioned glass filled with ice and a brown liquor. "No bourbon; try this."

He sipped it—strong and dark and peaty. "It's excellent, what is it?"

"Laphroaig—a single-malt Scotch whiskey from the island of Islay." (She pronounced it "Islah.")

"I'm not usually a Scotch drinker, but this will do just fine." He thought she seemed oddly cheerful and unaffected for a young woman who had had to leave her home on a moment's notice, for very odd reasons. "Are you doing all right?"

"Just fine. Lance will be off the phone in a minute, I'm sure; he's already been on it since we arrived here. Ali and Sheila are upstairs napping—or something." She smiled impishly.

Stone thought they must be napping, not something else, not after having seen their business explode before their eyes earlier in the day.

"Tell me about Ali and Sheila," Stone said. He wanted to hear what Erica had to say about them before Lance returned.

"They're just friends of Lance's," she said. "They have an antique shop in Chelsea."

Had, Stone thought. "What nationality are they?"

"Ali is Syrian, Sheila Lebanese, I think."

Syrian? Lebanese? Did they have something against the Greeks, or vice versa? He couldn't make any sense of this. "How did Lance meet them?"

"Business—some importing or exporting thing, I think."

"Does Lance have a lot of friends in London?"

"Just the ones you've met," she said. "Monica, Sarah, Ali, and Sheila. He's the sort of person who seems to have lots of acquaintances and few friends."

I'll bet, Stone thought. "Have you met a lot of his acquaintances?"

"Not really; once in a while someone will come to the house for a business meeting."

"To the house? Doesn't Lance have an office?"

"Not really; if he needs space for a meeting, he uses a club or a hotel meeting room."

"I guess Lance travels pretty light, then."

"Pretty light," Lance said from the doorway.

"Oh, you're finally off the phone," Erica said. "Would you like a drink?"

"Yes, some Scotch, please."

"Try the Laphroaig," Stone said, raising his glass. Stone opened his mouth to tell Lance what he'd experienced in his wine cellar, then changed his mind. So far, nobody knew he'd actually been at the house; perhaps it was better to keep it that way, at least, for the moment.

The three of them chatted idly for a while.

"Anybody hungry?" Erica asked.

"Now that you mention it," Stone replied.

"There's no food here; I guess we'd better go out somewhere."

"There's plenty of food back at Farm Street," Lance said. "Let's go back there and fix something. I've been on the phone with some people, and I think it's safe to go back now."

Stone wondered what kind of people could tell Lance that.

"Great!" Erica said. "I feel like cooking. Shall we wake Ali and Sheila?"

"Oh, I think they're down for the night," Lance said. "Let's leave them until morning." He drained his glass and got up.

Stone got up, too. He thought of begging off, but he was curious. "I'll see if I can find us a cab."

The rain had stopped. He found a cab almost immediately.

3 4

THEY GOT OUT OF THE CAB IN FRONT of the Farm Street house, and Stone paid the driver while Lance unlocked the door. Stone followed Lance and Erica up the stairs.

Lights were switched on and everything looked quite normal, Stone thought. Coats were hung up, and he followed them into the kitchen.

"Another drink, anybody?"

Stone nodded.

"We've got bourbon," she said, "or would you rather stick to the Laphroaig?"

"I'll stick with the Scotch, since I've started on it," Stone replied.

There was a banquette in the kitchen, and Erica made Stone and Lance sit down there, while she began to put some dinner together.

"How about spaghetti Bolognese?" she asked.

"Fine," Stone and Lance said together.

Erica put some ground steak on the stove to brown and a pot of water on to boil and began chopping an onion. After a few minutes she had all the ingredients in the pot; she covered it, poured herself a drink, and sat down next to Lance. "There," she said, "we'll let it simmer for a while; by the time the water has boiled and the pasta is done, it should be ready."

Nobody seemed to have anything to say. If Erica had had any questions to ask Lance about why they had so suddenly abandoned the house, and just as suddenly returned to it, she didn't ask them now, and neither did Stone, though he was dying to know. In his experience, Lance did not answer questions to which Stone wanted answers.

"What are you working on these days?" Stone asked Lance. Might as well try.

"Oh, this and that; nothing startling."

"Would you care to be more specific?"

Lance smiled a little smile. "Nope. What are you working on, Stone?"

"Zip," Stone replied. "This is now strictly vacation time."

"How long do you plan to stay in London?"

"Oh, I don't know, a few more days, to help Sarah get through James's estate stuff."

"Doesn't she have Julian Wainwright for that?" Lance asked.

"Yes, but she seems to want my advice, too. Anyway, I'm cheaper—couple of weekends in the country, a few good dinners."

The water began to boil, and Erica got up and put the pasta into the pot. "Six minutes for al dente," she said. She pointed to an empty wine rack. "Looks like a trip to the cellar is in order."

Stone gulped.

Lance sighed, reached into his pocket for the keys, and put them on the table. "Stone, will you bring up a few bottles? I have to go to the john."

Stone was reluctant but tried not to show it. "Where is the cellar?"

"The door is under the stairs. I'm sorry, but the bulb just inside is burned out, and we don't have a spare; be careful going down the steps. The cellar light is just inside the door; you pull a string."

Stone got up and took the keys. "Anything special you want?"

"There are two racks dead ahead. Those are my bottles; the rest belong to the house's owner. Bring a few bottles of the Italian stuff."

Stone nodded and walked into the hallway, pretending to find his way. Lance walked past him into the hallway powder room and closed the door behind him.

It was easier this time, with some light from the hallway, and Stone found his way to the bottom of the cellar stairs. He got the key into the lock and took a deep breath; this was going to require a performance; he would have to run back up the stairs, breathless, and report the presence of two corpses in the cellar. He got the door open and, in the dark, felt for the string to turn on the cellar lights. He found it, hesitated for a moment; should he yell out something, or just run back up the stairs to report the bodies? He pulled the string.

The lights came on to reveal the wine cellar as he had first seen it. No bodies. No bloodstains. No sign that anyone had ever been there, let alone been murdered there. How long since he had left the cellar? An hour and a half? Two hours? He thought about it for a few moments, then did as he had been told: He went to the wine racks dead ahead, the ones covering the office door, and chose four bottles of wine. Then, with two tucked under an arm, he switched off the light, locked the cellar door, and went back upstairs.

"Find everything all right?" asked Lance, who was back seated at the banquette.

"Sure," Stone replied, setting the bottles and the keys on the table. He sat down and resumed his drink.

Lance got up, found a corkscrew, and uncorked a bottle of Chianti Classico, then put the other three bottles into the kitchen wine rack. He got three glasses from a cupboard and set them on the table, then tasted the wine. "That should do the trick," he said, and sat down again.

Erica tasted the sauce, then began setting the table. A moment later, she poured the pasta into a collander in the sink, then, while it drained, switched off the stove. She got a large platter from a cupboard, emptied the pasta into it, then poured the sauce on top of it and set it on the table. She brought some Parmesan cheese from the fridge, grated it over the pasta, sat down, and began serving them.

"Buon appetito," Lance said, raising his glass.

They dug into the pasta.

Stone ate the food, which was very good, and wondered if Lance was the coolest person he'd ever met, or if he just had no idea what had occurred in his house a couple of hours before. "Who did you say owned the house?" he asked.

"A fellow in the Foreign Office, name of Richard Creighton; he's out in the East somewhere, I believe; I pay the rent directly into his bank account. It's quite a nice house, isn't it?"

"It certainly is. It's fairly lived in, for a house owned by someone who's never here."

"Well, I guess these diplomats have got to have some sort of home to come back to. Anyway, *I'm* living in it, and I suppose he rented it to others before me."

"I've done a few things to make it better," Erica said. "The living room curtains are mine, and I've replaced all the bedding in the master suite."

"Mmmm," Stone said. "Wonderful sauce."

"Thank you, sir."

"What plans do the two of you have for the next few days?" Stone asked, because he couldn't think of anything else.

"We're in London," Lance said. "Unless something comes up."

"What might come up?"

"Oh, you never know, sometimes a deal requires travel."

"What are Ali and Sheila going to do about their shop?"

Lance shrugged. "I suppose it's insured."

"The police are going to want to talk to them."

Lance stopped eating and looked as if he hadn't thought of that.

"I suppose you're right; Ali can call them in the morning. After all, they weren't in the shop at the time, so they can hardly be of much help."

"I can tell you from experience that the police are looking for them at this moment," Stone said. "They don't ignore bombings, and they'll want to hear who Ali and Sheila think might have done this."

"I expect so," Lance said, resuming his dinner. "Well, that's Ali's problem, not mine. I expect he'll handle it in the morning."

"The sooner, the better," Stone said. "Tell me, do you have a theory about who did it?"

"Not a clue, old bean," Lance said, looking perfectly innocent. "I hope Ali will leave me out of it when he talks to the cops."

"Do Ali and Sheila belong to some group that another group might be angry with?"

"What sort of group did you have in mind?"

"Well, they're Middle Easterners, aren't they?"

"Yes."

"I should think that would give you a variety of groups to choose from—Palestinian, Israeli, Osmin ben whatshisname?"

"I suppose so, but as far as I know, they're not into politics."

"What are they into?"

"Making money," Lance replied. "At least, until today. They may want to rethink their business after this; I'm sure they must have lost most, perhaps all, of their inventory."

"I expect so," Stone said. They continued eating their dinner, and Stone stopped asking questions; there seemed to be no point, what with the answers he was getting.

3 5

STONE SPENT THE FOLLOWING DAY IN
the most relaxed fashion possible. He was stuck in his
investigation, he had no theories, and he had always
found that was a good time to do nothing, to let the
brain work on its own.

He had breakfast in his room, then did the museums:
He started at the National Gallery, where he particularly enjoyed the Italian masters, went on to the National Portrait Gallery, which was fun but didn't take
long, then continued to the Tate, where he had lunch in
the excellent restaurant before taking in the exhibitions.
He walked slowly back to the Connaught—the rain
had cleared and the day was lovely—and he was back
in his suite when the satellite telephone rang.

"Hello?"

"It's Stan Hedger; do you possess a dinner jacket?"

"Yes."

"I mean, did you bring it with you? I can send over
something, if necessary."

"Yes, I brought it with me; where am I wearing a
dinner jacket?"

"To dinner at the American ambassador's residence;
I want you to look at some faces."

"All right; what time?"

"A car will pick you up at seven o'clock; when you get to the residence, don't recognize me; we'll talk later." He hung up before Stone could speak again. Stone shrugged and rang for the valet to press his tuxedo.

He was standing in front of the Connaught when a car pulled up to the entrance. Stone was startled because it was the car in which he had been abducted. The doorman went to the car window and briefly conversed with the driver.

"Mr. Barrington?" he said. "Your car, sir." He opened the rear door wide.

Stone inspected the interior before getting into the car.

"Good evening, Mr. Barrington," the uniformed driver said.

"Good evening." The car pulled away from the curb. "What kind of car is this?"

"It's a Daimler limousine, sir; made by Jaguar."

"And to whom does it belong?"

"It belongs to the embassy, sir; they have a small fleet of them; this particular one is assigned to the ambassador, but since he's entertaining at home this evening, he didn't need it."

"Are these cars common in London?"

"Oh, yes; many of the foreign embassies use them, as does the Royal Family."

Stone relaxed a little; he wasn't being abducted again. "Where is the ambassador's residence?"

"In Regents Park, sir; do you know it?"

"No, this is my first trip to London in many years, and I never got to Regents Park the first time."

"It's about a twenty-five-minute drive this time of day, sir."

"You're English?"

"Welsh, sir; the embassy employs quite a lot of locals. Cheaper than bringing over Yanks, I expect."

"I'm afraid I don't even know the ambassador's name."

"It's Sumner Wellington, sir; I'm told the name went down rather well with the Queen."

"Oh, yes, of course; he owns a big communications company," Stone said.

"That's correct, sir; it's said that American presidents always appoint very rich men to the Court of St. James, because they can afford to do all the necessary entertaining out of their own pockets. Ambassador Wellington has paid for a complete renovation of the residence, as well."

"Sounds like an expensive job."

"I expect so, sir."

"But Ambassador Wellington can afford it."

"Quite so, sir. You said you were in London once before?"

"Yes, as a student; I did a hitchhiking tour of Europe one summer, and I spent a week of it in London."

"I expect your accommodations this time are somewhat better than on your last trip."

"Oh, yes. I spent most nights at a youth hostel, and, on one occasion, I got back after curfew and was locked out, so I slept under a railway arch somewhere."

"So the Connaught is a big step upwards."

"You could say that." The man was awfully chatty for a Brit, Stone thought, especially for a chauffeur. "Are you the ambassador's regular driver?"

"No, sir, I'm just a staff driver; I've driven the ambassador on a few occasions, when his regular driver wasn't available."

"Do you like him?"

"Yes, sir, I do; I find self-made Americans are much nicer to staff than the upper-class British. Oh, we're in Regents Park, now."

They were driving along a wide crescent of identical buildings, with the park on their left. After a turn or two, the car glided to a stop before the residence, a very large Georgian house.

A U.S. marine opened the rear door of the car.

"Mr. Barrington?" the driver said.

Stone stopped getting out of the car.

"I was asked to give you a message."

"Yes?"

"If you recognize someone, be careful."

"That's it?"

"Yes, sir; I'll be waiting when you're ready to leave; just give your name to the marine on duty."

"See you later, then."

"Yes, sir."

Stone got out of the car and entered the house. In the huge foyer, there was a reception line that was moving slowly. Stone got into it, behind a very American-looking couple. He was short and pudgy; she was taller, very blonde, and expensive-looking.

"Hey," the woman said.

"Good evening," Stone replied.

"That's what I should have said, I guess; good evening."

"Hey works for me," Stone laughed.

She held out her hand. "I'm Tiffany Butts; this is my husband, Marvin."

Stone shook their hands.

"We're from Fort Worth, Texas," she said. "Are you an American?"

"Oh, yes; I'm from New York."

"I wasn't sure about your accent."

"I've been here a few days; maybe I'm picking up an English accent."

"Oh, shoot, no, it's just me."

"What business are you in, Mr. Barrington?" Marvin Butts asked.

"I'm an attorney."

"I'm in the scrap metal business," Butts said. "In a fairly big way."

I'll bet you are, Stone thought, or you wouldn't be at this party. "Sounds good."

"Good, and getting better," Butts replied.

They had been moving along the line, and suddenly they were before the ambassador and his wife. The ambassador was sixtyish, slim, and handsomely tailored. His wife was twenty-five years his junior, very beautiful and elegant. The ambassador greeted Marvin and Tiffany Butts warmly, then turned toward Stone.

"Good evening," he said. "Welcome to the residence."

"Good evening, Mr. Ambassador," Stone replied. "I'm Stone Barrington."

"Ah," the ambassador said, looking him up and down.

His wife gave Stone a broad smile. "We have a mutual friend, Stone," she said.

"And who would that be, Madame Ambassador?"

"Oh, please, I'm Barbara, among friends."

Friends? What was she talking about? An aide ushered Stone farther along before he could ask.

Stone found himself a few steps above a large hall, looking down on a very elegant crowd. Before he had moved a step, he recognized two people. The sight of either would have made his heart beat a little faster, but for very different reasons.

Arrington Carter Calder saw him almost at the same moment and held his gaze, expressionless. And just beyond her, Stone saw a short, bald, bullet-headed man he had met before.

3 6

THEN ARRINGTON SMILED WARMLY, and Stone's knees went a little weak. He experienced a series of vivid flashbacks: meeting her at a New York dinner party some years before, she in the company of America's biggest movie star, Vance Calder; taking her away from Calder, making love to her in his house and hers, falling desperately in love with her; then setting off on a sailing trip to the Caribbean, planning to meet her there; her not showing up, but writing to say she'd married Calder. Then there was the child, of course, Peter; born slightly less than nine months later: Calder's son, she said, and the tests had backed her up. Then, after Calder was dead, murdered, learning that the tests might have been rigged. She'd refused further testing. He'd seen her a few months before in Palm Beach, for a single evening, then he had been in the hospital with a bullet wound, then whisked back to New York. They had not spoken since.

Stone snapped back to the present and made his way down the steps toward her. She was tall, a little blonder than before, dressed in a long, emerald-green gown. Ravishing. To his surprise she met him halfway, embraced him warmly, and gave him a light kiss on the lips.

"Hello, Stone," she said, nearly laughing. "Are you surprised to see me?"

"I certainly am," he replied; "what brings you to London?"

"Barbara Wellington and I were roommates at Mount Holyoke; she invited me over to see what she's done with the residence. Isn't it beautiful?"

"Yes, it is." But he wasn't looking at the residence. "And you are more beautiful than I've ever seen you."

"Aren't you sweet! I saw your name on the guest list this afternoon, and I jiggled the place cards around so we're seated together." She stopped and looked at him. "I'm alone in London."

Stone was beginning to sweat a little, and he was grateful when a waiter showed up with a tray of champagne flutes. He took one and replaced hers with a full one. "I'll look forward to catching up," he said.

Then he remembered the other face he had recognized and looked for it. Gone. Lost in the crowd.

"Looking for someone?" Arrington asked.

"I thought I saw a familiar face, but no more."

She took his arm and led him across the room and out some French doors to a garden. "And what brings you to London?"

"A client asked me to come over and look into something for him."

"Sounds mysterious."

"It is."

"It's always mysterious when you're involved, Stone. Tell me about it."

"I'm afraid I can't. Maybe when it's over."

"Oh."

"How is Peter?"

"Growing," she said. "You must come and see him sometime."

"I'd like that very much," he said. "Where are you spending most of your time?"

"I've been dividing it between LA and Mother's house in Virginia. Peter is there for the summer with her, while I've been apartment hunting."

"In London?"

"In New York."

Stone began to sweat again and sipped the cold champagne. From inside the house a chime was being struck repeatedly.

"Sounds like dinner," Arrington said. "Shall we?"

"Let's do." The thought of Arrington living in New York again thrilled and frightened him. Immediately, his life seemed in turmoil.

They sat at round tables for ten, and there were at least twenty of them. Arrington knew some of the other guests, having "jiggled the place cards," and she chatted animatedly with them all, leaving Stone with a thousand questions and no opportunity to ask any of them. Dinner was good, for banquet food, and when dessert came, Stone excused himself and went to look for a men's room. A staffer showed him the way, and he went inside and stepped up to a urinal. A moment later, the door opened and someone walked behind Stone and around the room, then stepped up to the neighboring urinal.

"See anyone you know?" Hedger asked.

"Yes, Arrington Calder," Stone said.

"The movie star's widow? I think she killed him, don't you?"

"No."

"How do you know her?"

"We've been friends for a long time."

"Oh, wait a minute, I remember now; you were involved with her trial, weren't you?"

"She was never tried," Stone replied. "Her lawyer and I got it quashed at a hearing. She was plainly innocent."

"Yeah, sure," Hedger said.

Stone zipped up and went to wash his hands. Hedger was right behind him.

"I saw someone else," Stone said.

"Who?"

"The man who interrogated me. At least, I think it was he; I only got a glimpse of him, and he wasn't very well lighted the last time I saw him."

"Where is he sitting?"

"I don't know; when I looked for him again, he was gone."

"You mean, he left?"

"I don't know; he may have just moved elsewhere in the room."

"Did he see you?"

"I don't know."

"Try and spot him again, and find a way to let me know where he is. I'm at table sixteen."

"All right. There's something else we have to talk about, but we can't do it now."

"How about lunch tomorrow in the Connaught grill? One o'clock?"

"Fine, see you then."

Stone left first and went back to his table. He took the scenic route, wandering among the tables, and then, over near the doors to the garden, he saw the man, who was raptly listening to an elderly woman seated next to him. Table twelve, he noted. He looked at the man as closely as he dared. Was it his inquisitor, or was he simply a bald, bullet-headed man? Stone wished he could hear his voice; that would complete the identification. The man never looked at him, and he made his way back to his table and Arrington.

She was gone. Dancing had begun, and he spotted her on the floor with a man from their table. He took a cocktail napkin, drew a circle, and wrote on it, *Table Twelve*. He marked the bald man's position and gave it to a waiter. "Please take this to Mr. Hedger, at table sixteen; he's the one with the mustache."

The waiter departed, and Stone followed him with his gaze to Hedger's table. He saw Hedger read the note, then tuck it into a pocket. He didn't immediately look at table twelve, but a moment later he let his gaze run in that direction. Then he looked toward Stone and shrugged.

Stone looked back at table twelve, but the man was no longer there. He noticed a door to the garden open, near the table. Stone looked back at Hedger and shrugged.

Arrington came back to the table and took Stone's hand. "Come dance with me," she said. She led him to the floor, and the band was playing something romantic.

Stone held her in his arms, something he had always loved doing, and moved them around the floor.

"You were always a wonderful dancer," she said. "Vertically or horizontally." She kissed him on the neck.

"Let's get out of here," Stone said.

"I can't; I'm a guest of the ambassador, and it would be rude."

"Dinner tomorrow night?"

"Where?"

"The Connaught restaurant, at nine?"

"You're on."

She put her head on his shoulder, and he whirled her happily around the floor.

Stone looked back at table twelve; the man was still not there. "If you jiggled the place cards, you must have access to tonight's guest list," he said to Arrington.

"I suppose," she replied.

"Do you think you could get me a list of the people at table twelve, with their positions marked?"

"I suppose so, but not tonight."

"Will you bring it with you tomorrow evening? It's important."

"Anything for you," she said, and let her tongue play lightly over his ear.

Stone didn't complain.

3 7

STONE WAS ALREADY AT AN ALCOVE
table in the Connaught grill when Stanford Hedger arrived for lunch. Hedger sat down and ordered a pink
gin, something Stone had never heard an American do.

"What is a pink gin, anyway?"

"Gin with a dash of Angostura bitters," Hedger
replied. "I doubt if you'd like it."

"I doubt it, too," Stone replied, sipping his Chardon-
nay.

"Did you enjoy your evening?" Hedger asked. "I
saw you and Mrs. Carter dancing."

"Yes, thank you, and thank you, too, for the use of
the ambassador's car."

"Any time," Hedger replied. "When the ambassador's not using it, I use it myself, sometimes. Tell
me, is it hard to dance with someone's tongue in your
ear?"

"On the contrary," Stone replied. "It helps."

Hedger laughed. "I never saw your little bald man,
you know; are you sure he wasn't a figment of your
imagination?"

"Isn't his presence why you had me invited?"

"Well, yes; but I fully expected to see him, if you did."

"Why did you think he'd be there?"

"Just a hunch. Last night's dinner, if you didn't know, was for the foreign diplomatic corps. I reckoned if he was anybody important in an embassy, he'd be there."

"Good guess," Stone replied. "And why did you think he'd be somebody important in an embassy?"

"His accents, as you described them, one overlaid on the other. Eton is a very exclusive school, you know, and everybody who spends his youth there comes out with that accent, even the foreigners. Remember Abba Eban, the Israeli ambassador to the UN?"

"Yes."

"Same accent."

"Now that you mention it."

Hedger looked at the menu. "I'll have half a dozen oysters and the Dover sole," he said to the waiter, "off the bone, and I'd prefer a female, if there's one available."

"I'll have the cold soup and the sole," Stone said. "Should I order the female, too?"

"If you enjoy roe," Hedger replied.

Stone nodded to the waiter.

"And bring us a bottle of that lovely Sancerre," Hedger said. He turned to Stone. "Now, what's up? Why did you want to see me?"

"Things have taken a rather ominous turn," Stone said, "and I thought you might have some advice on how I should proceed."

"Tell me."

"I followed Lance Cabot yesterday from his house to an antiques market in Chelsea. Do you know his friends Ali and Sheila?"

"Oh, yes; he met them when we were in Cairo. I believe they were complicit in the bombing of my safe house there."

"Turns out they had a shop in the market. Also turns out that I wasn't the only one following Lance; so were the two men who abducted me and took me to the interrogation. They were in the same Daimler limousine."

"Did you make a note of the number plate?"

"No," Stone replied, a little embarrassed that he had not thought of that.

"Next time you get the chance," Hedger said. "It would help."

"Certainly. Anyway, the two men followed Lance into the building. I went inside and found Ali and Sheila's shop, phoned Lance there, and told them to get out. I got them into a cab, and as we drove around the building, a bomb destroyed the shop."

Hedger's considerable eyebrows went up. "Sounds like these people are getting serious."

"They're not the only ones," Stone said. "Lance called Erica and told her to get out of the house; then they went to the home of a friend, and I had a look around Lance's house; got the keys from Monica, Erica's sister."

"Oh, good," Hedger said, obviously pleased. "I assumed you searched it thoroughly."

"I did. There was absolutely nothing that revealed anything about Lance or whatever business he's conducting."

"I'm not really surprised," Hedger said. "Lance is too smart to leave sensitive materials lying around."

"Then I had a look in the wine cellar, where I found a small office, concealed behind a couple of wine racks." He gave Hedger a description of how he got in. "There was a desk, a computer, and filing cabinets, all secured. As I was trying to get into the computer, I heard someone entering the house; more than one person. I shut myself up in the office and waited for them to leave. After a few minutes, two men came into the wine cellar; a moment later, another person came in and shot them both." He had Hedger's undivided attention now.

Their first courses arrived, and Stone waited for the waiter to depart before continuing. "When I got out of the office, they were both dead—two small-caliber shots to the head, in both cases."

"I hope to God you didn't call the police."

"No, I got the hell out of there, after removing any fingerprints I might have left on various surfaces."

"Good," Hedger said, relieved.

"The two men were my former abductors."

Hedger looked surprised. "Oh, really?"

"They were carrying Greek passports."

"*Greek*?" Hedger grunted. "Probably false."

"They looked good to me."

"Would you recognize a false passport?"

"I've seen a few, but to answer your question, probably not a good one."

"Well, let's sum up," Hedger said.

"Not yet, there's more."

"More?"

"I went to find Lance and Erica; we had a drink, and then we returned to the Farm Street house. Erica cooked, and Lance asked me to go to the cellar and bring up some wine. I did, and the bodies were gone, everything cleaned up."

Hedger looked really interested. "How long were you out of the house?"

"An hour and a half, maybe two hours."

"Long enough for Lance to visit the house, clean up, and return to the other house?"

"If he hurried, and if he was very efficient. He was on the phone when I arrived at the other house, but I've no idea how long he had been there."

"Could Lance have had any idea you'd been to the Farm Street house?"

"Possibly, since I got the keys from Monica. Maybe she told him."

"So he sent you down to the cellar so you could see for yourself that everything had been cleaned up."

"Perhaps. I'll have to find out if Monica told him I had the keys."

"Do that. Now, as I said, to sum up, what does this tell us about Lance?"

"You tell me."

"It tells us that Lance is a part of something bigger than himself."

"How does it tell us that?"

"You obviously didn't read the papers this morning."

"Not thoroughly."

"Your two 'Greeks' were found in Hyde Park, in the trunk of a stolen car. The police are quite excited about it."

"Oh."

"I very much doubt if Lance had time to steal a car, load the bodies into it, and clean up the wine cellar, all on his own."

"You have a point. But what if it wasn't Lance?"

"Who else might it be?"

"The bald man?"

"They were his men; why would he shoot them in Lance's wine cellar, then clean up after himself? I could understand that he might wish to pin the murders on Lance, but in that case, he'd have left them where they lay, for somebody to find, wouldn't he?"

"I suppose so."

"The parties we know are involved in this are Lance, the bald man and his two companions, and the two

'Greeks,' and they're dead. If there's another party, I don't know about it, and neither do you."

"Lance would," Stone said. "If he knows anything. It's possible that another party murdered the two men, and Lance knows nothing about it."

"If you were the investigating officer, and you are, in a way, would you believe that?"

"It wouldn't be my first theory," Stone admitted.

"Now, back to the bald gentleman. I think he's a diplomat; how do we find out who he is?"

"Tonight, I'll have a list of the people at table twelve," Stone said. "We can begin there."

"Very good," Hedger said. The waiter arrived with their sole, and they tucked into it.

Stone liked the roe.

3 8

LATER THAT EVENING, MR. CHEVALIER, the maître d' in the Connaught restaurant, took note that Stone had arrived, for the second time that week, with a beautiful woman. He must have had a sense of humor, because he seated them at the same corner table that Stone had shared with Sarah.

Sarah had called that afternoon. "Why don't I cook you some dinner at my flat this evening?"

"I'm afraid I already have plans," Stone said.

"Anyone I know?"

Strictly speaking, no, though she knew about Arrington. "No."

"I'm not sure I like this."

"It's business," Stone said, falling back on the most convenient lie. He didn't like lying, but he was cornered.

"Oh."

"How's it going with James's estate?" he asked, wanting to remind her that she should, strictly speaking, be in mourning.

"Splendidly," she said. "Julian Wainwright has had a word with the conglomerate, and it looks as though they're still interested in buying the business."

"That's good news."

"Yes, it is."

There was an awkward silence.

"Will I see you this week?"

"Of course. Oh, by the way, do you know if Monica spoke to Lance the other night, after she gave me the keys to the Farm Street house?"

"I don't think so; we had dinner together, and I dropped her off at her place later. She didn't call anyone while we were together. Why?"

"I decided not to go to Lance's house, since it really isn't any of my business, and I didn't want Lance to think I had been there."

"I'm seeing Monica later today; I could mention that to her, if you like."

"I'd appreciate that. I put the keys through her mail slot not long after she gave them to me."

"All right, then, I'll see you later, I hope."

"Of course," Stone replied, and hung up feeling guilty.

Seated at the corner table, with Arrington beside him, in the warm glow of the Connaught restaurant, Stone no longer felt guilty. The difficult past he and Arrington shared had receded; all he could think about was here and now.

"It's so good to see you," Arrington said.

"And you."

"When I saw you in Palm Beach, you said you'd call me the next day. Why didn't you?"

He had called her in the morning and a man had answered, so he had hung up. "You'll recall the circumstances of the evening," Stone said. "I had to make a stop at the local hospital, and they got me out of there early the next morning on Thad Shames's jet." It had been from the jet that he had called her. "By the time I got to New York and the drugs had worn off, you had left Palm Beach." He was guessing that she had left.

"Yes, I left the next day," she said. "Oh, by the way, here's that list you asked for." She pulled a sheet of paper from her purse.

Stone looked at the list: the Swedish ambassador and his wife; the Belgian chargé d'affaires and wife; the Israeli cultural attaché and wife; the German military attaché and wife; the Australian head of chancery and wife. "There's no seating plan," he said.

"Sorry, I couldn't get that; some secretary had apparently shredded it, or something."

It was a start, Stone thought; he'd have to go over this with Hedger.

"Why did you want the list?"

"There was a man at the table I recognized, but I couldn't place him."

"You know a lot of diplomats, do you?"

"No, he just looked very familiar. It'll come to me."

"You're not losing brain cells, are you?"

He laughed. "Yes, but no more than usual."

They had a drink and ordered dinner. Stone didn't really care what he ate; he was happy just to be with her, with no strain, no conflict. Every time they had met during the past couple of years there had always been some problem that made the situation difficult.

"It's so nice to be back in London," Arrington said. "And I've always loved this room. Vance and I stayed here when we were in town, and we always had dinner here at least once."

That didn't improve the atmosphere much for Stone, but he let it pass.

"You're looking very beautiful tonight," he said, trying to get things back on track.

"You look pretty good yourself," she said.

Mr. Chevalier suddenly appeared at the table and handed Stone a small envelope. "A message for you, Mr. Barrington," he said.

"Thank you," Stone replied. "Sorry about this," he said to Arrington. He opened the envelope. On a sheet of the hotel's stationery was written, *I am in the hotel lounge; I must see you at once.* It was signed by Detective Inspector Evelyn Throckmorton.

"Oh, shit," Stone muttered.

"What is it?"

"There's someone here I have to see for a moment. Please excuse me."

"Not a woman, I hope," Arrington said.

"Fear not." He left the table and started toward the lounge. As he reached the central hallway, Monica appeared through the front doors.

"Hello, there," she said, taking him by the shoulders and giving him a kiss on the lips.

Stone could see Throckmorton waiting impatiently in the lounge across the hallway. "Hello; I dropped Lance's keys through your mail slot; did you get them?"

"Yes. Did you check out his house?"

"No, I decided it was none of my business, so I dropped off the keys. Why are you at the Connaught?"

"I'm having dinner with some friends in the grill; I'd better run." She repeated the warm kiss, then disappeared down the hall into the grill.

Stone walked into the lounge, wiping lipstick from his lips. Throckmorton and two men who were obviously detectives were waiting for him, seated in large chairs, still wearing their raincoats. The detective inspector looked grim. A raincoat was draped across his lap. "Sit down," he said. "I'm going to ask you some questions, and I want truthful answers," he said.

Stone sat down.

"Early this morning," Throckmorton began, "a police constable in Hyde Park found a stolen car abandoned there."

Stone tried to remain calm.

"In the boot were the bodies of two men who had been murdered, shot in the head with a handgun, obviously a professional job of work."

"I believe I saw something about that in the papers," Stone replied.

"They were of Mediterranean extraction, carrying Greek passports. Do you know anyone of that description?"

"No," Stone lied.

"Think carefully, Mr. Barrington; you don't want to make any mistakes."

"I do not think I am acquainted with them."

Throckmorton took the raincoat from his lap and held it out to Stone. "Then why was one of them wearing your raincoat?" He opened the coat and turned out an inside pocket. A label bore the name of Doug Hayward's shop and neatly printed inside, Stone's own name.

Stone was stunned; he struggled to remain calm. "I don't understand," Stone said. "My raincoat is upstairs."

"Let's go and see it," Throckmorton said, standing up.

Stone went to the concierge's desk, asked for his key, and led the way to the elevator. The four men filled it completely. Stone's mind was racing. When the two men had entered Lance's house, they must have hung their raincoats on the rack with Stone's: When he had left the house, he must have taken the wrong coat. Oh, shit, shit, shit! How was he going to explain this? And if he told Throckmorton everything, how would he explain not having told him earlier about the two corpses in the wine cellar?

The elevator stopped on Stone's floor, and he led them to his suite. He went to a closet, found the raincoat, and handed it to Throckmorton.

The two detectives peered over his shoulder at the two coats, comparing them. "They're nearly identical," one of them said, helpfully. "The linings look the same, too."

"Mmm, yes," Throckmorton agreed. He turned to Stone. "That doesn't explain how the two coats got exchanged," he said.

"I have absolutely no idea," Stone replied. "Perhaps in a checkroom somewhere?"

"Where? Where have you checked this coat?"

"Everywhere I've been," Stone replied. "Downstairs in the cloak room, in restaurants; I've also hung it on racks in pubs, set it down in shops."

"But where could you have taken this dead man's coat?"

"I don't know, it seems likely that he took mine and left his, doesn't it?"

Throckmorton turned to the two detectives. "Wait downstairs," he said. The two men left the room. "Sit down," he said to Stone. Both men took chairs.

"Evelyn . . ."

"It is only because of Lieutenant Bacchetti's recommendation of you that we are not having this conversation in an interrogation room, and that the interrogation is not being conducted by the two men who just left, who would be doing the job far less gently than I."

"I appreciate the consideration," Stone said, "but I have absolutely no idea when and where this exchange of raincoats happened."

"Let me tell you a bit more," Throckmorton said. "The passports found on the men were counterfeits. Does that help jog your memory?"

"I know nothing of false passports," Stone said.

"Let me see yours."

Stone went to his briefcase, got his passport, and handed it over.

Throckmorton examined it closely, then he took two passports from his pocket and compared them. "It says here that this passport was issued only a few days ago at the American Embassy in London."

"That's correct; when I arrived in this country, an immigration officer told me that my passport was expiring the following day."

"You didn't know that?"

"No. I hadn't used the passport for several months; it didn't occur to me to look at the expiration date. I went to the embassy, as the officer suggested, and got a new one."

"And where is your old one?"

"The passport office kept it."

"And I'm keeping yours," Throckmorton said, tucking all three passports into his pocket.

"Suppose I have to leave the country?"

"You will not leave the country until I say so," Throckmorton said, rising. "One last time, Stone; is there anything you wish to tell me?"

"No."

"I'll be in touch," Throckmorton said. He walked out of the room, taking both raincoats with him.

Stone sat down heavily and loosened his necktie. "Jesus Christ," he said aloud, "how could I have made such a stupid mistake?" He laid his head against the back of the chair and closed his eyes, trying to calm himself.

What seemed only a moment later, Stone jerked awake. Had he dozed off? Then he remembered that Arrington was downstairs in the restaurant. He ran to the elevator, buttoning his shirt and fixing his necktie; when he reached the ground floor, he tried not to run to the restaurant. From the door he could see that the table was empty.

"Mr. Barrington?" Mister Chevalier said.

"Yes? Where is Mrs. Calder?"

"I'm afraid she left a few minutes ago; she went to the lounge to look for you but could not find you, so she got her coat and left." Chevalier looked at his watch. "You were gone for nearly an hour," he said, with barely noticeable reproach.

"Oh, God," Stone moaned.

"We have kept your dinner warm," Chevalier said. "Would you still like to have it, or would you prefer to order something else?"

Stone stared at the paneling ahead of him, wondering how he was ever going to fix this.

"Mr. Barrington?"

"Oh. Will you send it to my suite, please?"

"Of course; and Mrs. Calder's dinner?"

"Give it to the cat," Stone said. He turned and trudged disconsolately to the elevator.

Upstairs, he got out the London telephone directory and looked for the ambassador's residence; he found it under U.S. Government and dialed the number.

"Good evening," a young male voice said, "this is the residence of the United States Ambassador." Probably a marine.

"My name is Barrington," Stone said. "May I speak with Mrs. Arrington Calder? She's a guest of the ambassador."

"I'm sorry, Mr. Barrington, Mrs. Calder has asked me not to put any calls through."

"Would you tell her I called, please?" He gave the Connaught's number.

"Of course, sir; good night."

There was a sharp rap on his door, and he went to answer it. His dinner had arrived, and he didn't feel like eating it.

3 9

STONE, HAVING LAIN AWAKE UNTIL the middle of the night, slept as if drugged. It was mid-morning before he woke up, and his first move was to call the embassy residence again and ask for Arrington. There was a long delay, then a woman came on the line.

"Stone?"

"Arrington, I'm so sorry, I—"

"Stone, it's Barbara Wellington."

"I'm sorry, I thought you were Arrington. I've been trying to reach her; she wasn't taking calls last night."

"I know; she came home very hurt and angry last night; she said you had abandoned her in the middle of dinner at the Connaught. What happened?"

"Some people showed up that I absolutely had to see, and—"

"She also said that when she got up to go to the ladies' she saw you kissing another woman in the Connaught lobby, so when you reach her, I don't think you ought to try and pass that off as business."

"It *was* business—not the woman—but three men I had to see, and—"

"And when she came back from the ladies' you had

disappeared, and the concierge said you had gone up to your suite with a guest."

"With three guests—they insisted. You see—"

"Stone, it's not I you have to convince, so save your strength."

"May I speak to Arrington, please?"

"I'm afraid that won't be possible."

"Barbara, please just tell her there's a perfectly reasonable explanation for—"

"Stone, Arrington has gone."

"Gone where? Where can I reach her?"

"To New York; she left here about twenty minutes ago for Heathrow. I think she'll be staying at the Carlyle. If I were you, I'd go after her, get the next plane."

"I'm afraid I can't do that—"

"You're going to have to resolve this face-to-face."

"How long did you say she'd been gone?"

"About twenty minutes."

"What airline?"

"British Airways."

"Do you know the flight number?"

"No, but it leaves around noon, I think. You have to be there early these days, because of all the security stuff."

"Thank you, Barbara." Stone hung up, then picked up the phone again. "Please ask the doorman to get me a cab for Heathrow immediately," he said to the operator. "I'll be right down."

He threw on some clothes and, unshaven and unshowered, ran for the elevator. The doorman had the cab door open as he came through the revolving door, and he dove into the rear seat.

"Heathrow, is it, sir?" the cabbie asked.

"Right, and hurry."

The driver pulled away and turned up Mount

Street, headed for Park Lane. "Shouldn't be too bad this time of day; what airline?"

"British Airways, first-class entrance."

"Righto."

Stone sat back and stared out the window, frequently glancing at his watch. Traffic wasn't bad, and after the Chiswick Roundabout, it became even better.

"Excuse me, sir," the driver said, "I don't want you to think I've come over all paranoid, but I'm quite sure there's a car following us."

Stone spun around and looked at the traffic behind them. "Which one?"

"It's a black Ford, the big one; at least two men in it, about four cars back."

"Are they staying back, or are they trying to overtake us?" Stone asked.

"They were closer before; now they're just lying back there, keeping us in sight." What now? he thought. Have the two big "Greeks" been replaced in the lineup?

"Is there any way you can shake them?"

"Not on this road; they're faster than I am. I could get off the motorway and try and lose them in Hammersmith."

He had no time for that. "Never mind, just get me to Heathrow as fast as you can."

"Righto."

The driver stayed in the center of three lanes, driving fast; the black Ford held its position, and when the cab left the motorway at the Heathrow turnoff, Stone saw the Ford's turn signal go on.

The driver followed the signs to the British Airways terminal, still driving fast. Stone reached into a pocket for money, and discovered he had none. He had nothing in his pockets.

The cab screeched to a halt. "Wait for me here," he said. "I'll be right back."

"I don't know if . . ."

But Stone was gone at a run. He did not see the black Ford stop fifty yards back and two men get out. He dashed into the terminal and ran for the first-class ticket counter. There were three people in line; he ignored them and went to the desk. "Excuse me, this is an emergency; can you tell me if Mrs. Arrington Calder has checked in yet?"

"Yes," the young woman said. "I checked her in no more than five minutes ago; she was headed for the security checkpoint when I last saw her."

"Thank you," Stone said, and hurried off, following signs to the checkpoint. The area was a zoo, with dozens of passengers lining up for the security check and X-ray machines. Stone jumped up and down, trying to see over their heads, and he saw Arrington pick up her hand luggage on the other side and start toward the gates. He didn't want to start shouting at her, and there was no way to break into the line, so he went to an exit, where a uniformed policeman was on guard.

"Excuse me," he said to the bobby, "I'm trying to catch up with a friend who has just gone through security; may I get in this way?"

"Do you have any luggage, sir?"

"No."

"May I see your ticket?"

"I don't have a ticket; I'm not flying today, she is."

"May I see your passport?"

The police had his passport. "I'm afraid I didn't bring it."

"Some other identification?"

Stone dove into a pocket, then remembered it was empty. "Oh, God, I didn't bring my wallet."

"I'm sorry, sir."

"This really is a sort of personal emergency."

"I'm very sorry, sir, but I can't let you through without a ticket or any identification."

Then Stone heard a voice behind him. "It's all right, mate, we'll deal with this."

Two men seized his arms and marched him back through the terminal. Stone looked at them and recognized the two detectives who had accompanied Evelyn Throckmorton the night before.

"Trying to catch a flight, were we, Mr. Barrington?" one of them said.

"No, I was trying to catch up with a friend who's leaving on a noon flight."

"Well, he'll have plenty of time to make it," the cop said.

"Do you think it might be possible for me to go after her? Can you vouch for me with the officer at the security gate? It's very important that I speak to her."

"I believe Detective Inspector Throckmorton told you last night that you were not to leave the country," the cop said.

"But I wasn't trying to leave."

"You wouldn't have made it without your passport, anyway."

"Honestly, I was just trying to catch up with my friend."

They were out the door, where Stone's taxi was still waiting for him.

"That cab is waiting for me to go back to the Connaught," he said.

"Never mind, we'll give you a lift," the cop replied.

"But I have to pay him."

The cop stopped. "All right, pay him."

"I don't have any money with me; it's back in my room at the Connaught."

The cop sighed wearily. "I suppose you expect me to pay him."

"Look, I'm not trying to leave the country; you can follow me back to the hotel."

"Just a moment." The cop produced a cellphone and stepped a few paces away. A moment later, he returned. "All right, Mr. Barrington, the detective inspector says you can return to the Connaught."

"Thank you."

"But don't give us any more chases, all right?"

"Thank you again." Stone got into the cab.

"Catch her, sir?"

"Not quite," Stone replied. "Take me back to the Connaught."

The black Ford followed them all the way back.

4 O

STONE GOT BACK TO THE CONNAUGHT,
went upstairs, got money, and paid the driver, tipping
him extravagantly. As he passed the concierge's desk,
he heard his name called.

"I'm very sorry, Mr. Barrington," the concierge said,
"but this message arrived for you last evening, and it
was somehow misplaced." He handed Stone a yellow
envelope.

Stone opened it and extracted the message. *I'm on
my way,* it said, and that was all. "Who is it from?" he
asked the concierge.

"I'm afraid that's just how it came, sir; there was no
name. We thought you'd know who it was from."

"Man or woman?"

"I'm sorry, sir, I wasn't on duty last evening, so I
don't know."

Stone stuffed it into his pocket and went upstairs. He
didn't care who the fuck it was from, he was too pissed
off. He let himself into the suite, hung up his jacket, and
picked up the London papers. He went quickly through
the *Times* and the *Independent*, looking for further mention
of the two dead "Greeks" but saw nothing. There was a
small piece about the explosion at the antiques market,
but it had, apparently, been attributed to a gas leak.

He soaked in a hot tub for nearly an hour, grateful for the solitude, then ordered some sandwiches from room service and turned on the TV. He watched CNN for a while and, after he began seeing the same stories for the third time, began channel surfing. There was an Italian soap opera, a bad 1930s movie, a children's show, and a soccer match. Stone had always thought that soccer would be a better spectator sport if the field were half as long and the goals twice as wide. Finally, he settled on a cricket match and for an hour tried to make some sense of it. He finally concluded that cricket was an elaborate joke that the Brits played on American tourists; that they probably played the same taped match over and over. He dozed.

He was awakened by a heavy knock on the door. Still in a stupor, he gathered the terrycloth robe around him and went to the door. Nobody there. The hammering came again, and it seemed to be coming from his right, where there was a door, always locked, apparently leading to a second bedroom adjoining his suite. He listened at that door and jumped back when the hammering started again. Very weird. Gingerly, he unlocked his side of the door and opened it. Behind it was another door, and someone hammered on it again. "It's locked on your side!" he yelled.

The latch turned, and the door opened. Dino Bacchetti stood in the adjoining room.

"Jesus," Dino said, "are you deaf? I've been knocking for ten minutes."

Stone was completely nonplussed. "What the hell are you doing here, Dino?"

"I'm hungry; get me a room-service menu."

"Press the button over there that says 'waiter,'" Stone instructed. Dino pressed it.

"Dino, what are you doing in London?"

"Didn't you get my message?"

"No. Well, yes, I guess so, but there was no name on it."

The waiter knocked on the door, and Stone opened it.

"Yes, sir; may I get you something?"

"What time is it in this country?" Dino asked.

"Nine-thirty P.M., sir," the waiter said, glancing at his watch.

"You want some dinner?" Dino asked Stone.

"Whatever you're having," Stone replied.

"Bring us a couple Caesar salads and a couple steaks, medium-rare, and a decent bottle of red wine," Dino said to the waiter.

"Of course, sir. Would you like some potatoes?"

"Sure, sure, whatever you've got," Dino said. "And bring him a double Wild Turkey on the rocks, and me a Johnnie Walker Black, fixed the same, right away, please." He closed the door behind the departing waiter.

"Dino, just once more, what are you doing here?"

Dino shucked off his coat, loosened his tie, and sank into an armchair. "What the fuck are they doing?" he asked, pointing at the TV.

"They're playing cricket," Stone replied. "It's been going on for at least six hours."

"What are the rules?"

"Nobody knows. What are you doing here?"

"Well, you're in trouble; somebody had to come over here and pull your ass out of the shit."

"I'm not in trouble."

"Oh? I hear you're looking good for a double murder."

"Oh, that; Throckmorton called you."

"Yep." He was still gazing, rapt, at the TV. "What kind of pitching is that?" he asked.

"They call it bowling."

"That's not what they call bowling in *my* neighborhood," Dino said.

"What did Throckmorton tell you?"

"Just that they found a couple of stiffs in a car trunk, and one of them was wearing your raincoat."

"That was an accident," Stone said.

"An accident? With two pops each in the head?"

"I mean the raincoat."

"An accidental raincoat? Hey, look at that; they don't run to first, they run to the pitcher's mound and back again. This is completely nuts!"

"I grabbed somebody's raincoat, and he apparently grabbed mine. Or rather, whoever shot him grabbed it and put it on him."

"Didn't want him to get rained on, I guess," Dino said. "Do you really expect anybody to believe a story like that?"

"Throckmorton doesn't believe it?"

"Of course not; who would?"

"Well, I didn't exactly tell him everything."

"I figured. You want to tell me?"

The waiter arrived with the drinks, and they sat down.

Dino raised his glass. "To your eventual freedom," he said, and took a long pull on his Scotch.

"I'm not under arrest," Stone said.

"No? Stick around. Now, you want to tell me what the fuck happened?"

"All right, but Throckmorton never hears this, okay?"

"Are you kidding? I came over here to get you out of this, not to send you to Wormy Scrubbers."

"Wormwood Scrubs."

"Whatever."

"All right, here's how it went," Stone said.

"You better start at the beginning, so we don't have to go backwards."

"All right; this guy showed up in my office, sent by Woodman and Weld." Stone began to take Dino, blow by blow, through what had happened since he'd arrived in London. He got as far as the explosion at the antiques market when dinner arrived. The waiter served it and left.

When he had gone, Stone continued with the events at the Farm Street house. When he got to the dinner of the night before, he stopped, not wanting to talk about Sarah or Arrington.

"So," Dino said, "how's Sarah? How's Arrington?"

"How did you know Arrington was here?"

"She called me a few days ago, said she was headed to London and how were you?"

"Why didn't she call me?"

"I guess she did, and you weren't there, so she called me. She's buying an apartment in New York."

"I heard."

"So tell me about Sarah and Arrington, and how you're keeping them both happy."

Stone did the best he could.

"So Arrington is on her way to New York?"

"Right."

"And Sarah is filthy rich, having knocked off her boyfriend?"

"She didn't knock him off, it was an accident; I was there."

"Sure, like Arrington didn't knock off Vance Calder."

"You don't really think she did that, do you?"

"Nobody's proved to me that she didn't."

"Dino, you're a very suspicious person, do you know that?"

"It's useful in my work; and if I weren't a suspicious person, somebody would have knocked you off by now."

"You're probably right," Stone admitted. Dino had gotten him out of the soup more than once.

"You know what I think?" Dino said, pushing back from the table.

"What?"

"I think I'm going to bed. I hear jet lag is a bitch if you don't get any sleep."

"So, you're going to bed without having solved any of my problems?"

"You betcha." He got up, went to the door of his room, and opened it. "I'll do that tomorrow." He closed the door.

"Christ, I wish somebody would," Stone said.

41

DINO WALKED INTO STONE'S ROOM AT 6:30 A.M., in his pajamas, whistling loudly. "Up and at 'em!" he shouted.

Stone groaned, rolled over, and pulled a pillow over his head.

"Don't you want to brush your teeth before breakfast?" Dino asked, ripping the covers off Stone.

"No," Stone replied, trying vainly to get the covers back.

"That's disgusting," Dino said. "You can't eat breakfast without brushing your teeth; it's unsanitary."

Stone peeped out from under the pillow. "What breakfast? I haven't ordered breakfast."

There was a sharp rap on the door.

"That breakfast," Dino said, opening the door and admitting the waiter.

Stone went and brushed his teeth; when he returned, an elaborate breakfast had been laid out.

Dino handed him a large glass of orange juice. "Come on, wake up."

Stone took the orange juice. "This must be what it's like to be married."

"Are you kidding?" Dino asked. "The day you get married is the last day you'll ever get breakfast in bed."

"I'm not in bed," Stone said, sipping the orange juice.

"Close enough. What's your plan for the day?"

"I'm planning for you to solve all my problems," Stone said.

"Okay, I can do that. Not Arrington, of course, or Sarah; you'll have to handle those yourself, though of course, I'll be there with lots of advice."

"I'd rather not hear it," Stone said, digging into his scrambled eggs.

"Man, these are really terrific eggs," Dino said. "How do they get them like this?"

"I asked about that," Stone replied. "Seems they cook them very slowly, with a lot of butter, in a saucepan, not a skillet, and they serve them on a hot plate, very soft, since they continue to cook on the plate."

"No kidding? I'll have to get Mary Ann to do them that way."

"Lots of luck. Your wife doesn't strike me as the kind of woman who would spend the early moments of her morning making you English scrambled eggs."

"Who would have thought the English could cook?"

"Someone, I think it was George Bernard Shaw, once said that you could eat very well in England, as long as you have breakfast three times a day." Stone was waking up now.

Dino laughed. "I gotta remember that one."

"Don't bother; it isn't true anymore; the Brits cook very well indeed these days. Okay, how are you going to solve all my problems?"

"I slept on your problems," Dino said, "and I think you can best solve them by leaving London and going back to New York. That would remove you from the evil influence of the people around you in this town."

"They aren't all evil," Stone replied.

"No? Name me one person you know in London that you can prove not to be evil."

"They're innocent until proven guilty," Stone said.

"Only in a court of law; in the court of *my* law, every fucking one of them is guilty of something."

"Demonstrate, please."

"Okay, let's take Bartholomew: Do you have any doubt that he's an evil son of a bitch?"

Stone thought about it for a moment. "No," he said, "none."

"And you're *working* for him. How about Lance?"

"Well, I think he may be mixed up in those two murders; and maybe a lot more, as well."

"Same for Sarah, except it's just one murder," Dino said. "Who's left?"

"Well, there's Erica and Monica, the sisters."

"Okay, I guess there have to be some innocent bystanders, but I'm not going to count on it."

"And there's Arrington."

"Arrington doesn't count; she's not in London."

"And Throckmorton."

"Throckmorton wants you to spend the rest of your life in an English prison, where they don't have toilets. How evil is that?"

"He doesn't believe for a moment that I killed those two men."

"He doesn't *care*," Dino said. "He just wants to clear these two killings; it doesn't make him look good for bodies to turn up in his nice, green park. If he can blame you, he's home free."

Stone thought for a moment. "They don't have toilets in English prisons?"

"No, they were all built before they had plumbing; you have to shit in a bucket and do God-knows-what with it."

"That's disgusting."

"My very point; it's why, among other reasons, you don't want to go to jail over here."

"So what is your solution to dealing with all this evil?"

"I told you: get out of town. You don't owe these people anything."

"I can't; Throckmorton has my passport. Yesterday, when I tried to see Arrington at the airport, two of his goons dragged me out of the place."

"I'll talk to him," Dino said. "If I can get your passport back, will you get out of here right away?"

Stone thought about that. "Maybe. But I have to admit, I'm pretty curious about what's going on. You have any thoughts about that?"

"Let's take these people one at a time, in reverse order of evilness," Dino said. "Monica: She just has a business here, and she's probably not involved. Erica: She may not be involved; she just wants to follow Lance around like a puppy, and she doesn't give a fuck what he's done or what he's doing. Sarah: If there were any justice, she'd be shitting in a bucket in an English prison, instead of collecting a huge inheritance. Ali and Sheila: They're in business with Lance, so they're just as evil as he is. That leaves us with Lance and Hedger, who are so obviously evil that it's hardly worth discussing."

"I want to know what it is that Lance and Hedger actually do that's so evil."

"Well, Hedger, for a start, killed that retired cop Bobby Jones."

"He just had him beaten up—not that that's a good thing."

"He's dead," Dino said. "Died of his injuries. Throckmorton told me on the phone; that's one of the reasons he's so pissed off with you."

"Oh, God," Stone moaned. "I didn't know; nobody told me."

"So that makes Hedger a murderer; Throckmorton wants him for Jones, but I get the impression that his investigation is being impeded by somebody in the British government."

"You two had quite a little heart-to-heart, didn't you?" Stone asked. "Why hasn't he told *me* any of this? He's certainly had the opportunity."

"Because he doesn't trust you, dummy; you work for Hedger, don't you? He'd like to have Hedger shitting in a bucket somewhere and you for an accessory. Jones and his buddy Cricket were apparently two of Throckmorton's favorite people."

"Jesus, I'm *never* going to get out of this country," Stone said.

"That's a possibility," Dino agreed. "What we've got to do is find out what's going on here, so we can tell Throckmorton, and then he can lock up the perpetrators, except for you."

"Hedger is my client; I can't help lock him up."

"What's the matter, don't you enjoy putting away bad guys anymore? Where's the cop in you?"

"He's still there, but so is the lawyer."

Dino sighed. "You're hopeless."

4 2

DINO WENT TO GET DRESSED, AND Stone shaved and showered. He was tying his tie when the satellite phone rang.

"It's Hedger."

"Good morning."

"You said you'd have a list of the people at table twelve."

"Right, let me get it." Stone retrieved the list, the only fruit of his aborted dinner with Arrington. "Want me to read you the names?"

"Yes."

Stone did so.

"It's the Israeli cultural attaché," Hedger said.

"Why do you think so?"

"Because the governments of Sweden, Australia, Germany, and Belgium do not usually participate in kidnapping innocent Americans off the streets of London. But I wouldn't put it past the Israelis. What's his name?"

Stone consulted the list. "David Beth Alachmy."

"Holy shit."

"Do you know him?"

"Just of him; he's very smart, very tough. And his very presence in London means that he's the new chief

of station for the Mossad, the Israeli intelligence service. He's so new in town that my people didn't know
yet."

"Then the two 'Greeks' were Israelis?"

"Probably. You said you had a contact in the London
police; why don't you ask him?"

"He and I are not on cordial terms at the moment."

"Why not?"

"He thinks I was involved in the murder of the two
Israelis."

"Why would he think that?"

"Because one of them was wearing my raincoat."

"How the hell—"

"I took off the raincoat when I was doing my little
survey of Lance Cabot's house, and apparently when I
left, I picked up the wrong coat. The murderer dressed
one of the two corpses in mine."

"Oh, swell, now you've come to the attention of the
local police."

"You could say that."

"That greatly reduces your value to me."

"You expect me to feel guilty about that? Let me remind you that I came to their attention while trying to
get information for you."

"In the old days, we'd have just shot you; as it is, I'll
have to fire you."

"As you wish—you'll recall that I've already resigned once."

"This time let's make it permanent; I can't have anything more to do with you."

"I'm afraid you're going to be stuck with a continuing hotel bill."

"Why is that? As far as I'm concerned, you can get
on the next airplane out of here."

"Not at the moment; the police have taken my passport. When I went to the airport yesterday to, ah, see off a friend, they dragged me out and sent me back to the Connaught."

"Well, as far as I'm concerned, pal, you're on your own."

"You can discuss it with the accounting department at Woodman and Weld," Stone said. "And while you're at it, remember that I've been on double my hourly rate for a while."

"Not anymore; as I said, you're fired." Hedger hung up.

Dino came into the room, dressed. "Who was that?"

"Hedger; when he heard the police were interested in me, he fired me."

"Well, I hope you don't still feel any loyalty to him."

"He's not my client anymore."

"So fuck him and the horse he rode in on."

"Yep."

"Let's call Throckmorton and tell him who beat up Bobby Jones."

"He already knows Hedger was behind it; Ted Cricket would have told him; he just can't prove that Hedger sicced the hoods onto Jones."

"Oh. Well, what are you going to do today?"

"I don't know; what were you going to do?"

"I was going to follow you around at a safe distance, to see if anybody else was following you."

"Good idea; I guess I'd better go somewhere."

"Got any ideas?"

"Why don't I take Lance Cabot to lunch?"

"Someplace good, I hope."

Stone picked up the phone and called Lance's number.

Erica answered. "Oh, hello, Stone," she said brightly. "How are you?"

"Very well, thanks; is Lance there?"

"Sure, just a minute."

"Good morning, Stone," Lance said.

"Good morning; are you free for lunch today?"

"Sure; where?"

"The Connaught grill, at twelve-thirty?"

"See you then."

Stone hung up.

"What do you hope to accomplish by having lunch with him?" Dino asked.

"A few days ago, he tried to bring me into some sort of business deal; I blew him off at the time, but now I feel more receptive. Also, it will give you a good look at Lance; I'll get you a table, too." He called downstairs and made the reservations.

Stone arrived in the grill on time; Dino was already seated a couple of tables away from his own; Lance showed up five minutes later.

"Well, what's up?" Lance asked, after they had ordered lunch.

"Last weekend, you asked me to do some legal work for you in New York."

"Yes, but you weren't interested; I accept that."

"Now I'm interested."

"What changed your mind?"

"I have some time on my hands here. I won't do the legal work myself, but I'll give you the name of a man who can handle it. I'm more interested in participating in the business end of the, ah, transaction."

"You mean you want a piece of the action?"

"If I like the action."

"I assume you'd be willing to make an investment?"

"That depends on what the deal is and how big an investment you want."

"Could you come up with a quarter of a million dollars?"

"If I were sufficiently motivated."

"What do you want to know?"

"Everything."

Lance laughed. "I'm not sure that *I* know everything."

"Let's start with what you know."

"All right; I propose to buy some items in England or elsewhere in Europe and sell them to someone in another part of the world for a large profit."

"How much will you pay for them and what will you sell them for?"

"I expect to pay in the region of half a million dollars for these items, and I expect to sell them for around two million, maybe a bit more."

"That is a very nice profit indeed. And exactly what are the items?"

"I'm not at liberty to tell you just yet."

"You understand that I will be unwilling to make the investment until I know?"

"Of course; I don't think you're a fool, Stone."

"Can you give me a general idea?"

"Let's just say that the goods are of a scientific nature, and that the buyers are lovers of science."

"Are Ali and Sheila part of this deal?"

"A very important part. They will act as liaison between the sellers and the buyers."

"Why can't you do it yourself?"

"Let's just say that I'm of the wrong nationality, ethnicity, and religion. Ali and Sheila are critical to the success of the transaction."

Stone took a card from his wallet and wrote a name and telephone number on the back of it. "This is a lawyer in New York who will handle your legal work.

But for the record, this is the only part of the transaction that I will ever admit taking part in—a simple reference."

"I quite understand."

"Apart from the nature of the goods and the name of the buyer, I will require a means of making my share of the profit bankable and spendable, without attracting the attention of any government agency anywhere."

"I quite understand. I have such an arrangement already in place, and you may avail yourself of it."

"When will this happen, and when can you tell me more about it?"

"Once I give the go-ahead, it will take only two or three days to conclude the transaction. The items in question have already been manufactured and will be transported as soon as I transfer the funds to the maker. How soon can you produce your quarter of a million?"

"What do you mean by 'produce'? Where and when?"

"I mean wire-transfer the funds to an offshore bank, which I will specify."

"As soon as I know all the details of what you're delivering and to whom. The funds are currently in a money market fund, awaiting investment. All it will take for delivery is a coded fax to my broker."

"I like your style, Stone."

"All we need to know now is if I like yours."

"I'll talk to some people and be in touch shortly."

They raised their glasses in a silent toast, then went back to finishing their lunch.

Stone glanced across the small room at Dino. He was enjoying his lunch immensely.

43

STONE SAID GOODBYE TO LANCE ON
the steps of the Connaught, then set off down Mount
Street toward Berkeley Square, walking slowly, so that
Dino could follow, window-shopping along the way.
It was time to see if anyone was following him.

He walked around the square, letting Dino follow
from a distance, and, on a whim, walked into Jack Barclay's, the Rolls-Royce dealer. A young man approached him immediately.

"Good afternoon, sir. May I help you?"

"I'd like to look at a Bentley, please." The showroom
was a good place from which to spot a tail, with its
large windows overlooking Berkeley Square. Stone
couldn't see Dino.

"The Arnage—that's the saloon car—or the con-
vertible?"

"The Arnage."

"This way." He led Stone across the large sales floor.
"Would this be for UK use or export?"

"UK," Stone lied, thinking that the young man would
send him to an American dealer if he said otherwise.

"Here we are," the salesman said, stopping before a
gleaming black example of the car. "This one is in
black with Autumn upholstery."

"May I see the engine?"

The salesman opened the car's hood to reveal a large engine bay, stuffed with equipment.

"What is the displacement and horsepower?" Stone asked, still unable to spot Dino.

"Six point eight liters, turbocharged; four hundred horsepower and six hundred and fifteen pounds of torque, available at low revs."

"Acceleration and top speed?"

"Zero to sixty miles per hour in five point nine seconds. Unfortunately, the top speed is electronically limited to a hundred and fifty-five miles per hour."

"Very impressive," Stone said, opening the driver's-side door and getting behind the right-side steering wheel. While the salesman droned on about the car's features, Stone was able to sweep the square from his seat, and he still could not spot Dino. Surely he hadn't walked too fast. He got out of the car.

"Would you like a brochure?" the salesman asked.

"Yes, thank you, and your card."

The salesman dropped both into an envelope and handed it to Stone. "We hope to hear from you," he said.

"Thank you." Stone walked out into the square; still no sign of Dino on the busy streets. Had he followed at all? He walked back to the Connaught and went up to his suite. He was relaxing, reading the Bentley brochure, when Dino let himself in from next door. Half an hour had passed since Stone returned to the hotel.

"Where have you been?" Stone asked. "Did I move too fast for you?"

"Nope, and not for the four-man team following you, either."

"There were *four men* following me?"

"Well, two of the men were women. They were very good, too, working both sides of the street, changing places. I don't know if I would have made them, if they'd been following me, but since I was following you, it was easier to see what was going on."

"Any idea of nationality?"

"They didn't appear ethnic, so I'd say English or American."

"What about the shoes?"

"The men wore expensive shoes with thin soles, so they're not cops, if that's what you're asking."

"No thick soles and white socks, then?"

"Nope."

Stone put down his brochure. "My guess is, it's Hedger's people."

"They must want Lance pretty bad."

"Then why aren't they following Lance?"

"Maybe they are."

"Maybe they are, at that; it's something to keep in mind. What did you think of Lance?"

"What struck me," Dino said, "was how much alike the two of you are."

"How do you mean?"

"Jesus, Stone, didn't you see the guy? He's waspy, blondish, beautifully dressed. He has that languid look that only very confident people have."

"Or very good actors."

"Well, you're not that confident, and you're not that good an actor; from my view of the conversation, you were the guy who wanted something, and he was the guy who was going to decide whether you get it."

"Just the opposite," Stone said. "He wants a quarter of a million dollars from me, and I'm demanding full disclosure; he's not ready to tell me yet."

"Do you have a quarter of a million dollars?"

"Yes, but I'm not about to give it to Lance; he doesn't know that, of course."

"You better be careful, Stone; you start promising people money, and they're liable to get very upset if you don't come through with it."

"You have a point."

"So what are you going to do?"

"I'm going to make a couple of phone calls."

"And the first one will be to Arrington, won't it?"

"Oh, shut up and get out of here; I'd like some privacy."

"I'll go to my room and see if there's a cricket game on TV."

"Cricket match."

"Whatever." Dino went to his own room.

Stone picked up the phone and dialed the number of the Carlyle hotel in New York, which was lodged in his memory, and asked for Mrs. Calder. The phone rang several times, and then the voice mail kicked in.

"Arrington, it's Stone. I want to apologize for the other evening; it was inexcusable leaving you like that, but I really didn't have a choice. I tried to catch up with you at Heathrow, but you got through security before I could. I'd like to explain, if you'll let me. I'd also like to see you again, but I won't be back in New York for at least a few more days. Please call me at the Connaught." He left the number and hung up, then he got out his address book and called Samuel Bernard at his home in Washington Square.

"Good morning, Stone," the old man said, "or good afternoon, if you're still in London."

"I'm still in London, sir, and I wanted to ask for some more advice."

"Go right ahead."

"Bartholomew is Hedger, as you suspected, and he and I have parted company."

"Why?"

"I've come to the attention of the local police on a related matter, and that put him off."

"I can see how it might," Bernard said.

"I had thought that Hedger was working outside his agency, for personal reasons, but today I was followed by a four-man team who seem to be either British or American, probably American."

"It's unlikely that he would have so many people at his disposal, if he were working on his own," Bernard said.

"That's what I figured. Now I have another problem: I've learned about something that I think should be brought to the attention of some authority, but I don't trust Hedger. Is it possible that you could connect me with someone at your former employer's that I could talk to without Hedger finding out?"

"I think that would be very dangerous, Stone; I don't know what's going on internally at the Company at this moment, so it's difficult to ascertain how much official support Hedger has. Even if I found someone for you to speak to, there's no guarantee that he wouldn't go straight to Hedger. And he wouldn't be in London, either. If anything happens in the London station, Hedger is going to know it, because if he's not actually station head, he'll be very close to whoever is. Why don't you want to go directly to Hedger?"

"I just don't trust him; he's lied to me a lot."

"That's what agents do; it's not surprising."

"I don't yet know enough about what's going on to know whether I might be hurting someone who's innocent of any wrongdoing."

"Can you give me a general idea of what's happening?"

Stone recounted his conversation with Lance, without mentioning names.

"It sounds as if your acquaintance is going to sell something important to a foreign government or more informal organization, that our government, or at least Hedger, doesn't want them to have. Are you actually going to put up this money?"

"I don't know."

"I warn you, if you do, you may involve yourself in this matter in an inextricable way."

"I'd much rather contact some agency that could support me in this."

Bernard was silent for a moment. "If you don't trust Hedger, then I think you should go to the British."

"Can you give me a name?"

"I'll give someone yours," Bernard said. "If you get a call from someone who says he's a friend of Sam's, see him."

"Thank you, sir," Stone said.

"Keep me posted," Bernard replied. "I'm beginning to enjoy this."

Stone hung up the phone, laughing.

4 4

STONE HAD EXPECTED TO GET A CALL
from someone soon, but it didn't come. He didn't see
any point in going out, just to be followed, so he
stayed home, looking in on Dino to find him snoring
away. Maybe he wasn't immune to jet lag, after all.
Stone found a movie on TV and settled in.

Early in the evening, Dino came into the suite, rubbing
his eyes. "I don't know what happened," he said. "I was
watching cricket, and then I practically passed out."

"Jet lag."

"If you say so. You hungry?"

"Almost. You want to order dinner now, or wait for
a while."

"You don't want to go out?"

"Not really."

Stone heard an odd noise, and he turned to see an
envelope being slid under the door.

"Looks like a message for you," Dino said.

"That's not one of the Connaught's message envelopes," Stone said, staring at it.

"Well, are you going to open it? The suspense is
killing me." Dino yawned.

Stone retrieved the envelope, which had nothing written on it. He opened it and took out a single sheet of paper. Written in block capitals was a message: AFTER TEN MINUTES TAKE THE WEST LIFT UP ONE FLOOR, TURN LEFT OUT OF THE LIFT, AND WALK TO THE END OF THE CORRIDOR. THE DOOR WILL BE AJAR. It was unsigned. He handed it to Dino, who read it and smiled.

"I love this kind of stuff," he chuckled. "You have any idea who it's from? A woman, I'll bet."

"I don't think so," Stone said. "I called a friend and asked to be introduced to somebody on this side of the water. I think this is it."

"Whatever you say; I still think it's a woman. It always is with you."

After ten minutes, Stone did as he was told. He figured out which sides of the hotel the two elevators were on, then took the west one up a flight and walked down the corridor. A door at the end was ajar. He rapped lightly and walked in. "Hello?"

He was standing in a small vestibule with three doors. One of them opened and a woman smiled at him. "Mr. Barrington?" She was of medium height, wearing a gray business suit and lightweight horn-rimmed glasses, dark hair. Stone thought she'd be quite pretty without the glasses and with a little more makeup. "Yes," he said.

She opened the door to reveal a large sitting room. "Please come in and have a seat; he'll be with you shortly. May I get you something to drink?"

"Some fizzy water would be nice," he replied.

She went to a cabinet at one side of the large room, opened it to reveal a full bar, and poured two glasses of San Pellegrino mineral water.

She returned to where Stone was sitting, handed

him a glass, and sat down. "My name is Carpenter,"
she said. Her accent was clipped, of indistinguishable
class, at least to him.

"How do you do?"

"Very well, thank you."

"For whom are we waiting?"

"For me, old chap," a voice said from behind him.
He turned to find a man in his mid-thirties entering the
room, apparently from the bedroom. He was dressed in
a severely cut pin-striped suit, and what Stone imagined was a club tie, though he didn't know which club.
It was dark blue or black, with a single sky-blue stripe.

"Thank you for coming up," he said briskly. "Sorry
to be so cloak-and-dagger, but from what our mutual
friend, Sam, told me, you've picked up a rather elaborate tail." His accent was terribly upper-class.

"It seems so."

"My name is Mason." He didn't offer to shake hands.
Instead, he went to the bar, poured himself a Scotch, no
ice, then sat down opposite Stone. "Sounds as though
you've gotten yourself mixed up in something."

"How much did our friend tell you?"

"Why don't you tell me the whole thing from the
very start?"

"Why don't you tell me what you already know? It
would save me repeating myself."

Mason smiled tightly. "You're a cautious chap,
aren't you?"

Stone shrugged.

"Apparently, you think somebody wants to sell
something he shouldn't be selling to someone who
shouldn't be buying it. That sum it up?"

"Pretty much."

"And you've fallen out with Stan Hedger, whom
you don't trust anymore, right?"

"Pretty much."

"But you came to London at his request."

"Yes."

"And you've attracted the attention of the police. How, may I ask?"

"You may have read in the papers about two gentlemen found dead in the trunk of a car in Hyde Park?"

"I heard of it less than an hour after they were discovered. Are you connected to that incident in some way?"

"One of them was wearing my raincoat."

Mason burst out laughing. "Goodness, that would put the coppers onto you, wouldn't it. Who's the man in charge, if you know his name?"

"Detective Inspector Evelyn Throckmorton."

"Oh, yes, he's all right."

"I was already acquainted with him."

"How?"

"I used to be a police detective in New York; a friend of mine on the force introduced me to him."

"Nice to have an introduction in a strange city, isn't it? Well, I think you should forget about the detective inspector and put your trust in me, from here on in," Mason said. "Sam thought so, too."

"All right."

Carpenter got up, went to a briefcase on a table, took out a small tape recorder, set it on the coffee table, and switched it on; then she sat back and prepared to listen.

Mason made a motion that Stone should continue.

Stone looked at the recorder, then at Carpenter, then Mason. He shook his head slowly.

Mason leaned forward and switched off the recorder. "My, my, you *are* cautious, aren't you?"

Stone nodded. "I wouldn't like to hear this conversation played back to me in a courtroom someday."

"Entirely understandable," Mason said. "You're a lawyer, Sam tells me."

"Right."

"Well, let me put your mind at rest, Mr. Barrington; Carpenter and I are not the police; the organization we work for conducts its business without reference to the police, unless we need them for some small chore or other. Tell me, just between us. Do you believe that you may have committed a crime while in Britain?"

"I didn't shoot those two men, if that's what you mean."

"Anything else? Drug smuggling? Rape? Incest? Cross the street without looking both ways?"

"No, nothing."

"You didn't boot poor James Cutler off that yacht, did you?"

"No."

"That's what I heard; heard you did your damnedest to save the poor chap."

"I got wet."

Mason leaned forward, his elbows on his knees, and his voice changed, lowered, became friendlier. "Relax, Stone," he said. "We're here to help. Start at the beginning, now."

Stone took a deep breath and, once more, started at the beginning.

4 5

WHEN STONE HAD FINISHED TELLING
them everything, Mason just stared at him for a long
moment. "Extraordinary," he drawled.

Stone looked at Carpenter; she nodded.

"Rather," she said.

He wasn't sure whether this meant they didn't believe him. "Do you have any questions for me?"

"Well, let me tell you a few things: First, David Beth
Alachmy is the new Mossad station chief in London;
old Stan was right about that; second, the two chaps in
the car were Beth Alachmy's men; third, the abduction
and interrogation of you by Beth Alachmy and his
thugs was way, way out of bounds, and I will see that
he is suitably punished for it."

"Thank you, but I don't really care about that,"
Stone replied. "I just want to get this thing over with
and get back to New York."

"Our sentiments exactly," Mason said. "I hope we
can have you out of here in just a few days."

"Thank you."

"We're aware of Lance Cabot and his little consulting
business, but this is the first we've heard of Ali and
Sheila; we'll be looking into them."

"Fine."

"Oh, I assume you do actually have the two hundred and fifty thousand dollars that Cabot wants for his project?"

"Well, yes, in a brokerage account in New York."

"I think the very first thing you'll want to do is have that transferred to the offshore account, as Cabot requested."

"But—"

"Oh, don't actually give it to him; just let him confirm that you've got it in the account. When we're done, you can wire it back to your brokerage account."

"I suppose—"

"Now, the first thing we've got to do is to get you out of this hotel."

"Why?" Stone asked plaintively. "I like it here."

"Because Stan's people know where to find you, and they can follow you anywhere from here," Mason said, as if he were explaining things to a child. "Do you have somewhere you can go?"

Stone thought for a moment. "Let me make a phone call."

"Of course."

He picked up a phone and called Sarah at her London flat.

"Hi."

"Well, hello; I was wondering when I was going to hear from you."

"Have our mutual acquaintances cleared out of James's house?"

"Yes, all gone."

"Do you mind if Dino and I move in there for a few days? I've got to get out of the Connaught; they're booked up, apparently."

"Dino's in London?"

"Yes."

"Well, of course you can stay there; when do you want to go?"

"Immediately."

"All right; why don't I cook us all some dinner over there? James has a decent kitchen, and I can pick up some things on the way."

"That would be wonderful."

"See you in an hour?"

"That's good. Bye." He hung up and turned to Mason. "We can go to James Cutler's house in Chester Street."

"Ah yes, good," Mason said. "Who is Dino?"

"Dino Bacchetti, my old partner at the NYPD. He got into town yesterday."

"All right, then; you go and get packed up, and I'll send someone for your luggage. I believe your bill is going to Stan Hedger?"

"Yes."

"Good, that solves that. We'll be taking you out of the hotel by a rear exit."

"Fine."

"Oh, by the way, Sam asked me to ask you if Hedger ever gave you any sort of electronic device—a radio, a pager, a clock—to carry around with you?"

"Yes, he gave me a satellite telephone."

"You'll want to give that to me; he's been using it to track your whereabouts."

Stone felt like a complete ass. "All right."

"I'll come and get you in, say, three-quarters of an hour."

"Good." Stone left the suite and went back to his own.

Dino was still watching cricket. "You know, I think I'm beginning to get the hang of this game."

"It's an illusion; no American will ever understand it."

"You ready for some dinner?"

"Yes, but Sarah is cooking it for us; get packed, we're moving out of the hotel."

"But I like it here," Dino said. "It's nice—you push a button and somebody comes to take care of you."

"I've just had a meeting with some British intelligence people, and they want us out of here; they say it's the only way we'll ever lose the tail that Hedger put on us."

"We're going right now?"

"Very shortly; just get your luggage ready to go."

Dino switched off the cricket match with reluctance.

At the appointed time, the porter rapped on their door. "Good evening, Mr. Barrington. I'm to take your bags down to the kitchen."

"There they are," Stone said, pointing to the pile. "Mr. Bacchetti's, too."

"There's a lady waiting for you at the lift."

Stone and Dino walked to the elevator, where Carpenter was waiting for them, the door open. He introduced Dino.

Once in the elevator, Carpenter inserted a key into a lock and turned it. "This will get us to the lower level," she said.

Stone watched her on the way down; she really was very attractive, in her muted way. The lift doors opened, and Carpenter led them down a hallway, past the kitchens, and out a rear door. There were three identical gray vans waiting outside, and the porter was loading their luggage into the middle one.

Mason appeared from behind them. "Give me Hedger's phone," he said.

Stone took the phone from an inside pocket and handed it to him.

Mason looked around him, then spotted a truck unloading seafood for the hotel. He tossed the phone over the crates of fish into the rear of the truck. "There," he said. "That will keep your tail busy. Get into the center van."

Stone and Dino climbed into the rear seat with Carpenter, while Mason got into the front.

"We'll wait until the fish lorry goes," he said.

As if on command, the truck started up and moved out of the mews, then turned right at the street.

"Wait," Mason said. "Let them register the move." He glanced at his watch. Two minutes passed, then Mason said, "Now; turn left at the end."

The three vans moved out.

"Why do I feel like a load of laundry?" Dino asked.

"This would be your policeman friend?" Mason asked.

"Yes," Stone said. "This is Lieutenant Dino Bacchetti, of the New York Police Department."

"Enchanted," Mason drawled, without turning around.

"Yeah, me too," Dino said.

The three vans drove into Grosvenor Square and at the next corner, each went in a different direction, none of them toward James's house.

"The house is in Chester Street, off Belgrave Square," Stone reminded Mason.

"I know, old chap," Mason said. "We're just going to lead any possible tail on a merry chase before we turn for home. I've visited the house, actually. James Cutler and I were at Eton together a couple of hundred years ago. He was a good chap, and I'm grateful to you for what you tried to do for him." He paused. "I'm not so sure about this Miss Sarah Buckminster."

Dino dug Stone in the ribs.

4 6

THEY ARRIVED AT THE CHESTER STREET house, and the van's driver set Stone's and Dino's luggage on the sidewalk.

"We won't come in," Mason said. He handed Stone a tiny cellphone, its charger, and an extra battery. "If anyone asks, you rented this through the concierge at the Connaught." He handed Stone an index card with a list of numbers written on it. "These are my and Carpenter's cellphone numbers," he said. "If there's no answer, you'll have an opportunity to leave a message, and one of us will get back to you quickly. I suggest you memorize them and destroy the card. Your number is there, too."

"All right," Stone said, pocketing the phone and the card.

"Tomorrow morning, call Lance Cabot and tell him you've arranged with your broker to have the quarter of a million transferred at a moment's notice, pending Cabot's satisfying you with the details of the transaction. When he tells you, I suggest you be somewhat less scrupulous than you've been so far; don't be shocked at what the goods turn out to be or to whom they're to be sold. The more of a buccaneer you seem to be, the more Cabot will be interested in doing business with you. Meantime, we'll be doing a complete background check on Cabot, Ali, and Sheila."

"Sounds good," Stone said.

"Don't leave the house without telling me, and on a few minutes' notice, I can provide any transportation you may need. From now on, I want your only tail to be my people."

"Thank you," Stone said. He and Dino got out of the van, and it drove away. They trudged up the steps with their luggage and rang the bell.

Sarah answered and threw herself at Dino. "How are you, darling?" she asked. "And how's Mary Ann?"

"We're all just great," Dino said, beaming at her.

"Come on in and get your things put away." She led them up the stairs. "Dino, you're in there, and Stone, you come with me." She led him to a rear bedroom, obviously the master, and then she gave him a long and tantalizing kiss. "Get unpacked and come downstairs; dinner will be ready in fifteen minutes."

Stone hung up his clothes and put his toiletries in the bathroom, which was large and old, wall-to-wall marble.

The three of them sat around the kitchen table eating lamb chops and drinking an outstanding claret from James's cellar.

"You won't believe the wine that's down there," she said. "I don't think that any lot of really fine wine passed through the business that James didn't grab a case or two of for himself."

Stone looked at the bottle: a Chateau Haut-Brion '66. "I never thought I'd be drinking this," he said.

"Stick around," Sarah said. "I'll ruin your liver for you."

"Sarah, you're not to tell anyone that Dino and I are staying here."

"And why not?"

"Because I don't want anyone to know."

"Dear, don't be so old-fashioned."

"That's not what I mean. I'm involved in some very delicate business, and the competition is unscrupulous. I don't want them to know my whereabouts. If someone should call you asking for me, you can tell them I've moved from the Connaught, but you don't know where."

"Oh, all right, if you say so. It's all very cloak-and-dagger, isn't it?"

"Yes, I suppose it is." More than she knew.

After dinner and brandy, Stone went upstairs and turned on the taps in the huge, old-fashioned bathtub. He had just settled in for a soak, with the lights dimmed, when Sarah came into the bathroom. She was quite naked, and it was the first good look he'd had at her that way for a long time.

"How about some company?" she said, sliding into the tub, facing him.

"Mmmm," he replied, closing his eyes.

A moment later, he felt her hand on his crotch.

"I think we have to get this clean," she said, and she began soaping it.

Stone held onto the sides of the tub.

"Now it's clean," she said, "and we have to get it warm." She climbed on top of him and brought him inside her. "There," she sighed. She began moving, slowly, in and out.

Stone responded favorably.

She reached behind her and took his testicles in her hand, still moving, now massaging gently.

Stone sat up and put his arms around her, cupping her buttocks in his hands, helping her move.

"Don't you dare come before me," she breathed, moving faster.

Stone ran a finger down between her cheeks, letting it pass lightly back and forth over her anus, then he inserted a finger.

Sarah came explosively, and he was right behind her. They writhed in the tub until they were both spent, then she put her head on his shoulder and wrapped herself around him. "I love a hot bath, don't you?" she said.

"Oh, yes," Stone replied. "I don't know why anyone ever bothered inventing the shower."

They stayed that way until the water began to get cold, then they dried each other and went into the bedroom, where they started over, this time with Stone on top.

Sarah lifted her legs and put her ankles on Stone's shoulders. "Now," she said, "all the way in."

Stone gave her everything. They lasted longer this time, changing positions, trying this and that—every orifice, every erotic pressure point, until in one final, earth-rocking spasm, they gave in to the climax, both crying out.

From down the hall, Stone heard Dino's voice.

"Can you two hold it down a little? A guy could get horny."

"Want me to go take care of that?" Sarah asked Stone from his shoulder.

"Remember Mary Ann," Stone said. "She'd track you down and kill you. Never underestimate a Sicilian woman."

"Good point," Sarah said, and they fell asleep.

47

AFTER BREAKFAST, SARAH LEFT THE house, and Stone called Lance Cabot.

"Hello?" He sounded sleepy.

"It's Stone; I'm ready to deal on this thing, if you're ready to talk."

"How soon can you get the money together?"

"I faxed my broker yesterday; the funds can be transferred with a phone call. But not until you've told me everything."

"Lunch?"

"Where?"

"At the Connaught again?"

"I've moved out of the Connaught."

"Why?"

"I discovered yesterday that Hedger had put a tail on me. Last night, I moved to another hotel, a lot farther from the embassy."

"Which hotel?"

"I'll keep that to myself."

"What's the matter, do you think Hedger and I are in league?"

"I doubt that."

"How can I reach you?"

"I've rented a cellphone." Stone gave him the number.

"All right, there's a restaurant out west of London called the Waterside Inn, in a village called Bray; do you know it?"

"I'll find it."

"I'll pick you up, if you like."

"No, I have some other things to do; I'll meet you there."

"One o'clock?"

"Fine." Stone hung up and called Mason's number.

"Yes?"

"I'm on for lunch with Cabot at one o'clock."

"I'll send one of our taxis."

"No, it's at a place called the Waterside Inn, in Bray."

"Oh, yes; I hope Cabot is paying; the Waterside is not in my budget."

"It's his turn. I'm meeting him there; I'll need a car that passes for a rental, but nothing cheap, please, since Cabot is buying lunch."

"The car will be outside the house at noon; do you know how to get to Bray?"

"Haven't a clue."

"I'll send along a map."

"Thank you."

"I'm also going to wire you."

"Oh, no you're not; with Cabot's background, he'll know what to look for."

"Not the way we do it, he won't; we have something quite new. Someone will be there at half past eleven to equip you; if you don't like the equipment, you don't have to wear it, but I urge you to; if Cabot is going to explain himself, we'll want it recorded."

"I don't want a tail of your people, either; he might spot it."

"There'll be a van tracking the car and listening to the wire, but it will be at least a mile away, so don't worry."

"I'll think about it."

"Good-bye." Mason hung up.

Dino, who had heard Stone's half of the conversation, spoke up. "I'll tail you."

"No, no; Mason is going to have a van tracking me from a mile away. You take the morning off."

"And do what?"

Stone tossed him the *Times*. "There's a very nice exhibition of Royal evening gowns at the Victoria and Albert Museum."

"Yeah, sure; where can I do some shopping? If I come home without something for Mary Ann, she'll kill me in my sleep."

"Try Harrod's; it's an easy walk from here." Stone found a London map in the kitchen and showed Dino Harrod's. "There's a really good pub right here, for lunch," he said, showing him the Grenadier, in Wilton Row. "King's Road is down here, if you want to do some further shopping; Hyde Park is up here, if you feel like a stroll. It's all very close together."

"Okay," Dino said. "It's Harrod's; anything else will have to wait until I see how my feet do. After walking a beat, I swore I'd never walk farther than to the can, if I could help it."

"There are taxis everywhere."

"Right. You got any English money? I didn't have time before I left New York."

Stone gave him a wad of notes. "Spend it in good health; it's Hedger's."

"That'll make it more fun," Dino said.

At eleven-thirty sharp, the doorbell rang, and Stone opened the door to find Carpenter standing there, holding a briefcase. "Come in," he said.

She smiled, the first time she had exhibited teeth, and they were very nice teeth, indeed. "Thank you." She stepped in and took a seat in the drawing room. "Horrible decor," she said, looking around.

"A dead man did it."

"I'm not surprised. Please bring me the jacket you're wearing to lunch."

Stone went away and came back with a blue blazer.

"Nothing with brass buttons," she said. "You should wear a suit, anyway; the Waterside Inn is quite elegant."

Stone went away and came back with a suit jacket. She examined the buttons and nodded, then opened her briefcase. She removed a small leather case, which held a selection of buttons. "Oh, good," she said; "an excellent match." She took some scissors and snipped off one of the four small buttons on Stone's left sleeve, then deftly sewed on one of her buttons. "There," she said. "Good match?"

"Excellent. Do you mean that tiny button is a bug?"

"In conjunction with this," she said, holding up a fat Mont Blanc pen, made of sterling silver. She clipped it into Stone's inside left-hand pocket. "The button transmits to the pen, and the pen transmits up to three miles, but we'll keep the van within two, just to be sure. They pick up the transmission and record it." She took out the pen and unscrewed the cap. "It's a working pen, too."

Stone examined the pen and tried to unscrew the other end.

"You can't do that without a special tool; don't worry, it has a fresh rollerball refill inside; you won't run out of ink."

"Good," Stone said, replacing the pen in the jacket pocket.

"The only limitation is that the button has to be within six feet of whoever you're talking to. I used a sleeve button because you can put your hands on the table and get it closer to Cabot. Don't have any conversations with him from across the room."

"I'll remember that," he said. "Tell me, how did a nice girl like you get into this business?"

"Isn't that what you're supposed to ask a whore?" she asked wryly.

"Spies, too."

"I'm not a spy; I catch spies."

"Come on, how?"

"I was recruited my last year at Oxford; my father had worked for the same firm, but he was killed in the line of duty when I was sixteen. I suppose I wanted to finish his job. How did you get from being a cop to being a lawyer?"

"I was recruited for the police department my last year in law school," Stone said. "Fourteen years later, I was retired for medical reasons. I took the bar exam, and a friend found a place for me with his law firm."

"You look pretty healthy to me," she said, looking him up and down.

"It was a bullet in the knee. I got over it, except in cold weather."

"Oh," she said, retrieving a map from her briefcase. "Sit down, and I'll show you how to get to the Waterside Inn."

Stone sat on the arm of her chair and caught a faint whiff of perfume. He wondered if intelligence agents often wore perfume to work.

"Here we are, in Chester Street; you go down to the corner, turn left at Hyde Park Corner, that's the big roundabout, here, and go straight out Knightsbridge, past Harrod's, straight on out, as if you were going to

Heathrow. You'll end up on the M4 motorway; get off at the Bray exit and follow the signs to the village. You'll see signs for the inn once you're in the village. It's at the end of a street that runs dead into the river, on your left."

"What river?"

"The Thames; it's pretty much *the* river around here. Have you driven on the right side before?"

"No, but it doesn't look too hard."

"It isn't, but watch out for the first right-hand turn you make. Americans invariably turn into the right lane, instead of the left. The streets are littered with smashed rental cars." She stood up. "Well, I have to go. Your car should be here shortly; I'd allow three-quarters of an hour for the drive; it could take an hour if traffic is bad."

He walked her to the door, and with a final, fleeting glance at him and a little smile, she left. He wished he had more time to get to know her.

4 8

AT TWELVE O'CLOCK, THE DOORBELL rang again. A man Stone had never seen before held out a set of car keys. "It's the Jaguar S-type, parked along there, British Racing Green," he said. "Here's a car rental receipt from a firm in Knightsbridge; sign it here and here, and fill in your American driver's license number. Ring Mason when you're finished with the car and someone will collect it."

"Thank you," Stone said. The man left. Stone filled out the form, then turned to Dino. "You want a lift to Harrod's? I'm going right past it."

"Yeah, sure."

"Let's go, then." Stone put on his jacket, checked to be sure the pen was still in place, and led the way out the door, locking it behind him. Sarah had given them each a key.

"Here we are," Stone said, climbing into the Jaguar and adjusting the seat.

Dino got into the passenger seat, and Stone pulled out of the parking place, went to the corner, and turned left.

"Isn't there supposed to be a steering wheel over here?" Dino asked.

"Nope, it's over here."

"It's very weird sitting here with no controls," Dino said. "I keep wanting to put on the brakes."

"Relax," Stone said, negotiating Hyde Park Corner. "That's the Duke of Wellington's house over there," he said, pointing, "and that's Hyde Park behind it."

"Got it," Dino said.

They drove a couple of blocks through heavy traffic, and Stone pulled over in front of the department store. "Here's Harrod's," he said.

Dino looked out at the line of store windows. "Which one?"

"The whole block," Stone replied. "It's the largest store in the world."

"Jesus," Dino said, "I'll need a map."

"Just wander, and ask somebody if you get lost."

"Okay, pal; when will I see you?"

"I'll come back to the house after lunch; if anybody calls and asks for me, except Sarah, you don't know me."

"I might be better off," Dino said.

"Maybe, but you wouldn't have nearly as much fun."

Dino closed the door and walked into Harrod's.

Stone drove on out Knightsbridge, which became the Cromwell Road, and soon he was on a four-lane highway, and soon after that, on the M4 motorway. Traffic was heavy, but he made good time. He got off the motorway at the prescribed exit and took the opportunity to check the traffic behind him. No one exited after him that he could see, and he felt tail-free, except for Mason's van, which was nowhere to be seen.

He followed the signs to the village and the restaurant and parked the car. The Thames was before him, broad and slow-moving, with pretty houses on the other side. He went into the restaurant; it was precisely one o'clock. Lance was not there yet, and the maître d' seated him outside on the terrace, under an elm tree. He ordered a kir royale and sipped it. Lance, he figured, was driving around the village to see if either he or Stone had a tail. Another fifteen minutes passed before he entered the restaurant.

Stone shook his hand. "A very elegant place," he said.

"Wait until you taste the food."

They had only desultory conversation until the food arrived, then Lance took a look around to be sure they were not being overheard. "I'm going to have to pat you down," he said to Stone.

Stone laughed. "Don't worry, I haven't worn a wire in years, not since I was a cop."

Lance got up, walked behind Stone and, on the pretense of pointing at something on the river, ran his hands expertly over Stone's body, down to the crotch.

"Don't have too much fun there," Stone said.

"What's this?" Lance asked, patting Stone's jacket pocket.

Stone removed the pen and handed it to him.

Lance inspected it closely and unscrewed the cap.

Don't try to unscrew the other end, Stone thought.

Lance didn't; he returned the pen, and Stone put it back into his pocket.

"Now," Lance said.

Stone leaned forward, as if to listen closely, putting his left hand on the table.

"I'm going to tell you everything I think you need to know."

"If it's everything *I* think I need to know, we'll be fine."

"There is a company west and south of here, in Wiltshire, a very secret company that makes very, very high-tech parts for the British military. We're talking very specialized metallurgy, machine tools, incredibly tight tolerances, and computerized design. For the past year, a man who works there, making these parts, has managed to make a duplicate of one extremely important component."

Stone interrupted. "Surely parts of that kind are stringently catalogued and accounted for."

"This man has been working in this facility for nearly thirty years, and he has accumulated a reservoir of trust, which leads his employers and colleagues to give him wide latitude. He's brilliant, and he's crotchety, and nobody likes to piss him off, so they leave him pretty much to himself."

"I see."

"This gentleman is nearing retirement, and he feels that his pension plan and what he has managed to save are insufficient to keep him in the style to which he would like to become accustomed. You see, he has a little horse-betting habit, which, over the years, has taken its toll on his nest egg."

"Do you mean to tell me that an important employee of a high-security facility could be betting the ponies and losing and not be noticed?"

"Apparently, he has been very discreet, and he has not been noticed," Lance replied. "In any case, he has made it known to someone who knows someone I know that he has built this very special device, and that it is for sale. I have bid on it, and he has accepted my offer. All that remains to be done is to meet with him, retrieve the device, pay him half a million dollars in cash, and pass the device on to someone else."

"It sounds too simple," Stone said.

"Believe me when I tell you, there has been nothing

simple about it. I have known about this for seven months, and it has taken nearly every day of that time to set this up—retrieval of the device, payment, shipping, and finally, collecting payment."

"And with all that time to prepare, why do you suddenly need my money?"

"Because the investor who was to have provided it last week met with a fatal accident, and his funds are no longer forthcoming. You happened to arrive at a moment when you could be useful."

"Why me?"

"Because you're *here,*" Lance said emphatically. "The people to whom I'm to deliver the device are not the kind who take disappointment lightly; they get ugly quickly. I have given them a schedule, and they expect me to keep it."

"Why don't they deal directly with your man? Why do they need you?"

"Because they don't know who he is or how he came by the device. Only I know that, just yours truly, and no one else. By the way, *you* are not going to know that, either. You will know only what I tell you, and if that's not enough for you, then—"

"Then you'll have to disappoint your buyers, won't you?" Stone asked coldly.

That stopped Lance in his tracks. "I have another source for the funds, but it is a less attractive one, which will cost me too much in interest. If you don't want into this, say so, and lunch is on me and we won't meet again."

Stone stared at him for a long moment. "What is the device? What does it do?"

"Please believe me, Stone, you *do not want* that information. In the unlikely event that this should go awry, you will be grateful for not knowing."

Stone thought he had shown a sufficient amount of reluctance to be convincing. "When does the transaction take place?"

"Within the next forty-eight hours," Lance replied, "after your funds are safely in a Swiss account."

"Whose account?"

"Yours; I've brought the paperwork with me; you can instruct the bank not to proceed at any time you choose. But if you're in, then the transfer has to be received in Zurich by the close of business tomorrow, which is noon in New York."

Stone looked at his watch. "I can transfer the funds today. But first, when do I get paid, and how much?"

"We're paying half a million dollars for the device, and I have negotiated a final sales price of two million, two. Your cut of that is one million dollars. I get more, because I set it up."

"How and when will I be paid?"

"The device will be transported to a secure location, a bank in southern Europe, where the exchange will take place. The buyers' funds will be transferred to your Zurich account and mine, in the appropriate amounts, before the device is handed over. It's as foolproof as a transaction of this sort can be. I've done a number of them, I know. I much prefer doing business in the conference room of a bank, instead of in a back alley."

"What about the arrangement you mentioned that will keep this transaction away from prying eyes, such as the Internal Revenue Service?"

"I also have the documentation for an account in the Cayman Islands. You sign both sets of documents— Swiss and Cayman—and I'll fax them to the respective banks, along with a code word. You can then transfer from the Swiss Bank to the Cayman one with one phone call. Once it's in the Cayman bank, you can draw on the account anywhere in the world—cash can be transferred to you, you can write checks, and you can have a credit card which is paid directly from the Cayman account. Thus, no transaction ever goes through an American bank, and you come to the attention of no one."

"I like it," Stone said. "Give me the documents."

Lance produced a thick envelope from an inside pocket and showed Stone where to sign. "Write your code word—any combination of letters and numbers, up to twelve characters."

"I don't like the idea of your having the account numbers and the password," Stone said.

"It's the only way I can transfer your share of the funds to your account. Once I've done that, you can change the account number and the password." Lance tore off a copy of each account application and handed them to Stone.

Stone put the papers into his pocket. "Where do I transfer my funds?"

"To your account in Zurich, which will be open in an hour; I'll let you know where and when to send them from there."

Stone stuck out his hand. "I'll speak with my broker as soon as I get back to my hotel; I'll have to fax him, too. The funds will be in Zurich before the day is over." He glanced at his watch; he had three hours to get it done.

He and Lance parted at the restaurant door.

"I'll call you on your cellphone tomorrow morning, with further instructions," Lance said. "Make sure it's turned on; from here on in, everything has to be done in a precise manner."

"Good," Stone said. Driving back to London, he wondered if he would have gone for this deal if he'd been on his own. Certainly not, he decided. Too risky.

4 9

STONE DROVE BACK TO LONDON AND
Chester Street; as soon as he was in the house, he
called Mason's cellphone. No answer; he left a message. As an afterthought, he called Carpenter's number.

"Yes?" She sounded harried.

"It's Stone Barrington. Did you get it?"

"Hold on," she said, and covered the phone, so that
he could hear only muffled voices. She uncovered it in
time for Stone to hear her say, "Find out why, and do
it *now*." There was real authority in the voice. She came
back to Stone. "Are you in Chester Street now?"

"Yes."

"I'll be there in twenty minutes."

Stone was going to ask what the hell was going on,
but she had already hung up.

Dino let himself in through the front door; he was
carrying two large Harrod's shopping bags. "Hey," he
said.

"I take it you got Mary Ann something."

"Yep; how'd your lunch go?"

"Just as it was supposed to, I think."

"Good." Dino stretched. "I think I'm going to take a
nap."

"It's jet lag," Stone said.

"I never get jet lag."

"Whatever you say. You want me to wake you up later?"

"Not unless it gets to be dinnertime. Do we have any plans?"

"Not yet; I'll call Sarah later."

Stone read the papers for ten minutes, then the doorbell rang. He let Carpenter and Mason into the house.

"Come and sit down," she said. "We have a lot to ask you."

They all went into the drawing room and took seats.

"Did you get everything?" Stone asked.

"We got almost nothing," Carpenter replied.

Mason seemed uncharacteristically quiet; usually, he did the talking.

"Your brand-new bug didn't work?"

Now Mason spoke. "There was something in the neighborhood interfering with it," he said petulantly. "As soon as you left the restaurant, we could clearly hear the sound of your car; it was just in the restaurant that it didn't work. Must have been something in the walls."

"We lunched outdoors," Stone said. "It sounds as if Lance Cabot is smarter than you gave him credit for."

"What do you mean?" Mason demanded.

"He searched me for a wire," Stone replied, "which means he was suspicious. My guess is he had something in his car that would interfere with any radio transmissions in the immediate vicinity."

"Shit," Mason said, with disgust.

"Don't worry about it," Carpenter said. "We have Stone to tell us." She turned to him. "Tell us."

"Someone who works in what sounds like the factory of a defense contractor has made a duplicate of the device he builds every day. He's going to sell it to Lance for half a million dollars in cash, and Lance is going to resell it to an unknown party for two million, two."

"What details did he give you about the device?"

"The device is something that requires exotic metallurgy and special machine tools to make. It's made to extremely tight tolerances. Sounds as though it's small enough to carry around."

"What else did he tell you about this man?"

"He has worked in the same facility for nearly thirty years and is about to retire. Apparently, he's frittered away his savings on the ponies, and he wants to sell the device to make his retirement comfortable."

"Ponies?" Mason asked, baffled. "Polo?"

"Horse racing," Carpenter said to him sharply.

"This gives us nothing to go on," Mason said. "There are factories and laboratories all over the country doing classified work. How are we going to find this man?"

"Lance said that the facility was very secret, and that it's south and west of the restaurant, in Wiltshire," Stone replied.

"Oh, Christ," Carpenter said, turning pale.

"Eastover?" Mason asked.

"Shut up!" Carpenter said sharply.

Stone had the distinct impression that, for some reason, Carpenter was now in charge. Perhaps she had been from the beginning.

"What's Eastover?" Stone asked.

"You don't need to know," Carpenter replied. She turned to Mason. "Listen to me very carefully: I want you to call someone in our tech department and have him call someone eminent in the related sciences that we know well. Have that person call the director at Eastover and tell him that someone is coming to see him for some advice on a technical matter. I don't want the director to have any idea what's going on, until you get there."

"I understand."

"When you arrive and are alone with the director, ask him who fits this description: long-time employee, highly classified work, a builder of devices rather than a designer, close to retirement. If he can't come up with answers based on his own knowledge, have him call in his director of security to go through the personnel files, until you've identified the man. This must be done softly, softly, in such a way that does not create any alarm or gossip in the labs." She turned to Stone. "When is the buy supposed to take place?"

"Within forty-eight hours of the time I transfer my funds to a Swiss account, which Cabot has already opened."

Carpenter turned back to Mason. "We have forty-eight hours, probably less, to place our suspect under the most stringent surveillance—electronic, sonic, anything we can scrape up, but I don't want any bodies anywhere near him or his residence, because if Cabot is as smart as he appears to be, that might alert him. Now, get on the phone."

Mason whipped out a cellphone and walked into the dining room, pressing buttons.

Carpenter turned back to Stone. "When did you say you would transfer the funds?"

"Before the day was out."

"Have you done it?"

"No."

"Then you'd better get moving, hadn't you?"

Stone went into the kitchen and used the phone there to call his broker in New York.

"Richardson."

"Hank, it's Stone Barrington."

"Hi, Stone, what's up? Got some more money for me?"

"No, I'm taking some out."

"How come?"

"I can't explain right now. How much have I got in my money market account?"

"Hang." Stone could hear computer keys clicking. "Three hundred and ten thousand, give or take. The way the market is going, I'm getting ready to start investing it."

Stone took out the document from the Swiss bank. "Got a pencil?"

"Yep."

"I want you to transfer two hundred and fifty thousand to the following account number at the Charter Bank in Zurich." He read the account number twice. "Got that?"

"I've got it. Listen, Stone, I can do as well for you as the Swiss, you know, probably better."

"This is a short-term thing, Hank; I'll have the money back in my account with you in a couple of days."

"Is this ransom money, Stone? Has somebody been kidnapped?"

"No, nothing like that. Just do it, Hank."

"I'm going to need written confirmation; can you fax me something?"

"In five minutes; go stand by the fax machine." Stone hung up, then went upstairs to his room and opened his briefcase. He took out a sheet of his letterhead, wrote a letter of instructions, then took it down to James Cutler's study and faxed it to Richardson. Then he went back into the drawing room.

Carpenter was on her cellphone, and she waved him

to a seat. She ended the conversation, snapped the phone shut, and turned to Stone. "Did you get it done?"

"The money will be in Zurich within the hour."

"Good. What are you supposed to do when it's there?"

"Lance is to phone me on my cellphone tomorrow morning and tell me where to transfer it. I'm not going to do that, of course."

"Why not?" she asked, alarmed.

"Are you kidding? It's a quarter of a million dollars that I worked very hard for. You think I'm going to flush it down some cockamamy security operation I don't really give a damn about?"

She looked miffed. "I quite understand; I'll do something about getting hold of some funds tomorrow. Obviously, if we don't transfer the money, Cabot isn't going to go through with the buy."

"He said that everything will have to be done at precise times from then on."

"Don't worry, I'll get the money. And we'll put someone on his house, to keep track of him."

"I wouldn't do that; he might spot your people, no matter how good they are. He's been trained for that, you know."

"Yes, you're probably right," she said.

"Why did you want me to think Mason was in charge?"

She smiled. "The less you know, the better."

"Carpenter and Mason," Stone said. "I'll bet you have a colleague named Plumber."

She laughed. "Let's just stick with those names for the moment, shall we?"

"What are you doing for dinner, Carpenter?"

She blushed. "Maybe when this is over," she said. She stood up. "Now I have to go find that money." She walked into the dining room, dialing her cellphone.

5 0

CARPENTER AND MASON MADE MORE
phone calls, then Mason made ready to leave. "I can be
in the director's office at Eastover by five," he said.

"Wait until half-past. Give the building time to
empty out after work," Carpenter said. "Is everything
in motion?"

"Our people are meeting at a country hotel a few
miles from Eastover," he said. "When we've identified
our man, I'll get them cracking."

"Good. Call me if there are any problems."

"Where will you be?" he asked.

"At the end of my cellphone," she replied.

"All right; will you need transport?"

"If I do, I'll use Barrington's Jaguar."

Mason nodded and left.

"He's really quite good," she said to Stone. "If a little short of imagination sometimes. I'm not sure that
can be cured. Now, I have some phoning to do; may I
use something besides the dining room?"

"Yes, Cutler's study, right through there." He
pointed at the door.

"Maybe we should plan on dinner," she said. "It
wouldn't surprise me if Lance Cabot decided to rush
things a bit."

"All right."

She disappeared into the study. Stone called Sarah at her studio.

"Hey, there," she said brightly. "Are we on for dinner and, you know?"

"I'm afraid not; some business has come up, and I'm going to be tied up all evening. Maybe all night. How about tomorrow night?"

"Oh, all right," she said, sounding disappointed. "I must have worn you out last night."

"Not entirely."

"Good; well, you have until tomorrow evening to rest. I'll see you then."

"Until then." He hung up. With nothing else to do, he read the papers until Carpenter emerged from the study around six.

"Well, I've done all I can do until we hear from Mason," she said. As if on cue, her cellphone rang. "Yes?" She listened intently. "Do you have enough people for that? Well, get more; then call Portsmouth, if necessary. Do you want me to call them? All right, get back to me." She hung up. "A complication," she said.

"What is it?"

"There are, believe it or not, *two* people who fit the description of Cabot's contact at Eastover. One of them is a woman."

"Lance always referred to his contact as 'he.'"

"But 'he' could be a woman, so we have to surveil them both; there's no way around it. Mason is getting more help."

"What happens at Eastover?"

"Eastover is a code word for a government facility on an army base in Wiltshire, north of Stonehenge."

"And what do they make there?"

"*Very* serious items," she said. "Things that are shared only with your government, things that are vital to both our defenses."

"Were they able to recognize the device from what Lance said about it?"

"As there are two people, there are two devices, made in separate departments; it could be either of them."

"Is there nothing else you can tell me?"

"Suffice it to say that, if either of the devices fell into the hands of an unstable government or a terrorist organization, it might give them capabilities that neither my government nor yours would like them to have."

"Weapons capabilities?"

She nodded. "Now, don't ask me any more."

"All right."

"Do you like Chinese food?"

"You betcha."

"I know a place; we'll order in. It's all right, is it, that we have dinner here?"

"Yes, of course, but order for three; my friend Dino is upstairs asleep."

"May I use the phone? My department frowns on the use of secure cellphones for ordering Chinese."

"Sure, there's one in the kitchen."

"It will be an hour or so," she said. "The restaurant is in Gerard Street, in Soho, not far from my, ah, place of business; they'll send it over in a taxi."

"Do I pay the driver when he arrives?"

"No, it's already been charged to a business account."

"For future reference, what's the restaurant?"

"The Dumpling Inn. It's good for a quick before-the-ater dinner, a short block off Shaftsbury Avenue."

"I'll make a note," he said, "for a future trip. Would you like a drink while we wait?"

"Thank you, yes; is there any bourbon?"

Stone went to a liquor cabinet across the room and found a bottle of Knob Creek. "Yes, and a good one. Where would a proper, Oxford-educated Englishwoman acquire a taste for bourbon?"

"I did some training in Virginia, near Washington."

"At the Farm?"

"How did you know that?" she demanded.

"Lance Cabot told me he spent some time there."

"True; he was in the class just a year ahead of mine; we heard about him."

"Was Stan Hedger running the place then?"

"Yes; you do know a lot, don't you?"

"Not a lot. Just enough to sound knowledgeable. Ice?"

"Yes, please; I learned that in Virginia, too."

There was an ice machine built into the cabinet; Stone returned with the two drinks and sat down. They clinked glasses.

"Mmmm, good one," she said. "I've never heard of it."

"It's one of a rash of boutique bourbons that have cropped up the past few years. Sort of like your single-malt Scotches."

Her cellphone rang. "Yes? Well, give the man priority. Try and have it done before he gets home. You'll just have to do the other one while the house is occupied; it *must* be done as soon as possible." She hung up. "Mason is bringing more personnel up from our Portsmouth office, but right now we've only enough people to wire one house, and I've chosen the man, since he's working late in the lab."

"Probably getting his device ready to sell."

"Probably."

"Did you enjoy the training at the Farm?"

She smiled. "I *adored* it, the rougher the better. I'm quite a tomboy, you know. I grew up outdoors, around horses, played polo. At school, I was a *vicious* lacrosse player; had a terrible reputation among our opponents."

"I expect your people liked that about you, when you were being considered for your work."

"No, I think they would have preferred me working in a code room, or something else less masculine. Mason has been working for me for two years, and he's never really become accustomed to being bossed around by a woman. That's one reason I let him take the lead with you; good for his ego."

"You're not married?"

She held up a bare ring finger. "How very observant of you."

"Oh, I'm real quick."

"Marriage would be difficult. If I married inside my organization there would be the problem of arranging compatible postings, office politics, all that. If I married outside, I'd probably have to resign."

"Why?"

"Oh, many of our male employees are married to civilians, their wives having been well vetted, of course. But for our management, it doesn't seem to work both ways. There'd still be the problem of postings, and they'd be fearful of an officer having to rush home and cook dinner for her husband. And, of course, children would be an unbearable complication. I love the work so much, I rather think I won't marry."

Dino appeared, rubbing his eyes. "What's going on?" he asked.

"Not a lot. You up for Chinese?"

"I'm always up for Chinese," Dino replied.

5 1

THEY DINED FROM CARDBOARD CAR-
tons on Wedgwood plates. The food was superb, and
Stone had found a dry, white Bordeaux in James Cutler's cellar that was a perfect companion to Chinese
food. Among the three of them, they managed two
bottles.

Stone's cellphone rang. "Hello?"

"Hi, it's me," Lance's voice said.

"Lance," Stone mouthed to Carpenter. She came and
put her ear next to his.

"What's up? Everything on schedule?"

"Did you wire the funds into the Swiss account?"

"Yes; they would have been there before the close of
business."

"Good; then we're a go."

"When is the buy going to take place?"

"The evening of the day after tomorrow. Tomorrow
morning I have to arrange for the cash to be transported from Zurich to England. You'll wire it to an account in Belgium, and it will be across the Channel as
quickly as possible. I'll give you the wiring instructions tomorrow morning, so don't be far from your
cellphone."

"Lance, I want to be there for the buy."

Lance was quiet for a moment. "That isn't necessary," he said.

"It's necessary for me. I don't want to be separated from my money."

Lance laughed. "All right; we'll arrange to meet west of London; I'll give you an address."

"Why don't you just pick me up?"

"Because I won't be returning to London after the buy; you'll need transportation. Believe me, this is the best way to do it."

"If you say so."

"I'll call you at nine o'clock tomorrow morning with the wiring instructions."

"All right, good night."

"Good night."

Stone punched off the phone. "What do you think?"

"I'm not sure," she said. "Let's wait until you hear from him with the wiring instructions. By that time, I'll have the funds available to make the transfer. We'll wire them to your Swiss account, and then you can forward them to the Belgian account. That way it will look entirely kosher. You'll have to sign for the funds, of course." She smiled. "We can't have you running off with our money."

"Suppose I did?"

"I'd hunt you down; you couldn't hide for long."

"I don't think I'd want you on my trail," Stone said.

Carpenter looked at her watch. "I have to go home and get some sleep."

"Can I drive you?"

"I'm within walking distance."

"Then I'll walk you."

"That won't do, I'm afraid. You get some sleep; I'll be back here by eight in the morning." She stood up.

Stone walked her to the door and said good night.

Stone went back to the kitchen, where Dino was polishing off a final dumpling.

"She doesn't want you to know where she lives," Dino said.

"I guess not."

"Or her name."

"I guess not."

"It's a shame; she's quite a broad; I've never met anybody like her."

"Neither have I," Stone admitted.

"What did you tell Sarah about tonight?"

"Business."

"I suppose that wasn't too much of a lie."

"I try never to lie."

"The best policy," Dino agreed.

They had a brandy, then went to bed.

Stone was already up and dressed the following morning, when Carpenter rang the bell.

"Good morning," she said. Today she was dressed more informally, in a cotton pantsuit that complemented her figure.

"Come in," Stone said.

"Heard anything from Cabot?"

"No, not yet. He said he'd call at nine. Have you had breakfast?"

"No."

"Come to the kitchen; I'll make you some eggs."

Carpenter followed him into the kitchen, where Dino was making coffee. Stone scrambled some eggs, English-style, and fried some superb smoked Irish back bacon. They were just finishing when nine o'clock came.

Stone looked at his watch. "Any minute," he said.

"My funds are ready to go," Carpenter said. "The minute you have the wiring instructions."

By ten o'clock, Stone had still not heard from Lance.

"Call him," Carpenter said.

Stone dialed the Farm Street house; Erica answered.

"Hi," Stone said, "may I speak with Lance?"

"He's not here," she said, and she sounded upset.

"What's wrong?" Stone asked.

"He left in the middle of the night; I didn't wake up until Monica called a few minutes ago."

"You sound a little groggy."

"I know; I can't seem to wake up."

"Did Lance leave a note?"

"No, nothing; and all his clothes are gone. I mean, everything, and all his luggage, too."

"I'll call you back," Stone said, and hung up. He turned to Carpenter. "Sounds like Lance drugged Erica last night, then packed up and decamped. Does this change anything?"

"No," she said. "It makes sense that he'd not tell her where he's going, and he wouldn't want to return to the house after the buy."

"But why would he go two days before the buy?"

"This leads me to think that the exchange will be tonight, rather than tomorrow. It can't happen any earlier than that, because his man at Eastover will be working all day; if he didn't show up for work, our people would be all over him."

"Then why hasn't Lance called with the wiring instructions?" Stone asked. "He can't make the buy without the funds, and he made the very good point last night that the cash would have to be transported to England. This doesn't make any sense."

Carpenter got out her cellphone and went into the study. She came back a few minutes later. "Both our suspects at Eastover are at work, as usual," she said. "We'll be notified if they leave the installation for any reason, and there are people there to keep track of them if they do."

Stone was suddenly struck with an odd feeling. "Excuse me a minute, will you?" He went upstairs and retrieved his copy of the Swiss bank documents. There was an account manager's name at the top of the first page, and a telephone number. Stone dialed the number.

An operator answered, repeating only the number.

"May I speak with Dr. Peter von Enzberg?" Stone asked.

"Who is calling, please?" the operator asked in stiff English.

"My name is Stone Barrington."

"One moment." There was a brief pause, followed by several clicks.

"This is Peter von Enzberg," a deep voice said, sounding very English. "Is that Mr. Barrington?"

"Yes, Doctor. I opened an account yesterday and transferred some funds from New York."

"Of course, Mr. Barrington; we received the funds in good order."

"Can you tell me the current balance in my account?"

"May I have your code word, please?"

Stone gave it to him.

"One moment." Stone could hear computer keys clicking. "Your current balance is one hundred dollars, Mr. Barrington."

Stone felt suddenly ill. "What was the amount you received from New York?"

"Two hundred and fifty thousand dollars."

"Then why isn't it in the account?"

"A request was made to transfer the funds shortly

before closing yesterday. It was very late, but the request was urgent, so we accommodated Mr. Cabot."

"Mr. Cabot had access to my account?"

"Why, yes, Mr. Barrington; his signature was on the account application, and he knew the code word."

Stone felt frozen. "Where were the funds transferred?"

"To an account in Hong Kong," the account manager replied.

"Thank you, Dr. von Enzberg." He hung up and trudged down the stairs.

"What's wrong?" Carpenter asked. "You look ill."

"I've been had," Stone replied.

52

STONE SANK HEAVILY INTO AN ARM-
chair in the drawing room.

"Explain," Carpenter said.

"Lance transferred all the money out of the account yesterday, to a bank in Hong Kong."

"How could he do that?"

"Apparently, he had access to my account."

Carpenter stared at him. "Did you sign the account application, then give it back to Lance?"

"Yes."

"Then he simply added his own signature to the document. Did he know your code?"

"I wrote it on the form. How could I have been so stupid?"

"An expensive oversight," Carpenter said.

"I could get the Hong Kong account number, and we could trace the funds," Stone said.

Carpenter shook her head. "Remember the time difference; Cabot has had plenty of opportunity to re-transfer the funds half a dozen times; he was probably at it all night. We'd never find it."

"But your people will reimburse me?"

"I can't make any promises; my management are likely to take a dim view of all this."

"I worked very hard to earn that money," Stone said, though he'd really made it in the market. "You can't let them hang me out to dry."

"If it were our funds he'd stolen, that would be one thing, but your funds are quite another." She looked at her watch. "We have to get going," she said.

"To where?"

"To Wiltshire; obviously, the timetable has been accelerated. I hope we're not too late."

Stone grabbed a tie and his suit jacket and they met downstairs.

"We'll take your Jaguar," Carpenter said. "But you can't go," she said to Dino.

"I go where he goes," Dino replied.

Carpenter looked at Stone, who nodded. "Oh, all right. Let's get out of here," she said.

Carpenter drove, fast and expertly.

Stone glanced at the speedometer, which was glued to a hundred and twenty miles an hour. "Aren't you worried about being stopped by the police?"

"The number plate is a special one; they'll know to leave us alone," she replied. She fished her cellphone out of her bag and dialed a number, driving with one hand, making Stone nervous. "It's Carpenter," she said. "Cabot has bolted with Barrington's money, we don't know where. We have to assume that his timetable has changed. I'm on the way, and I'll be there in an hour." She punched off.

Stone called the Farm Street house again. Erica answered.

"Are you all right?" he asked.

"I've had three double espressos, but I'm still a little fuzzy around the edges."

"Write down this number," Stone said, and gave her his cellphone number. "If Lance should call, tell him I called and want to speak to him urgently. When he hangs up, you call me immediately."

"What's going on, Stone?" Erica asked.

"I'm not sure," he said, "but don't leave the house; stick by the phone."

"All right," she replied.

Stone hung up. "Should I call her back and have her check the office in the wine cellar?"

"Don't bother," Carpenter said. "It isn't Cabot's office."

Stone looked at her. "Then whose is it?"

"It belongs to the owner of the house," she said. "He's one of ours."

"Why would Lance rent a house from one of your people?"

"He doesn't know. We've been keeping track of Cabot ever since he arrived in London last year. He was followed to an estate agent's, where he was looking for houses to rent, and we, in effect, made him an offer he couldn't refuse. The rent and the location were irresistible."

"Who shot the two Israelis?"

"Not our people; maybe Stan Hedger."

"Why?"

"He may have read them as a threat to Cabot, and he didn't want anything to happen to Cabot, at least not yet."

"This is way too complicated for me," Stone said.

"Then don't try to figure it out."

"Makes perfect sense to me," Dino chipped in from the backseat.

"What does?"

"The whole thing. Hedger hires you to look into

Cabot because he's afraid if he uses his own people Cabot will figure it out, because, having been one of them, he knows how they operate. Cabot researches you, figures you were telling the truth when you said you were no longer working for Hedger."

"I did tell the truth," Stone said. "Eventually."

"Yeah. Once Cabot thinks you're not working for Hedger, he figures you for a mark."

"God knows, that's true."

"The Israelis obviously want whatever Cabot is buying, and so does Hedger."

"But the American government already has access to this technology, doesn't it?" Stone asked Carpenter.

Carpenter looked momentarily uncomfortable. "Not necessarily," she said.

Dino continued. "Makes even more sense," he said. "The Brits build this . . . *thing* . . . and they don't share their little secret with the Americans, so Hedger and his people are pissed off."

"But why me?" Stone asked.

"You're not some unknown person," Dino said. "You get your name in the papers now and then. That's probably how you came to Hedger's attention—that, or your old professor buddy down at NYU dropped your name on somebody he used to know."

"And who would the professor be?" Carpenter asked.

"Samuel Bernard," Stone replied. "He was one of my professors in law school."

"That bloke is a bloody *legend*," she said, wonder in her voice.

"I knew he had a lot of connections, but I didn't know he qualified as a legend."

"He was offered the directorship of central intelligence at one time; turned it down and went to NYU, but word is, he kept his hand in. Once you've been at that level in the agency, you don't just get put out to pasture." She whipped off the motorway, made a left, drove another half a mile, and turned onto a smaller road, keeping her speed at what Stone figured was about twenty miles an hour more than the car was capable of on that road.

Stone hung onto the door handle and tried not to look at the winding black tarmac rushing at him. Dino, on the other hand, seemed perfectly awake.

"Looks like everybody knows what's going on here except you, Stone," he said.

"Oh, I think you've explained it to him very well, Dino," Carpenter said, whipping around a hairpin turn. "You missed your calling; you're wasted as a policeman."

"Don't you believe it," Dino replied. "I wouldn't get mixed up in your business for anything. You can never trust *anybody*."

"Not a bad policy," she replied. "Is it any better on the NYPD?"

"Marginally," Dino said.

"Where are we going?" Stone asked.

"Right up there," Carpenter replied. They had emerged from a stand of trees onto an open, rolling plain with few trees. Ahead of them a mile or so, at a crossroads, was a three-story stone building, which got larger fast. Carpenter skidded into the parking lot, which was nearly full, and got out of the car. "Come on," she said.

Stone saw two men on a ladder stringing a cable from a utility pole on the road to a corner of the building. He looked at the sign: THE BREWER'S ARMS, it read. He followed Carpenter inside.

5 3

THEY WALKED UP TO THE THIRD FLOOR of the country inn, past a guard, and into a roomy, two-bedroom suite, which contained half a dozen men, most in their shirtsleeves, and several pieces of electronic equipment—radios, computers, and two large, flat-screen monitors. Thick wires ran from the equipment out a window, where Stone had seen the two men stringing wire, and he could see a small satellite dish mounted to the windowsill.

"What's happening?" Carpenter said to one of the men. "Oh, this is Barrington and Bacchetti; they're with me. Gentlemen, this is Plumber."

"We're just about set up," Plumber said. "We're expecting satellite contact any moment, and we've got great weather for it."

"What have you done with the two subjects' homes?"

"We couldn't get anything decent with sonic equipment," Plumber said. "They both live in official housing, and double glazing was installed a few months ago, so we can't get anything off the glass. We've tapped both phones from the exchange, but since they're both at work, we're not getting anything."

"Eyeball surveillance?"

"Nothing within five miles," Plumber replied. "We

figure that when Cabot arrives in the area he'll canvass the neighborhood, looking for anything that might be surveillance, so we're going to rely on satellite, until dark. After that, we'll have taxis with local numbers painted on, but we'll keep our distance. We're going to place satellite tracker marks on both subjects' cars, so we needn't stay within sight."

"Where's Mason?"

"He's running the on-ground operation; he'll be in touch when something happens."

"Anything else?"

"Bad news; Portsmouth let us down."

"*What?*"

"Something about a suspect merchant ship in the harbor; they've put all their people and equipment on that."

"Do we have enough resources on the ground here to cover both subjects?"

"Maybe; that's the best I can tell you."

"Isn't there anything else we can draw on?"

"No. Another team is on its way to Scotland, looking for a suspected terrorist who is supposed to be arriving in the Clyde on a tanker."

"Shit," she muttered.

"Satellite's up," a young man at a computer station said.

Everyone gathered around him. The image on the big monitor was of a building and a carpark. "Eastover internal security gave us the position of the two subjects' cars." He moved the cursor to a small car and clicked on it: an *A* appeared on the car's roof. He moved the cursor to another, larger car and clicked again. A *B* appeared on the car. "*A* is Morgan, our male subject; *B* is Carroll, our female. The equipment will move the ID letter with the cars, so we won't lose them in traffic."

"How about the houses?" Carpenter asked.

The tech tapped some more keys, and the screen divided into thirds. "Now you can see both Eastover and the two houses," he said. "Neato, huh?"

"Stop speaking American," Carpenter said.

Plumber spoke up. "Internal security at Eastover is tracking both Morgan and Carroll inside the building. They'll know if either tries to take something out."

"Tell them not to stop either one," Carpenter said. "I want to bag Cabot and find out from him who his buyer is."

"Righto."

"Well," Carpenter said, "we've nothing to do until the end of the workday, when our two subjects will leave the building. We might as well order some lunch." She went to a desk and found a room-service menu.

By half-past five, they were ready for some action. Stone was reading an elderly copy of *Country Life*, and Dino was in one of the bedrooms, glued to a cricket match. Carpenter merely paced.

"We've got movement," Plumber said. It was one minute past five-thirty, and people were streaming out of the Eastover building.

"Typical civil servants," Carpenter said. "Leaving on the stroke of quitting time."

"We can't identify individuals by satellite, but look, A's car is on the move. There—so is B's." The cars pulled out of the carpark and turned in opposite directions.

A cellphone rang, and Plumber answered it. "Righto," he said, then hung up. "We've got word from internal security that both subjects have left the building."

"Were they carrying anything?" Carpenter asked.

"A wore a loose raincoat, and B had a bakery box, looked like a cake."

"Did they search them on the way out?"

"I asked them not to, as per your instructions."

Carpenter watched the screen as it divided in two, each displaying a car with a letter on top.

Five minutes passed. "They're home," Plumber said. "Both cars are garaged. The houses are virtually identical."

"Government-issue," Carpenter said.

"Right, but they're on opposite sides of the village; both back up onto Salisbury Plain."

"What now?" Stone asked.

"We wait," Carpenter replied.

They did not have long to wait. "We've got movement on A, Morgan," Plumber said. "He's backed his car out of the garage, now he's loading something, can't tell what."

Everybody gathered around the screen to see the man putting several items into the back of what seemed like a small station wagon.

"What kind of car is that?" Stone asked.

"Morris Minor Estate," Plumber replied. "It's from the fifties, and Morgan has carefully restored it himself; looks new."

Across the room a man wearing headphones shouted, "B's getting a phone call!" He flipped a switch, and, over a speaker, they could all hear the phone ringing.

There was a click, and a woman's voice said, "Hello?"

From the other end of the connection came not a voice, but a whistle. The whistler performed a few bars of *"Rule Brittania,"* then hung up. The woman hung up, too.

"That's a signal," Plumber said. "Everybody alert; she's going to move now."

On the split screen they watched Morgan back his Morris Minor out of his driveway and head off down the street, his car still marked with an A.

"Oh, shit," Plumber said, pointing at the other side of the screen. B was coming out of the garage, too, but not in her car; she was pushing a bicycle. On the back, a large pair of saddlebags could be seen. "We can't put a tracker mark on her bicycle—not enough area showing to the satellite. This is going to be dicey."

"Don't you lose that bicycle," Carpenter warned.

"I'll do my best," the tech said, "but with the marked car, the tracking would have been automatic. With the bike, I'm going to have to do it manually, and it's the toughest computer game you ever saw."

"Cabot is very smart," Carpenter said. "But we knew that; we should have suspected something like this. Where's Morgan going?"

"I'll put him on the other screen," the tech said. "It'll be easier to track B if we devote a whole screen to her." He tapped in a command, and the second screen came to life.

"He's leaving the village," Plumber said. "We've got fewer houses, now. He's headed west, toward the Plain. Wait a minute, he's turning into some woods. Shit, we won't be able to see him under trees."

Then the Morris Minor emerged from the trees and stopped. Morgan got out of the car, opened the rear doors, and began unloading.

"What's he doing?" Carpenter asked.

"Equipment of some sort," Plumber replied.

"It's an easel," Stone said. "Look, he's setting it up."

"He's going to paint?" Plumber asked.

"Looks like it," Carpenter replied.

Morgan set up a camp stool, opened what looked like a toolbox, and placed a canvas on the easel.

"He's going to paint the sunset," Plumber said.

"I've got trouble here," the tech said suddenly, pointing to the screen before him. "Carroll is approaching a roundabout, and so are some other bikes." They watched as B moved into the roundabout, merging with half a dozen other bicycles. Then they began exiting.

"Which one is she?" Carpenter demanded.

"You got me," the tech replied. "There are two roads off the roundabout, and we've got two bikes on one and four on the other. We can't track them all."

"It's B, Carroll," Carpenter said. "Use both views to track the cyclists, until we can identify her. Morgan's going to be there awhile; we'll let him be. It's Carroll, I know it."

Stone watched as both screens began displaying cyclists on country roads. His last view of Morgan was of the man painting away.

5 4

THEY SPLIT INTO TWO GROUPS, EACH watching the cyclists. "There," Stone said. "The saddle-bags; there's only one bike with large saddlebags."

"You're right," Carpenter said. "And none of the other bikes has saddlebags at all. That's Carroll!"

Then the bicycle with the large saddlebags split off from the other three and turned onto a dirt lane.

"Okay," Carpenter said to the tech, "follow her, ignore the others, and let's get Morgan back on the other screen."

The tech got the bicycle in his sights. "It's going to be easier now, since she's on that little lane."

"Show me Morgan," Carpenter said.

The tech tapped more keys, and the image popped back onto the second screen.

"Where is he?" Carpenter asked.

"Let me pan around," the tech replied.

"It's the same spot," Stone said, "but Morgan's car isn't there; he's gone."

"Find that car," Carpenter said, "and be quick about it."

"It's not so easy," the tech said. "It's one thing to track the A car when you've got him in your sights, but finding him in a landscape is going to be nearly impossible."

"I don't care, do it!"

Stone watched the lone cyclist as she pedaled down the little lane. "Anybody got a map of the area?" he asked.

"Here," Plumber replied, spreading a large-scale map of the area on a table. "She came up here from her house to the roundabout," he said, pointing, "and then she left it here." He ran his finger up the road. "She exited the paved road here, and she's going up this lane."

"What's this?" Stone asked, pointing to a green area up the lane.

"It's a copse of trees, with a clearing in the middle."

"Look at this," Carpenter said, pointing at the trees.

Carroll had cycled into the clearing, and a car was waiting for her. A man got out.

"Here's the buy," Carpenter said. "Get me Mason." Somebody handed her a cellphone. "Mason? Close on the following map coordinates." She read them off.

"We've got a problem here," Plumber said, pointing at the map. Everybody gathered around him. "There are three roads out of the clearing, in different directions."

"Dammit," Carpenter said. She spoke into the cellphone again. "Mason, check the coordinates; there are three exits from the clearing; you've got to cover them all. I don't care, pull your men off Morgan's house and get them out there; I am *not* going to lose the device, and I am *not* going to lose Cabot. Do it!"

Stone went and stood behind the tech. "Are you having any luck locating Morgan?"

"Not yet," the young man said.

"I think it's very important that you find his car." He turned to the other screen. "What's Carroll doing?"

"See for yourself," Carpenter said. Carroll and the

man she had met were embracing. "Looks as though Cabot gives this lady a lot of personal attention. Any luck on Morgan's car?"

"Not yet."

"Zero in on Morgan's house," she said. "Let's see if he returned home."

"That's easy," the tech replied, tapping his keyboard. "Here we are; all is quiet."

"Work outward from the house in circles; see if you can find him in the neighborhood. Maybe he stopped at the pub, or for groceries."

"Will do," the tech replied.

Carpenter moved back to Carroll's screen. She stared at it for a moment, then laughed. "I don't believe it!"

"What?" Stone asked.

"They're fucking." She pointed at the screen. They had spread out a blanket, and the principal view was of a man's bare back.

Then the tech widened the view. "Here come our people," the tech said. Cars could be seen approaching the copse from three directions.

Mason drove the lead car, and he was moving fast up the unpaved lane. Ahead, the trees beckoned, and inside them, the clearing. He was going to make this bust himself, he thought; it was going to be the high point of his career. He entered the trees, and ahead, he could see the clearing in the evening light. Simultaneously, three cars entered the clearing from each access road. A couple were lying on a blanket, naked, and they looked up. "Oh, God," he moaned. He picked up the cellphone.

Carpenter's eyes widened. "I don't believe it. He's

who?" She snapped the phone shut. "Carroll is fucking her immediate superior at Eastover."

"Then Morgan is our man," Stone said.

"Find him!" Carpenter said to the tech.

"He's not in the neighborhood," the young man replied.

"Get somebody over to Morgan's house," Carpenter snapped at Plumber.

"We don't have anybody; they're all on Carroll."

She picked up the cellphone. "Mason? It's Morgan, no doubt, and we've lost him. Get over to his house and arrest him. Report back."

"How long will it take him to get there?" Stone asked.

Plumber spoke up. "Four, five minutes."

"I don't believe it," Carpenter was saying. "All this bike ride was in aid of was fucking her boss!"

"They couldn't meet at either of their houses," Plumber said. "These facilities frown on extramarital relationships."

"Carroll is married?"

Plumber was checking a list. "Divorced, but her boss is married."

"How about Morgan?" Stone asked.

Plumber checked his list again. "Never married."

"So he lives alone?"

Plumber checked his sheet again. "No; he has a cat."

Carpenter was back on the cellphone. "Mason, where are you? Well, hurry up!" She closed the phone. "He says he's two minutes out."

"Morgan won't run," Plumber said. "He has no idea we're onto him. He plans to take his retirement on schedule, then retire somewhere with his new money, probably Spain, where we can't get at him. I'll bet he's home watching telly right now."

Dino came out of the bedroom. "What's happening?"

"Lots," Stone replied. "Who won the cricket match?"

"I have no idea," Dino said. "Bring me up to date."

Stone gave him a sixty-second recap.

"Mason's at the house," Carpenter said. "Get it on-screen," she said to the tech.

The tech had it up in seconds; two cars pulled into Morgan's driveway, and men spilled out of them. One opened the garage door; the others ringed the house, while someone at the front kicked in the door.

"Mason, report," Carpenter said into the cellphone. "Mason? Where are you?"

Stone stared at the screen. He didn't like this at all.

"Mason!" Carpenter shouted. "What? What's happening?" She listened. "It's still there?"

"The car," Dino said. "I'll bet it's in the garage."

Stone held up a hand for silence; he was listening to Carpenter.

She closed the phone. "Morgan's gone," she said. "His luggage is gone, and most of his clothes. The Morris Minor is in the garage, empty."

"Is it a two-car garage?" Stone asked.

"Yes."

"Then he had another car. The device was in the back of the Morris Minor; while Morgan painted, Lance took it and left the money in the car. Morgan drove home, garaged his car, then got into the other car, which was packed and ready to go, and just drove away."

Carpenter turned to Plumber. "Full-scale alert—every airport, every seaport, every police patrol car. Photographs of Cabot and Morgan faxed everywhere, the continent, too. Call Interpol and explain the situation. I want them both back, and the device, too. Especially the device. What's the longest Cabot and Morgan could have been gone?"

Plumber looked at his watch. "Forty minutes for Cabot; Morgan would have needed another, say, fifteen minutes to return to the house and leave again."

"Establish a perimeter at eighty miles," Carpenter said. "Right now, Cabot could be, say, forty miles away, driving fast, and Morgan less. Every road blocked; turn out the local police, but don't tell them why we want these two."

Stone picked up a photograph. "Is this Morgan?"

"Yes," Plumber replied.

"I want to see his house."

"Me, too," Dino said.

Carpenter handed Stone the keys to the Jaguar. "Give them a map," she said. "I can't spare anybody to go with you, Stone."

Stone took the keys and ran for the car.

"I want to drive," Dino said.

5 5

DINO GOT THE CAR STARTED AS STONE got in. "Don't waste any time," Stone said.

Dino hung a right out of the carpark and found himself staring at a moving van coming straight at him in his lane. "Shit!" he yelled, whipping to the other side of the road and nearly running into the ditch.

"Sorry, I forgot to warn you about that first right turn."

"Maybe I don't want to do this after all," Dino said.

"Shut up and drive," Stone said. "Just remember which side of the road you're supposed to be on."

"Very weird, driving on the left," Dino said. "But I'll get the hang of it."

"Soon, please."

They followed the map into the small village and to Morgan's street. All the houses seemed identical.

"It's gotta be the one with no front door," Dino said, whipping into the driveway.

They walked into the house to find Mason and his people pulling the place apart. A man appeared from the kitchen. "I found a safe in the garage," he said.

Everybody trooped through the kitchen to the garage. There was, indeed, a safe, the door open, empty.

"He put that in for the device," Mason said. The group started to pull the garage apart.

Stone motioned Dino back into the house.

"What are we looking for?" Dino asked.

"Anything that might give us a hint where Morgan has gone—travel brochures, reservation forms, anything. You take the desk."

Dino began going through the desk drawers, while Stone walked around the living room slowly, looking at everything. He didn't know exactly what he was looking for, but he would know it when he saw it. There was a large television set, and an easy chair and ottoman parked in front of it. On the ottoman was a stack of magazines; Stone began to go through them.

A television guide, a well-marked racing form, a couple of girlie magazines, and a travel magazine. Stone flipped through the travel magazine twice before he found something. A corner of one page had been dog-eared, then flattened again. The page was a continuation of an article on country inns that began earlier in the magazine; there was only one ad. "Take a look at this," he said to Dino.

"Nothing in the desk," Dino said. "No secret compartments, no travel receipts, nothing."

Stone held out the magazine. "This page has been marked," he said.

Dino looked at the ad in the lower right-hand corner. A photograph of a large country house dominated it. "What's Cliveden?" he asked, pronouncing it with a long *i*.

"Cliveden, with a short *i*, was the country house of Lord Astor, before the war. His wife, an American woman named Nancy, who was a member of parliament, ran a very big salon there. Everybody who was anybody showed up at one time or another—George Bernard Shaw, Charlie Chaplin—and every literary or political figure of the time."

"How do you know this stuff?"

"I read a book about it."

"So why is this important?"

"It's a hotel now, and it's near Heathrow. Suppose Morgan wanted to lie low for a few days, until the heat was off at the airports, then beat it out of the country? He's got to know everybody will be looking for him."

"Could be," Dino said. "You want to check it out?"

"Have we got anything else to do?"

"Nope."

"Then let's do it."

They were on the M4 motorway, driving fast.

"Why aren't we looking for Lance instead?" Dino asked.

"Two reasons: First, Lance is a lot smarter than Morgan, I think, and he's going to be a lot harder to find; second, Morgan has my money."

"And that's the important one, huh?"

"You bet your ass; I don't give a damn about the device, whatever it is, but Carpenter and her people don't give a damn about my money, either."

Following a small map in the magazine ad, they found the house.

"Jesus Christ," Dino said, as they drove up the drive and came to the place. "I didn't expect it to be so big."

"Neither did I," Stone said, getting out of the car. He took the photograph of Morgan from his pocket and showed it to Dino. "This is our guy." Morgan was late fifties, heavyset, balding, with graying hair and a military mustache.

"I'll bet he shaved before he left the house," Dino said.

They walked into the building, into an enormous living room, ornately decorated.

"Wow," Dino said under his breath. "This Astor guy knew how to live, didn't he?"

They approached the reception desk. "Show them your badge," Stone whispered.

"May I help you, gentlemen?" the young woman behind the desk asked.

Dino flashed his badge. "We're looking for a man," he said.

Stone handed her the photograph. "His name is Morgan, although he may be using an alias. It's possible he's shaved his mustache, too."

"Oh, yes," she said. "Sir William Mallory, and no mustache; he booked in a week or so ago, sent a cash deposit, checked in half an hour ago."

"Where can we find him?"

"I'm afraid I don't know," the young woman said.

"What's his room number?"

"He didn't check all the way in," she replied.

"Pardon?"

"He came to the desk; a porter brought his luggage; he registered, then he left. He seemed very nervous; he was sweating, I remember."

"Did he show you any kind of identification?"

"Yes; he didn't want to use a credit card, insisted on paying cash in advance, so I asked him for identification. He showed me a British passport."

"Did he say anything?"

"He said he'd forgotten something at his London house; he'd have to go back for it."

"How was he dressed?"

"A raincoat and a trilby hat, which I thought was odd, since the weather is so nice at the moment."

"How much luggage did he have?"

"Two large cases and a sort of canvas bag."

"Describe the canvas bag, please."

"A kind of satchel, roomy, like a Gladstone. The porter told me after he'd gone that he'd insisted on carrying it himself."

"Where would I find the porter?"

The young woman raised a finger and beckoned a man in a uniform. "These gentlemen have some questions about Sir William Mallory," she said.

"Yes, sir?" the porter said.

"How did he arrive?"

"By car, sir."

"What kind of car?"

"A Jaguar from the sixties—dark blue—quite beautifully restored, inside and out. His luggage was fitted to the boot, except for the valise."

"Did you, by any chance, take note of the number plate?"

"It was a vanity plate, sir; B-R-A-I-N."

"Did he say where he was going?"

"Back to London; he said he'd forgotten something important."

"Thank you very much," Stone said. He and Dino went back to their car.

"Good call, Stone," Dino said, "but now we're going to have to get Carpenter's people on the case; he could be anywhere."

Stone dialed Carpenter's cellphone.

"Yes?" She sounded harried.

"It's Stone. Morgan drove to Cliveden, a country house hotel; do you know it?"

"Yes, it's famous, but how did you know he went there?"

"He left a travel magazine at his house with a page marked with an ad for the hotel."

"Is he still there?"

"No, he came over all nervous while checking in, and left, telling the desk clerk that he'd forgotten something in London and had to go back for it."

"Anything else?"

"Yes; he's traveling under the name of Sir William Mallory, and he has a British passport in that name. Cabot got it for him, I expect. He's driving a sixties-vintage Jaguar, dark blue, restored, with the number plate B-R-A-I-N. Should be easy to spot."

"Stone, that's very good. Would you like a job?"

"I'd like my money back," Stone replied. "And if I were you, I'd double your effort at Heathrow; it's very near here, and that's where I'm going. Can you have somebody from airport security meet me at the departures entrance?"

"Which terminal? There are four."

"International departures?"

"Terminal four; I'll find a man for you."

"Tell airport security he's shaved his mustache, and he'll be carrying a canvas valise; he won't check it."

"Right."

Stone hung up. "Heathrow, my man."

"This is a long shot," Dino said.

"It's the only shot we've got."

5 6

LANCE CABOT LEANED INTO THE WIND
and accelerated. The big BMW motorcycle tore along
the country road, making a steady eighty miles per
hour, taking the curves as if glued to the road. From a
hilltop, he spied the airfield, a disused World War II
training facility. There was no longer an entrance; the
road had been plowed up and now sported a crop of
late wheat. Lance stopped the motorcycle, went to the
fence along the road, pulled up a post, and laid it flat.
He got back onto the bike, drove over the fence, then
stopped and returned the post to its hole. Then he
started, overland, for the field, driving as fast as he
could without capsizing the big machine.

The two old runways were potholed, and there were
many weeds growing up through the tracks. The field
was empty. Lance looked at his watch: The son of a
bitch was late, and it was getting dark. He drove up
and down both runways, checking for holes that
might wreck an airplane; he took note of the wind,
then he drove to the end of one runway, shut down the
engine, and got off the motorcycle, searching the skies.
He saw it before he heard it, a black dot, steadily getting bigger.

Lance stood at the end of the selected runway, holding

his arms straight above his head, the airport lineman's signal for "park here." The Cessna circled once, then set down on the correct runway, slowing, then taxiing toward him. It stopped, but the engine kept running.

Lance unstrapped a salesman's catalogue case from the rear rack of the BMW, opened a door, and placed the case on the rear seat, securing it with the passenger seat belt. He looked over the rear seat at the luggage compartment; his bags were already aboard. He got into the airplane, closed the door behind him, and fastened his seat belt.

"Beautiful bike," the pilot said. He rubbed the thumb and first two fingers of his right hand together, the ancient code. Lance took a stack of fifty-pound notes from an inside pocket and handed it to him. The pilot did a quick count, tucked the notes into a pocket, and grinned. "Where to, old sport?"

"That way," Lance said, pointing south. "I'll direct you."

"Any particular altitude?"

"Ten."

"Ten thousand?"

"Ten feet; fifteen, if ten makes you nervous."

"We'll attract attention that low, and besides, there are a lot of trees between here and the Channel. I'd suggest a thousand feet."

Lance reached forward and switched off the transponder. "Good; when you get to the Channel, descend to minimum altitude, and fly a heading of one eight zero."

"Below the radar? I could get into trouble."

Lance held up the keys of the motorcycle. "You like the BMW?"

The pilot pocketed the keys, lined up on the runway, and pushed the throttle to the firewall. Two minutes later, they were at a thousand feet. "How far we going?" he asked. "Will I need to refuel?"

"Less than two hundred miles," Lance replied. "If you topped off as requested, you'll have fuel for there and back."

The pilot nodded. After a few minutes he pointed to a blinking light. "Lighthouse," he said, and started a descent.

"Careful you don't bump into any shipping," Lance said.

"A hundred feet will keep us below the radar and above anything but the QE2," the pilot said. "What line of work are you in?"

"I'm a salesman," Lance replied.

"What do you sell?"

"Whatever's in demand."

They flew on in silence, at one point steering around a big tanker plowing up the Channel, then the shore lights of Normandy came into view.

"Come right to one niner five degrees," Lance said. He reached forward and turned a knob on the Global Positioning Unit in the panel, selected "create user waypoint," and entered some coordinates. "Climb back to a thousand feet," he said.

The pilot leveled off at a thousand feet, and Lance reached forward, switched on the autopilot, and pushed the NAV button. The airplane swung a few degrees onto a new heading. "Let it fly the airplane for now," he said. He checked the distance to waypoint; one hundred eight miles.

"What are we landing on?" the pilot asked.

"A farmer's field," Lance replied. "You've got about three thousand feet of length and all the width you need."

"Any lights?"

Lance pointed to the rising full moon. "That," he said, "and some car headlights." He tuned the number one communications radio to 123.4 MHz and held the microphone in his lap.

Forty-five minutes later, Lance spoke again. "Descend to five hundred feet." He spoke into the microphone. "It's me; you there?"

"I'm here," Ali's voice said.

"Wind?"

"One eight zero, light. I'm already parked."

"Switch on your headlights, and put them on bright; turn them on and off, once a second." Lance scanned the horizon.

"Five hundred feet," the pilot reported.

"We're five miles out," Lance said. "Look for headlights, flashing on and off, and land into them, on a heading of one eight zero."

The pilot leaned forward and searched the ground ahead of him.

"Four miles," Lance called out.

"I don't see anything."

"They're there. Three miles."

"Nothing."

"Dead ahead, see them?"

"Got them!"

"A mile and a half; get lined up; can you see the tree line?"

"Yes, the moonlight is good."

"Just miss the trees and aim for the car. You should have a soft touchdown."

The pilot punched off the autopilot, swung right, then back left, lining up on the headlights. He put in full flaps and reduced power.

"Minimum speed, and for God's sake, don't hit the trees," Lance said.

The pilot switched on both the landing and taxi lights, faintly illuminating the grass beyond the trees. He floated over the treeline, chopped the throttle, and put the airplane firmly down on the field, standing on the brakes. He swung around in front of the car and stopped.

"Keep the engine running," Lance said, reaching behind him for the catalogue case. He got out, opened the door to the luggage compartment, and started handing bags to Ali. "Tell Sheila to turn off the headlights," he said.

Ali went to the car, and a moment later, the lights went off.

Lance leaned into the airplane. "Wind's light," he said to the pilot; "you should be able to take off due north. Keep it low all the way."

The pilot nodded. "Good luck," he said.

"Enjoy the bike," Lance replied. "The registration's in the saddlebags." He closed the door and watched as the pilot ran the engine up to full power, then released the brakes. Lance winced, thinking he might not make the trees, but then the little airplane was off the ground and climbing steeply. He ran back to the car and got into the passenger seat, while Ali got into the rear.

Sheila put the car in gear and drove slowly off the field. When she was into the trees, she switched on the headlights and found the track through the woods.

"How long until we hit the autoroute?" Lance asked.

"Less than half an hour. Driving at a steady eighty we should be at the Swiss border before dawn."

"Got the passports?" he asked Ali.

Ali handed the three forward, and Lance inspected them. "Good," he said.

Ali handed him a small leather case. "Here's your makeup and beard," he said.

He had tried out the makeup and beard when they had taken the passport photographs. He'd apply it after they were on the smooth autoroute. Then he would be Herr Schmidt.

"Meine damen und herren," he said, *"mach schnell!"*

Sheila joined the paved road, put her foot down, and the car roared off into the European night.

57

MORGAN PARKED HIS CAR IN THE short-term lot at Heathrow, fastened his luggage to a folding hand trolley, and walked into terminal four. He found a men's room, let himself into the handicapped toilet stall, then took off his hat, got out of the raincoat, and began unbuttoning his shirt. He opened his small suitcase, took out a loud Hawaiian shirt and put it on, followed by a tweed cap and sunglasses with heavy black rims. He wadded up his shirt and wrapped it in the raincoat, then stuffed the bundle behind the toilet. He left the stall, dug into his bag, and found a small bottle of pills marked VALIUM 5MG. He took one, then looked at himself in the mirror. "Keep calm," he said. He grabbed his luggage cart, left the men's room, and walked to the ticket counters.

From the departure board, he chose a flight, and, a minute later, he was standing in a ticket line. Then it occurred to him that he was going to have to go through security, and that the money in his valise might be discovered. As he stepped up to the counter, he made a snap decision. "Check everything," he said to the ticket agent.

"Of course, sir," she replied. "You're going to have

to hurry; your flight leaves in twenty-five minutes, and it's already boarding."

"I'll hurry," Morgan replied, accepting his ticket and boarding pass.

Dino screeched to a halt in front of terminal four. Before Stone could open his door, a man clutching a handheld radio opened it for him.

"My name's Bartlett," he said. "Heathrow security."

Stone introduced himself and Dino, then showed him the photograph of Morgan.

"I've already circulated it," Bartlett said.

"He's shaved the mustache, and he's wearing a raincoat and a trilby hat," he said. "And he'll be carrying a canvas valise, I'm sure of that. He's calling himself Sir William Mallory, and he has a British passport in that name."

Bartlett used his radio, passing on the new description. "Let's go," he said to Stone.

"How many people have you got working right now?" Stone asked, hurrying to keep up.

"I'm afraid I can't tell you that, but I've pulled every available man and woman off nearly everything else. We're concentrating on the security checkpoint, since every passenger has to pass through it."

"Let's start there," Stone said.

With Bartlett leading the way, they made off across the busy terminal.

Morgan reached the security checkpoint, and immediately he was approached by two men in suits, one of whom flashed an ID card.

"Please step over here, sir," one of them said, taking his arm and moving him out of the line.

"What's going on?" Morgan asked, as innocently as he could.

"May I see your passport and ticket, please?"

Morgan produced both.

"You are . . ." The officer looked at the passport. "Mr. Barry Trevor?"

"That's right," Morgan said. "What's this about?"

"Just a routine security check, sir. And is this your current address?" The officer held up the passport.

"Yes, it is, and I've got a plane to catch."

"We won't be a moment, sir. Would you remove your sunglasses, please?"

Morgan took them off and gave the officers a big smile. He knew his security photograph at Eastover made him look dour.

The officers compared him to a photograph one of them produced. They looked at each other; one shook his head. The officer handed back Mr. Barry Trevor's passport and ticket. "Thank you, sir; sorry for the inconvenience. Here, let me get you through security." He led Morgan to one side of the checkpoint and signaled to the officer on station, who ran a detector wand over Morgan's clothes, then waved him through.

Morgan headed for the gate. With a little luck, his timing would be perfect.

Stone arrived at the security checkpoint, and Bartlett called two men over.

"Any sightings?" he asked.

"No; we've checked three men, but all seemed okay."

"Any of them carrying a canvas valise?"

"No; one of them had a briefcase, but there were only business documents inside."

"Any of them wearing a raincoat and a trilby hat?"

"No, sir."

Bartlett turned to Stone. "Anything else you want to try?"

Stone nodded. "I hear Spain is a favored destination for fugitives."

"That's right; we've no extradition treaty with them."

"Let's go to the gates that have flights departing for anywhere in Spain."

Bartlett looked up at a row of monitors next to the security checkpoint. "Three, no, five flights departing in the next two hours, from three gates." He led the way through the checkpoint, then flagged down an oversized golf cart driven by an airport employee. Bartlett, Stone, and Dino boarded the vehicle, and, on Bartlett's instructions, it began to move down the long corridor.

Morgan walked along the people mover, dodging other travelers who were happy to stand still and ride. He tried to move quickly, without looking as though he was hurrying. He checked his watch; seven minutes to go.

Bartlett was on the radio, summoning officers to the three gates with departing flights to Spain. "I want two men at each gate, scrutinizing every male passenger even remotely resembling the photograph." He turned to Stone. "If he's bound for Spain, we'll get him at the gate." His radio squawked, and he held it to his ear. "Say again?" He turned back to Stone. "One of my men has found a raincoat, a shirt, and a trilby hat, discarded in a men's room. A British passport bearing the name Sir William Mallory was in the raincoat pocket."

"Costume change," Stone said. "This guy is starting to do everything right."

The cart pulled up to a gate, and Stone got out, followed by Dino and Bartlett. The first person he saw was Stan Hedger.

Hedger walked up to him. "What the hell are you doing here?" he demanded.

"It's a public airport; none of your business."

"Have you seen Lance Cabot?"

"Is that why you're here? You're looking for Cabot?"

"That's right."

"So is half the country, from what I hear."

"I thought you had gone back to the States, Stone. Why are you involved in this?"

"It's personal," Stone said. "See you around, Stan."

"Come on," Dino said, "we're wasting time."

Morgan reached his gate two minutes before the flight was scheduled to take off. He went to the counter for a seat assignment.

"You'll have to hurry, Mr. Trevor," the young woman said. "We're about to button up the airplane."

"I'll hurry," Morgan said, and made for the boarding ramp. There was no line, and a moment later he was strapping himself into a first-class seat.

Stone, Dino, and Bartlett made their way quickly from gate to gate, coming up empty-handed at each one.

"That's it," Bartlett said. "We know he's in the airport, but we don't—"

"What are other likely destinations for fugitives?" Stone asked.

Bartlett shrugged. "Could be anywhere. There are more than a hundred international flights taking off in the next two hours; I don't have the manpower to cover them all, and I'm not about to shut down this airport, unless I get a personal call from the Home Secretary."

"Shit," Stone said.

"My sentiments exactly," Bartlett replied. "But let's keep looking."

"Good evening, ladies and gentlemen," the flight attendant said. "We are now pushing back from the gate, and in a few minutes we'll be taking off for our flight to Honolulu. While we're taxiing, we direct your attention to the video, which will explain the emergency procedures for this aircraft."

Morgan picked up a magazine. Fuck the emergency procedures, he thought. He wanted a double Scotch.

Stan Hedger left the airport in disgust, along with one of his people, and got into a waiting car. He did not notice, nor did his driver, that the car was followed by another, which kept a respectful distance.

Stone and Dino stuck it out until nearly midnight, when departures slowed dramatically, then they drove back to the Brewer's Arms.

Carpenter, Mason, and Plumber were all in the suite

when they arrived. "Anything?" Carpenter asked.

"Morgan was at the airport," Stone said. "One of the security people found his discarded hat, coat, and passport in a men's room. We covered the departures for Spain all evening, but there were too many departing flights to cover them all. What have you heard about Lance?"

"A farmer about eighty miles west of here reported that a light airplane landed and took off again at a disused RAF airfield near his house. Two local police officers found a brand-new BMW motorcycle abandoned there."

"You think it was Lance's?"

"It was wiped completely clean of fingerprints," she said, "and it was properly registered to someone in London. We're checking it out now, but who else would abandon an expensive motorbike at an old airfield and wipe off the prints?"

"I doubt if he's coming back for it," Stone said.

"The police are keeping a watch, to see if anyone picks it up."

Stone sank into a sofa. "This hasn't gone well, has it?"

Carpenter sat down next to him. "No, it hasn't, but it's not your fault; you were a big help. And you've lost all that money."

Stone raised a hand. "Please, don't mention that again."

"I'll do what I can to get you reimbursed, but I'm not very hopeful. My management are very annoyed that we've let these people get away."

"Can I give you a lift back to London?"

"I have to stay here, but I'll walk you downstairs."

They walked through the inn to the parking lot, and Dino got behind the wheel.

"I don't suppose we'll be seeing each other again," Carpenter said.

"Oh, I don't know; I might get to London, from time to time." He handed her his card. "You might even get to New York."

"Possible, I suppose. Let me give you a telephone number; memorize it, don't write it down." She gave him the number, then repeated it. "If you call that number at any hour of the day or night, you'll hear a beep; leave a message for Carpenter, and I'll get back to you when I can."

"I'm sorry about the device," he said.

"Spilt milk," she replied. "They don't have the electronics to make it work, and they don't have the software—especially the software. It will take them months, hopefully years, to figure out how to use it, and by that time we'll have something better."

Stone offered her his hand, but she snaked an arm around his neck and planted a wet kiss on his ear. "Hope I'll hear from you," she said, then she turned and walked back into the Brewer's Arms.

Stone got into the car, and Dino drove off. "Two hundred and fifty thousand dollars, gone," he sighed.

Dino laughed. "And I was looking forward to a finder's fee."

As they drove back along the M4, Stone looked out at the rolling landscape. He'd heard that the road had been planned to show off the countryside. "I love this country," he said. "I feel as though I've been here forever."

"A pretty short forever," Dino replied.

5 8

LANCE CABOT WOKE UP IN HIS ZURICH
hotel room at noon, wakened by his travel alarm. He
showered, shaved, dressed, and applied his false
beard, which on inspection in the mirror, he thought
very becoming. Maybe he'd better grow one, he
thought, since he was going to be hot for a while, even
though no one had anything on him. Stan Hedger was
his only real worry; Hedger wanted him badly, and he
wouldn't stop looking. He felt sorry about Erica, but
he couldn't contact her for a long time, he knew.

He called Ali's room. "I'm off," he said. "As soon as
the transaction is complete I'll pick you up here. Our
flight to Cairo isn't until five o'clock. We'll change
passports again." He hung up.

Lance arrived at the bank on time. He gave the appropriate name to an officer and was escorted into a conference room. Two men of Middle Eastern appearance
sat at the large table. They stood up when he arrived.

"There's a buzzer on the table, there," the bank officer said. "Ring when you need me."

Lance nodded and sat down.

"You have the item?" one of the men asked.

Lance set the catalogue case on the table and opened it. He handed over the device, wrapped in tissue paper.

Nervously, the man on the other side of the table tore away the paper, then held the device in his hands and weighed it. "It's very light," he said.

"Very advanced metallurgy," Lance said. "Are you ready to make the transfer?"

"How do we know this is the device you promised?"

"I would have thought that your people would have been smart enough to send someone with the skills to authenticate it."

He handed the device to his companion, who inspected it for, perhaps, two minutes, then nodded.

"All right," the first man said, "we are ready to make the transfer."

"I think, perhaps, you should put that away," Lance said, nodding at the device and pushing the catalogue case across the table. When the device was safely in the case, Lance pressed the button.

The bank officer returned with a file folder and sat down at the table. "Have you successfully completed your transaction?" he asked.

"We will have when the funds have been transferred," Lance said.

"I have made out the paperwork as per your instructions," the banker said. "Five million dollars to be transferred to your numbered account."

"That's correct," Lance said.

The banker laid the documents before the two Middle Easterners. They examined them, and one of them signed.

"I'll just be a moment," the banker said. He took the documents and left the room.

Lance sat and looked at the two men, who impassively returned his gaze. No one said anything.

Presently, the banker returned. "Gentlemen, your transaction is complete."

The two men rose and left the room without a word.

"Will there be anything else, sir?" the banker asked Lance.

Lance thought for a moment. "Yes," he replied.

Ted Cricket stood in a light rain outside the Guinea pub and restaurant, in a mews off Berkeley Square. It was nearly eleven o'clock. The door to the restaurant opened, and Cricket stepped back into the shadows and looked around. The mews was empty.

Hedger left the restaurant alone, weaving a little, and started up the mews toward Berkeley Square. He walked right past Cricket, no more than six feet away.

Cricket stepped from the shadows, reached out, cupped a hand over Hedger's mouth, and ran the slim blade into his back, thrusting upward. Hedger's knees gave way, and when Cricket released him, he collapsed onto the wet cobblestones.

Cricket looked up and down the mews again; empty. He rolled Hedger over, switched on a tiny flashlight, and shone it into Hedger's face. He was still alive. "This is for Bobby Jones," Cricket said. He placed the knife point on Hedger's chest, over the heart, shoved it through the flesh, twisted it ninety degrees, and pulled it out, wiping the blade on Hedger's fine Savile Row jacket. Hedger coughed up some blood, then was still.

Cricket walked up the mews into Berkeley Square, then around the square and into the warren of streets that was Mayfair. He waited until he reached Park Lane before hailing a taxi.

*   *   *

The telephone was ringing as Stone let himself into the house.

"Hello?"

"It's Sarah," she said. "I'm at Monica's gallery; Erica is here, and she's very upset."

"Bring her here for the night," Stone replied. "Don't take her back to the Farm Street house for any reason."

"What's going on?" Sarah asked.

"I don't want to tell you on the phone," Stone said. "Get here as soon as you can; I'll wait up for you."

The two women arrived in a rush, carrying Erica's luggage.

"I moved out of the house," Erica said. "It seemed very strange with Lance not there, and I was hearing clicking noises on the phone."

"You did the right thing," Stone replied. "I think you should fly back to New York tomorrow."

"It seems the only thing to do," Erica said.

"Stone, what is going on?" Sarah demanded.

"Lance has been involved in some sort of smuggling, I think, and they're looking for him."

"Who's looking for him?"

"Just about everybody."

"Good God."

"I'm going home tomorrow, too," he said. "Dino, will you call British Airways and book the three of us on the Concorde?" He still had some of Stan Hedger's money.

Dino went into the kitchen to use the phone.

"Why don't you get Erica to bed?" Stone asked Sarah. "I'm pretty bushed myself."

By the time Sarah crawled into bed with him, he was out.

5 9

STONE AND DINO WERE HAVING BREAK-
fast when the doorbell rang. Stone answered it, to find
Detective Inspector Evelyn Throckmorton standing
there with another officer, looking grim.

"Good morning," Stone said.

"No, it isn't," Throckmorton replied, brushing past
him and walking into the drawing room. "Come in
here and sit down."

"I was about to call you; how on earth did you find
me here?" Stone asked.

"I had Miss Burroughs followed," Throckmorton
replied, "and my people weren't the only ones doing
so. Where is she?"

"Upstairs, asleep," Stone replied.

"No, I'm not," Erica said from the doorway.

Stone introduced her to the two men.

"I have only a few questions for you, Miss Burroughs," Throckmorton said, and he proceeded to ask
them. Ten minutes of grilling her produced nothing,
and he told her she could go.

"Get some breakfast," Stone said to her. "I'll be a few
minutes."

"Well, Barrington," Throckmorton said, "you've certainly managed to mix in a number of things, haven't you?"

"I suppose I have," Stone replied.

"How about Stanford Hedger's death; did you mix in that?"

Stone had no trouble looking surprised. "He's dead?"

"Knifed outside a Mayfair restaurant late last evening."

"I saw him at Heathrow earlier in the evening," Stone said, "and he was perfectly fine."

"He was looking for Lance Cabot?"

"Yes."

"And so were you, I suppose."

"No."

"Look, I know very well that you're up to your ears in the Eastover matter, and I'm not in the least convinced that you had nothing to do with Hedger's death."

"May I speak to you alone for a moment?" Stone asked.

Throckmorton motioned for the detective to leave them.

"I think we both have a pretty good idea who might have dispatched Hedger, don't we?" Stone asked when they were alone.

Throckmorton sighed. "Yes, I suppose I do. He had all the skills; he was ex–Special Air Services, you know."

"I didn't know, but I'm not surprised. I don't suppose there's anything but suspicion to link him to Hedger's death?"

"He has half a dozen witnesses, all retired policemen, who swear he was in a card game at the time."

"Then I suppose you'll have to leave it."

"I wish I could; the Americans are very upset."

"Then let them solve it; they don't seem to have any compunctions about operating on your soil."

"No, they don't, do they?"

Stone didn't say anything for a moment. "May I have my passport back, please?"

"Oh, yes." Throckmorton stood up, took it from his pocket and handed it to Stone.

"And my raincoat?"

"No. That's evidence. You'll be returning to New York, then?"

"Yes, today."

"Thank God," Throckmorton said. "I hope you never come back." He walked out of the room and the house without another word, followed by his detective, bumping into Mason as he entered the house. The two men exchanged a long glance, but said nothing to each other.

"Good morning," Stone said to Mason. "Any news?"

"None I can give you," Mason replied. "I've come for your car, your pen, and your button."

"Oh, yes." He had forgotten. He went into the kitchen, found a knife, and cut the button from his sleeve.

"What are you doing?" Dino asked.

"I'll tell you later." He went back into the drawing room and handed Mason the button, pen, and car keys.

"Thank you," Mason said, then turned to go.

"There's nothing you can tell me?" Stone asked.

"It's not my place," Mason replied. "Thank you for your assistance; you got your passport back?"

"Yes."

"I shouldn't delay leaving the country, if I were you."

"I'll be gone before sundown," Stone replied.

"Yes, sundown; that's when you Americans get out of town, isn't it?"

"Only in Westerns."

"Well, I suppose this has been a sort of Western, hasn't it? Except we didn't get the bad guy in the end."

"Will you?"

"A personal opinion?"

"Sure."

"We'll get Morgan one of these days. As for Cabot, I doubt if Morgan can identify him, so we don't actually have anything concrete on which to base a prosecution. And to tell you the truth, I doubt if my management would prosecute him if we did. This whole business has been terribly embarrassing for them, as well as for Carpenter and me."

"I'm sorry," Stone said.

Mason shook his hand. "Don't be; in a week or two, the whole thing will have blown over for us. Take care."

"You, too." Stone showed him out.

Stone went into the kitchen, where Sarah had joined everybody. "I want everybody ready to leave for Heathrow in an hour," he said, checking his watch.

Sarah drove them, and walked Stone as far as the security checkpoint. "I had hoped you might stay for a long time," she said.

"I'm an American and a New Yorker. As much as I like it here, I know where home is."

"And after I went to all that trouble," she said.

Stone frowned. "Trouble?"

"Well, I had to, didn't I? Daddy is nearly broke, and if he'd lost any of the lawsuits, he'd lose everything,

even the house. I had to do something; then you
turned up, and it became even more imperative."

Stone stared at her. "Jesus, Sarah, you didn't . . ."

"Didn't I?" she asked. She kissed him and walked
away.

Dino and Erica joined Stone. "You don't look so
hot," Dino said.

"Just a little shaken," Stone said.

"What, she told you the truth?"

"Yes, in a way; nothing that I could testify to,
though."

"Jesus, Stone, I knew all that; why didn't you?"

"I guess I didn't want to know."

"Yeah, you're good at that. Come on, we've got a
rocket ship to catch."

As the Concorde roared down the runway, Stone
looked at Erica sitting beside him, reading a magazine.
"You don't seem terribly upset about Lance," he said.

She shrugged. "He told me something like this
might happen someday. I'll hear from him, eventually."

Stone reflected that he was finally doing what "John
Bartholomew" had hired him to do: bring home Erica
Burroughs. He settled into his seat. What with the time
change, they'd arrive in New York before they left
London.

6 0

STONE WAS AWAKENED EARLY THE following morning by the telephone. For a moment he was disoriented, thinking he was at the Connaught or in the late James Cutler's bed. He glanced at the clock; he had slept for twelve hours. "Hello?" he croaked into the phone.

"It's Carpenter," she said. "You sound awful."

"I was asleep," he said.

"Oh, yes, the time difference; it's lunchtime here."

"Right."

"Mason said you wanted an update?"

"Yes, thanks."

"There's good news and bad news; which do you want first?"

Stone groaned. "The bad news."

"My management have categorically refused to reimburse you for your monetary loss. They feel no responsibility."

"That's sweet of them. Tell me the good news."

"It comes in two parts: first, we caught Morgan in Hawaii."

Stone sat up in bed. "Did he have my money with him?"

"No, he didn't."

Stone fell back into the bed. "Why are you torturing me?"

"I said the good news came in two parts."

"All right, what's part two?"

"Morgan checked in for his flight only shortly before it departed, so his luggage didn't make it aboard the aircraft."

Stone sat up in bed again. "The valise?"

"Heathrow security found it, waiting patiently to be put aboard the next flight. There was nearly half a million dollars in it."

"Yeeessss!" Stone shouted, punching the air.

"It will take a little sorting out, but I imagine that, in a few days, I can transfer it to your New York bank. Do you have the account number?"

Stone gave her his brokerage account number. "Send it there," he said, "back where it came from."

"Well, I suppose you'll be able to buy me dinner the next time I'm in New York."

"Yes, I suppose I will be able to afford that. Soon, I hope."

"You never know."

"What about Lance Cabot? Any word on him?"

"He was too slick for us. The motorcycle turned out to be his; we picked up his pilot when he returned for the machine; Cabot had given it to him, apparently."

"What did the pilot tell you?"

"He delivered Cabot to a farmer's field in France, he isn't sure where, since Cabot erased the coordinates from his GPS computer before leaving the airplane. He was met by two people, one of them answering to the description of Ali. We haven't been able to trace him from there, so we have to assume that both he and, ah, his luggage reached their destination. We don't know where that was."

"Mason said he probably wouldn't be prosecuted."

"That's right, but we would certainly make it difficult for him if he ever returned to Britain. I expect that he won't; he'll enjoy his ill-gotten gains in a more hospitable climate." She paused. "Well, I must run."

"May I know your name, now?"

She laughed. "All in good time. You take care of yourself."

"Listen, when do you think . . ." But she had gone.

Stone got out of bed, and by the time he had dressed and breakfasted, his secretary was at her desk, working away.

"Good morning!" she said. "And welcome back!"

"Thank you, Joan," he said. "Will you let my broker know to expect the return of some funds I took out of my account? In a few days, I think."

"Of course," she said. She handed him a stack of message slips. "Here are your phone calls, and this was in the fax machine when I came in yesterday."

Stone looked at the paper. It was from his Swiss banker.

Sir, it read, *I take pleasure in reporting the receipt of the following funds into your account.* Stone looked at the bottom of the form. The amount was one million dollars.

"Good God!" Stone said.

"What's the matter?"

"Nothing; Lance kept his word."

"Who?"

"Never mind." Stone stood and thought about the ramifications of receiving this money. Should he return it? If so, to whom?

"You look puzzled," Joan said.

Stone nodded. "I think you'd better get my accountant on the phone."

"That doesn't really mean what it says, does it?" she asked, nodding at the document in his hand.

"I'm afraid it does."

She picked up the phone. "I'll get your accountant," she said.

"You know," Stone said to her, "it's amazing what can happen in a short forever."

She stopped dialing. "What?"

"Never mind," Stone said. He was trying to figure out how he was going to explain all this to his accountant.

He'd had worse problems.

ACKNOWLEDGMENTS

I want to express my thanks to my editor, David High-fill, for making this the first manuscript in my career where an editor asked for no revisions whatever. It takes a highly discerning editor to know when something doesn't need fixing.

I am very grateful to my publisher, the remarkable Phyllis Grann, now gone on to other things, for her interest in my career and for her efforts to do the best for each of my titles that she published. I wish her well in whatever she undertakes.

My agents, Morton Janklow and Anne Sibbald, and all the people at Janklow & Nesbit, continue to manage my career with care and thoughtfulness, and always produce excellent results. I am very appreciative of all their efforts.

I thank Maldwin and Gilly Drummond for lending me the site of their wonderful house, if not the house itself, to use for the Wight home.

And I am always grateful to my wife, Chris, for her acute observations when reading my manuscripts and for her affection.

AUTHOR'S NOTE

I am happy to hear from readers, but you should know that if you write to me in care of my publisher, three to six months will pass before I receive your letter, and when it finally arrives it will be one among many, and I will not be able to reply.

However, if you have access to the Internet, you may visit my website at www.stuartwoods.com, where there is a button for sending me e-mail. So far, I have been able to reply to all of my e-mail, and I will continue to try to do so.

If you send me an e-mail and do not receive a reply, it is because you are among an alarming number of people who have entered their e-mail address incorrectly in their mail software. I have many of my replies returned as undeliverable.

Remember: e-mail, reply; snail mail, no reply.

When you e-mail, please do not send attachments, as I *never* open these. They can take twenty minutes to download, and they often contain viruses.

Please do not place me on your mailing lists for funny stories, prayers, political causes, charitable fund-raising, petitions, or sentimental claptrap. I get enough of that from people I already know. Generally speaking, when I get e-mail addressed to a large number of people, I immediately delete it without reading it.

Please do not send me your ideas for a book, as I have a policy of writing only what I myself invent. If you send me story ideas, I will immediately delete them without reading them. If you have a good idea for a book, write it yourself, but I will not be able to advise you on how to get it published. Buy a copy of *Writer's Market* at any bookstore; that will tell you how.

Anyone with a request concerning events or appearances may e-mail it to me or send it to: Publicity Department, G. P. Putnam's Sons, 375 Hudson Street, New York, NY 10014.

Those ambitious folk who wish to buy film, dramatic, or television rights to my books should contact Matthew Snyder, Creative Artists Agency, 9830 Wilshire Boulevard, Beverly Hills, CA 90212-1825.

Those who wish to conduct business of a more literary nature should contact Anne Sibbald, Janklow & Nesbit, 445 Park Avenue, New York, NY 10022.

If you want to know if I will be signing books in your city, please visit my website, www.stuartwoods .com, where the tour schedule will be published a month or so in advance. If you wish me to do a book signing in your locality, ask your favorite bookseller to contact his Putnam representative or the G. P. Putnam's Sons Publicity Department with the request.

If you find typographical or editorial errors in my book and feel an irresistible urge to tell someone, please write to David Highfill at Putnam, address above. Do not e-mail your discoveries to me, as I will already have learned about them from others.

A list of all my published works appears in the front of this book. All the novels are still in print in paperback and can be found at or ordered from any bookstore. If you wish to obtain hardcover copies of earlier novels or of the two nonfiction books, a good used-book store or one of the on-line bookstores can help you find them. Otherwise, you will have to go to a great many garage sales.

Please turn the page
for a preview of Stuart Woods's
new Stone Barrington novel

DIRTY WORK

available in April 2003
from Putnam

ELAINE'S, LATE.

A big night—a couple of directors, a couple of movie stars, half a dozen writers, an assortment of journalists, editors, publicists, cops, wiseguys, drunks, hangers-on, women of substance, and some of considerably less substance. And this was just at the tables; the bar was a whole other thing.

Stone Barrington pushed his plate away and sat back. Gianni, the waiter, snatched it away.

"Was it all right?" Gianni asked.

"You see anything left?" Stone asked.

Gianni grinned and took the plate to the kitchen.

Elaine came over and sat down. "So?" she said. She did not light a cigarette. To Stone's continuing astonishment, she had quit, cold turkey.

"Not much," Stone replied.

"That's what you always say," Elaine said.

"I'm not kidding; not much is happening."

The front door of the restaurant opened, and Bill Eggers came in.

"Now something's happening," Elaine said. "Eggers never comes in here unless he's looking for you, and he never looks for you unless there's trouble."

"You wrong the man," Stone said, waving Eggers over to the table, but he knew she was right. For ordinary work, Bill phoned; for more pressing tasks, he hunted down Stone and usually found him at Elaine's.

"Good evening, Elaine. Stone," Eggers said, "your cellphone is off."

"It didn't work, did it?" Stone replied.

"I gotta be someplace," Elaine said, getting up and walking away. She got as far as the next table.

"Drink?" Stone asked.

Michael, the headwaiter, materialized beside them.

"Johnnie Walker Black, rocks," Eggers said.

"I have a feeling I'm going to need a Wild Turkey," Stone said to Michael.

Michael vanished.

"How's it going?" Eggers asked.

"You tell me," Stone said.

Eggers shrugged.

"If I had to guess," Stone said, "I'd say, not so hot."

"Oh, it's not so bad," Eggers replied.

"Then what drags you away from home and hearth, into this den of iniquity?"

"You remember that big Irish ex-cop, used to do little chores for you from time to time?"

"Teddy? He dropped dead in P. J. Clarke's three months ago."

"From what?"

"How many things can an Irishman in an Irish bar drop dead of?" Stone asked rhetorically.

"Yeah," Eggers admitted.

"And why would I need somebody like Teddy?" Stone asked.

"You remember telling me about that thing Teddy used to do with the water pistol?" Eggers asked.

"You mean, after he kicked down a door and had his

camera ready, how he squirted his naked subjects down low, so they'd grab at themselves and leave their faces open to be photographed in bed with each other?"

Eggers chuckled. "That's the one. I admire that kind of ingenuity."

The drinks came, and they both sipped for a long, contemplative moment.

"So, you're in need of that kind of ingenuity?" Stone asked at last.

"You remember that prenup I tossed you last year?" Eggers asked. Bill Eggers was the managing partner of Woodman & Weld, the very prestigious New York law firm to which Stone was of counsel, which meant he sometimes did the work that Woodman & Weld did not wish to appear to be doing.

"Elena Marks?" Stone asked.

"The very one."

"I remember." Elena Marks was heiress to a department store fortune, and she had married a member in high standing of the No Visible Means of Support Club.

"You remember that funny little clause you wrote into her prenup?"

"You mean the one about how if Larry got caught with his pants around his ankles in the company of a lady other than Elena, he would forfeit any claim to her assets or income?" Lawrence Fortescue was English—handsome, well-educated, and possessed of every social grace, which meant he didn't have a receptacle in which to relieve himself.

"The very one," Eggers said.

"Has Larry been a bad boy?" Stone asked.

"Has been, is, and will continue to be," Eggers replied, sipping his Scotch.

"I see," Stone said.

"Now that Teddy has gone to his reward, who do you use for that sort of thing?"

"It's been quite a while since that sort of thing was required of me," Stone replied edgily.

"Don't take that tone with me, young man," Eggers said, raising himself erect in mock dudgeon. "It's work, and somebody has to do it."

Stone sighed. "I suppose I could find somebody."

Eggers looked at him sharply. "You're not thinking of doing this yourself, are you? I mean, there are heights involved here, and you're not as young as you used to be."

"I am *not* thinking of doing it myself, but I'm certainly in good enough shape to," Stone said. "What kind of heights are we talking about?"

"The roof of a six-story townhouse. Shooting photos through a conveniently located skylight."

"There is no such thing as a conveniently located skylight, if you're the one doing the climbing," Stone said.

"You'd need someone . . . spry," Eggers said, "and the term hardly applies to the cops and ex-cops you mingle with."

At that moment, as if to make Eggers's point, Stone's former partner from his NYPD days, Dino Bacchetti, walked through the front door and headed for Stone's table.

"If you see what I mean," Eggers said.

Stone held up a hand, stopping Dino in his tracks, then a finger, turning him toward the bar.

"I get your point," Stone said. "I'll see who I can come up with."

"You don't have a lot of time," Eggers said. "It's at nine o'clock tomorrow night."

"What's at nine o'clock tomorrow night?"

"The assignation. Larry Fortescue has an appointment with a masseuse, who, I understand, routinely massages more than his neck muscles. Elena would like some very clear photographs of that service being performed."

"Let me see what I can do," Stone said.

Eggers tossed off the remainder of his Scotch and placed a folded sheet of paper on the table. "I knew you would grasp the nettle," he said, standing up. "The address of the building is on the paper; I'll need the prints and negatives by noon the day after tomorrow."

"What's the rush?"

"Elena Marks is accustomed to instant gratification."

"But not from Larry?"

"You *are* quick, Stone. Nighty-night." He slapped Dino on the back as he passed the bar on his way to the door.

Dino came over, licking Scotch off his hand, where Eggers had spilled it. He flopped into a chair. "So what was that about?" he asked, pointing his chin at Eggers's disappearing back.

"Dirty work," Stone said.

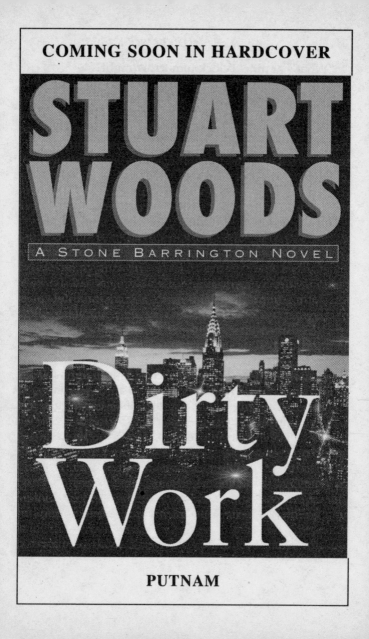

SOPHISTICATED SUSPENSE

From The New York Times Bestseller

STUART WOODS

BLOOD ORCHID

CHIEF OF POLICE HOLLY BARKER RETURNS in her third suspenseful adventure—along with her father Ham and Daisy the Doberman. This time, they get introduced to the cutthroat world of Florida real estate...and uncover a scam as dangerous as it is lucrative.

"Stuart Woods, famous for his Stone Barrington private eye novels, has created a whole new series with it's own unique voice. The Holly Barker police procedurals are fun to read because the author imbues a subtle sense of humor in many of the characters...Mr. Woods just keeps getting better with each book he writes." **—BookBrowser**

0-451-20881-1

COMING SOON IN PAPERBACK

To order call: 1-800-788-6262